"GET OUT AND STAY OUT OF MY AFFAIRS . . . OR ELSE!"

These were Mr. X's orders to Nero Wolfe. Mr. X's affairs included extortion, mayhem, killing for hire, traffic in women, weapons and drugs. Murder was obviously the least of Mr. X's crimes.

THE SECOND CONFESSION

Nero Wolfe discovers just how dangerous being the world's greatest detective can be, when he commits himself to destroying the most deadly adversary he has ever faced . . .

A NERO WOLFE NOVEL

THE SECOND CONFESSION

By REX STOUT

This low-priced Bantam Book has been completely reset in a type face designed for easy reading, and was printed from new plates. It contains the complete text of the original hard-cover edition.
NOT ONE WORD HAS BEEN OMITTED.

THE SECOND CONFESSION
A Bantam Book / published by arrangement with The Viking Press, Inc.

PRINTING HISTORY
Viking edition published September 1949
2nd printing .... October 1949
Dollar Mystery Guild edition published December 1949
Bantam edition published September 1952
New Bantam edition published May 1961
2nd printing .... December 1968
2nd new Bantam edition published January 1975
2nd printing .... November 1980

Condensations appeared in the MONTREAL STANDARD, NEWARK EVENING NEWS, *and* CHICAGO SUN-TIMES *1950*

Published simultaneously in the United States and Canada
ISBN 0-553-14448-0

Bantam Books are published by Bantam Books, Inc. Its trademark, consisting of the words "Bantam Books" and the portrayal of a bantam, is Registered in U.S. Patent and Trademark Office and in other countries. Marca Registrada. Bantam Books, Inc., 666 Fifth Avenue, New York, New York 10103.

PRINTED IN THE UNITED STATES OF AMERICA

11 10 9 8 7 6 5 4 3 2

THE SECOND CONFESSION

1

"I didn't mind it at all," our visitor said gruffly but affably. "It's a pleasure." He glanced around. "I like rooms that men work in. This is a good one."

I was still swallowing my surprise that he actually looked like a miner, at least my idea of one, with his big bones and rough weathered skin and hands that would have been right at home around a pick handle. Certainly swinging a pick was not what he got paid for as chairman of the board of the Continental Mines Corporation, which had its own building down on Nassau Street not far from Wall.

I was also surprised at the tone he was using. When, the day before, a masculine voice had given a name on the phone and asked when Nero Wolfe could call at his office, and I had explained why I had to say never, and it had ended by arranging an appointment at Wolfe's office for eleven the next morning, I had followed up with a routine check on a prospective client by calling Lon Cohen at the *Gazette*. Lon had told me that the only reason James U. Sperling didn't bite ears off was because he took whole heads and ate them bones and all. But there he was, slouching in the red leather chair near the end of Wolfe's desk like a big friendly roughneck, and I've just told you what he said when Wolfe started the conversation by explaining that he never left the office on business and expressing a regret that Sperling had had to come all the way to our place on West Thirty-fifth Street nearly to Eleventh Avenue. He said it was a pleasure!

"It will do," Wolfe murmured in a gratified tone. He was behind his desk, leaning back in his custom-made chair, which was warranted safe for a quarter of a ton and which might some day really be put to the test if its owner didn't level off. He added, "If you'll tell me what your problem is perhaps I can make your trip a good investment."

Seated at my own desk, at a right angle to Wolfe's and not far away, I allowed myself a mild private grin. Since the condition of his bank balance did not require the use of sales pressure to snare a client, I knew why he was spreading the sugar. He was merely being sociable because Sperling had said he liked the office. Wolfe didn't like the office, which was on the first floor of the old brownstone house he owned. He didn't like it, he loved it, and it was a good thing he did, since he was spending his life in it—except when he was in the kitchen with Fritz, or in the dining room across the hall at mealtime, or upstairs asleep, or in the plant rooms up on the roof, enjoying the orchids and pretending he was helping Theodore with the work.

My private grin was interrupted by Sperling firing a question at me: "Your name's Goodwin, isn't it? Archie Goodwin?"

I admitted it. He went to Wolfe.

"It's a confidential matter."

Wolfe nodded. "Most matters discussed in this office are. That's commonplace in the detective business. Mr. Goodwin and I are used to it."

"It's a family matter."

Wolfe frowned, and I joined in. With that opening it was a good twenty-to-one shot that we were going to be asked to tail a wife, and that was out of bounds for us. But James U. Sperling went on.

"I tell you that because you'd learn it anyhow." He put a hand to the inside breast pocket of his coat and pulled out a bulky envelope. "These reports will tell you that much. They're from the Bascom Detective Agency. You know them?"

"I know Mr. Bascom." Wolfe was still frowning. "I don't like ground that's been tramped over."

Sperling went right on by. "I had used them on business matters and found them competent, so I went to Bascom with this. I wanted information about a man named Rony, Louis Rony, and they've been at it a full month and they haven't got it, and I need it urgently. Yesterday I decided to call them off and try you. I've looked you up, and if you've earned your reputation I should have come to you first." He smiled like an angel, surprising me again, and convincing me that he would stand watching. "Apparently you have no equal."

Wolfe grunted, trying not to look pleased. "There was a man in Marseille—but he's not available and he doesn't speak English. What information do you want about Mr. Rony?"

"I want proof that he's a Communist. If you get it and get it soon, your bill can be whatever you want to make it."

Wolfe shook his head. "I don't take jobs on those terms. You don't know he's a Communist, or you wouldn't be bidding so high for proof. If he isn't, I can't very well get evidence that he is. As for my bill being whatever I want to make it, my bills always are. But I charge for what I do, and I can do nothing that is excluded by circumstance. What I dig up is of necessity contingent on what has been buried, but the extent of my digging isn't, nor my fee."

"You talk too much," Sperling said impatiently but not impolitely.

"Do I?" Wolfe cocked an eye at him. "Then you talk." He nodded sidewise at me. "Your notebook, Archie."

The miner waited until I had it ready, open at a fresh page, and then spoke crisply, starting with a spelling lesson. "L-o-u-i-s. R-o-n-y. He's in the Manhattan phone book, both his law office and his home, his apartment—and anyway, it's all in that." He indicated the bulky envelope, which he had tossed onto Wolfe's desk. "I have two daughters. Madeline is twenty-six and Gwenn is twenty-two. Gwenn was smart enough to graduate with honors at Smith a year ago, and I'm almost sure she's sane, but she's too damn curious and she turns her nose up at rules. She hasn't worked her way out of the notion that you can have independence without earning it. Of course it's all right to be romantic at her age, but she overdoes it, and I think what first attracted her to this man Rony was his reputation as a champion of the weak and downtrodden, which he has got by saving criminals from the punishment they deserve."

"I think I've seen his name," Wolfe murmured. "Haven't I, Archie?"

I nodded. "So have I. It was him that got What's-her-name, that baby peddler, out from under a couple of months ago. He seems to be on his way to the front page."

"Or to jail," Sperling snapped, and there was nothing angelic about his tone. "I think I handled this wrong, and I'm damned sure my wife did. It was the same old mistake, and God only knows why parents go on making it. We even told her, and him too, that he would no longer be admitted into our home, and of course you know what the reaction was to that. The only concession she made, and I doubt if that was to us, was never to come home after daylight."

"Is she pregnant?" Wolfe inquired.

Sperling stiffened. "What did you say?" His voice was suddenly as hard as the hardest ore ever found in any mine. Unquestionably he expected it to crush Wolfe into pretending he hadn't opened his mouth, but it didn't.

"I asked if your daughter is pregnant. If the question is immaterial I withdraw it, but surely it isn't preposterous unless she also turns her nose up at natural laws."

"She is my daughter," Sperling said in the same hard tone. Then suddenly his rigidity gave way. All the stiff muscles loosened, and he was laughing. When he laughed he roared, and he really meant it. In a moment he controlled it enough to speak. "Did you hear what I said?" he demanded.

Wolfe nodded. "If I can believe my ears."

"You can." Sperling smiled like an angel. "I suppose with any man that's one of his tenderest spots, but I might be expected to remember that I am not just any man. To the best of my knowledge my daughter is not pregnant, and she would have a right to be astonished if she were. That's not it. A little over a month ago my wife and I decided to correct the mistake we had made, and she told Gwenn that Rony would be welcome at our home as often as she wanted him there. That same day I put Bascom onto him. You're quite right that I can't prove he's a Communist or I wouldn't have had to come to you, but I'm convinced that he is."

"What convinced you?"

"The way he talks, the way I've sized him up, the way he practices his profession—and there are things in Bascom's reports, you'll see that when you read them—"

"But Mr. Bascom got no proof."

"No. Damn it."

"Whom do you call a Communist? A liberal? A pink intellectual? A member of the party? How far left do you start?"

Sperling smiled. "It depends on where I am and who I'm talking to. There are occasions when it may be expedient to apply the term to anyone left of center. But to you I'm using it realistically. I think Rony is a member of the Communist party."

"If and when you get proof, what are you going to do with it?"

"Show it to my daughter. But it has to be proof. She already knows what I think; I told her long ago. Of course she told Rony, and he looked me in the eye and denied it."

Wolfe grunted. "You may be wasting your time and money. Even if you get proof, what if it turns out that your daughter regards a Communist party card as a credential for romance?"

"She doesn't. Her second year in college she got interested in communism and went into it, but it didn't take her long to pull out. She says it's intellectually contemptible and morally unsound. I told you she's smart enough." Sperling's eyes darted to me and went back to Wolfe. "By the way, what about you and Goodwin? As I said, I looked you up, but is there any chance I'm putting my foot in it?"

"No," Wolfe assured him. "Though of course only the event can certify us. We agree with your daughter." He looked at me. "Don't we?"

I nodded. "Completely. I like the way she put it. The best I can do is 'a Commie is a louse' or something like that."

Sperling looked at me suspiciously, apparently decided that I merely had IQ trouble, and returned to Wolfe, who was talking.

"Exactly what," he was asking, "is the situation? Is there a possibility that your daughter is already married to Mr. Rony?"

"Good God, no!"

"How sure are you?"

"I'm sure. That's absurd—but of course you don't know her. There's no sneak in her—and anyhow, if she decides to marry him she'll tell me—or her mother—before she tells him. That's how she'd do it—" Sperling stopped abruptly and set his jaw. In a moment he let it loose and went on, "And that's what I'm afraid of, every day now. If she once commits herself it's all over. I tell you it's urgent. It's damned urgent!"

Wolfe leaned back in his chair and closed his eyes. Sperling regarded him a while, opened his mouth and closed it again, and looked at me inquiringly. I shook my head at him. When, after another couple of minutes, he began making and unmaking fists with his big bony hands, I reassured him.

"It's okay. He never sleeps in the daytime. His mind works better when he can't see me."

Finally Wolfe's lids went up and he spoke. "If you hire me," he told Sperling, "it must be clear what for. I can't engage to get proof that Mr. Rony is a Communist, but only to find out if proof exists, and, if it does, get it if possible. I'm willing to undertake that, but it seems an unnecessary restriction. Can't we define it a little better? As I understand it, you want your daughter to abandon all thought of marrying Mr. Rony and stop inviting him to your home. That's your objective. Right?"

"Yes."

"Then why restrict my strategy? Certainly I can try for proof that he's a Communist, but what if he isn't? Or what if he is but we can't prove it to your daughter's satisfaction? Why limit the operation to that one hope, which must be rather forlorn if Mr. Bascom has spent a month at it and failed? Why not hire me to reach your objective, no matter how—of course within the bounds permitted to civilized man? I would have a much clearer conscience in accepting your retainer, which will be a check for five thousand dollars."

Sperling was considering. "Damn it, he's a Communist!"

"I know. That's your fixed idea and it must be humored. I'll try that first. But do you want to exclude all else?"

"No. No, I don't."

"Good. And I have—yes, Fritz?"

The door to the hall had opened and Fritz was there. "Mr. Hewitt, sir. He says he has an appointment. I seated him in the front room."

"Yes," Wolfe glanced at the clock on the wall. "Tell him I'll see him in a few minutes." Fritz went, and Wolfe returned to Sperling.

"And I have correctly stated your objective?"

"Perfectly."

"Then after I've read Mr. Bascom's reports I'll communicate with you. Good day, sir. I'm glad you like my office—"

"But this is urgent! You shouldn't waste an hour!"

"I know." Wolfe was trying to stay polite. "That's another characteristic of matters discussed in this office—urgency. I now have an appointment, and shall then eat lunch, and from four to six I shall be working with my plants. But your affair need not wait on that. Mr Goodwin will read the reports immediately, and after lunch he will go to your office to get all required details—say two o'clock?"

James U. Sperling didn't like it at all. Apparently he was set to devote the day to arranging to save his daughter from a fate worse than death, not even stopping for meals. He was so displeased that he merely grunted an affirmative when, as I let him out the front door, I courteously reminded him that he was to expect me at his office at 2:15 and that he could save himself the trouble of mailing the check by handing it to me then. I took time out for a brief survey of the long black Wethersill limousine waiting for him at the curb before I returned to the office.

The door to the front room was open and Wolfe's and Hewitt's voices came through. Since their mutual interest was up in the plant rooms and they wouldn't be using the office, I got the bulky envelope Sperling had left on Wolfe's desk and made myself comfortable to read Bascom's reports.

2

A couple of hours later, at five to two, Wolfe returned his empty coffee cup to the saucer, pushed his chair back, got all of him upright, walked out of the dining room, and headed down the hall toward his elevator. I, having followed, called to his half an acre of back, "How about three minutes in the office first?"

He turned. "I thought you were going to see that man with a daughter."

"I am, but you won't talk business during meals, and I read Bascom's reports, and I've got questions."

He shot a glance at the door to the office, saw how far away it was, growled, "All right, come on up," and turned and made for the elevator.

If he has his rules so do I, and one of mine is that a three-by-four private elevator with Wolfe in it does not need me too, so I took the stairs. One flight up was Wolfe's bedroom and a spare. Two flights up was my bedroom and another spare. The third flight put me on the roof. There was no dazzling blaze of light, as in winter, since this was June and the shade slats were all rolled down, but there was a blaze of color from the summer bloomers, especially in the middle room. Of course I saw it every day, and I had business on my mind, but even so I slowed up as I passed a bench of white and yellow Dendrobium bensoniae that were just at their peak.

Wolfe was in the potting room, taking his coat off, with a scowl all ready for me.

"Two things," I told him curtly. "First, Bascom not only—"

He was curter. "Did Mr. Bascom get any lead at all to the Communist party?"

"No. But he—"

"Then he got nothing for us." Wolfe was rolling up his shirt sleeves. "We'll discuss his reports after I've read them. Did he have good men on it?"

"He sure did. His best."

"Then why should I hire an army to stalk the same phantom, even with Mr. Sperling's money? You know what that amounts to, trying to track a Communist down, granting that he is one—especially when what is wanted is not presumption, but proof. Bah. A will-o'-the-wisp. I defined the objective and Mr. Sperling agreed. See him and get details, yes. Get invited to his home, socially. Meet Mr. Rony and form an opinion of him. More important, form one of the daughter, as intimately and comprehensively as possible. Make appointments with her. Seize and hold her attention. You should be able to displace Mr. Rony in a week, a fortnight at the most—and that's the objective."

"I'll be damned." I shook my head reproachfully. "You mean make a pass at her."

"Your terms are yours, and I prefer mine. Mr. Sperling said his daughter is excessively curious. Transfer her curiosity from Mr. Rony to you."

"You mean break her heart."

"You can stop this side of tragedy."

"Yeah, and I can stop this side of starting." I looked righteous and outraged. "You've gone a little too far. I like being a detective, and I like being a man, with all that implies, but I refuse to degrade whatever glamour I may—"

"Archie!" He snapped it.

"Yes, sir."

"With how many young women whom you met originally through your association with my business have you established personal relationships?"

"Between five and six thousand. But that's not—"

"I'm merely suggesting that you reverse the process and establish the personal relationship first. What's wrong with that?"

"Everything," I shrugged. "Okay. Maybe nothing. It depends. I'll take a look at her."

"Good. You're going to be late." He started for the supply shelves.

I raised my voice a little. "However, I've still got a question, or two, rather. Bascom's boys had a picnic trying to tail Rony. The first time out, before anything could have happened to make him suspicious, he had his nose up and pulled a fade. From then on not only did they have to use only the best, but often even that wasn't good enough. He knew the whole book and some extra chapters. He may or may not be a Communist, but he didn't learn all that in Sunday school."

"Pfui. He's a lawyer, isn't he?" Wolfe said contemptuously. He took a can of Elgetrol from the shelf and began shaking it. "Confound it, let me alone."

"I will in a minute. The other thing, three different times, times when they didn't lose him, he went into Bischoff's Pet Shop on Third Avenue and stayed over an hour, and he doesn't keep any pets."

Wolfe stopped shaking the can of Elgetrol. He looked at it as if he didn't know what it was, hesitated, put the can back on the shelf, and looked at me.

"Oh," he said, not curtly. "He did?"

"Yes, sir."

Wolfe looked around, saw the oversized chair in its place, and went to it and sat down.

I wasn't gratified at having impressed him. In fact, I would have preferred to pass the chance up, but I hadn't dared. I remembered too well a voice—a hard, slow, precise voice, cold as last week's corpse—which I had heard only three times altogether, on the telephone. The first time had been in January 1946, and the second and third had been more than two years later, while we were looking for the poisoner of Cyril

Orchard. Furthermore, I remembered the tone of Wolfe's voice when he said to me, when we had both hung up after the second phone call, "I should have signaled you off, Archie, as soon as I recognized his voice. I tell you nothing because it is better for you to know nothing. You are to forget that you know his name. If ever, in the course of my business, I find that I am committed against him and must destroy him, I shall leave this house, find a place where I can work —and sleep and eat if there is time for it—and stay there until I have finished."

I have seen Wolfe tangle with some tough bozos in the years I've been with him, but none of them has ever had him talking like that.

Now he was sitting glaring at me as if I had put vinegar on his caviar.

"What do you know about Bischoff's Pet Shop?" he demanded.

"Nothing to speak of. I only know that last November, when Bischoff came to ask you to take on a job, you told him you were too busy and you weren't, and when he left and I started beefing you told me that you were no more eager to be committed for Arnold Zeck than against him. You didn't explain how you knew that that pet shop is a branch of Zeck's far-flung shenanigans, and I didn't ask."

"I told you once to forget that you know his name."

"Then you shouldn't have reminded me of it. Okay, I'll forget again. So I'll go down and phone Sperling that you're too busy and call it off. He hasn't—"

"No. Go and see him. You're late."

I was surprised. "But what the hell? What's wrong with my deducting? If Rony went three times in a month to that pet shop, and probably more, and stayed over an hour, and doesn't keep pets, and I deduce that he is presumably an employee or something of the man whose name I forget, what—"

"Your reasoning is quite sound. But this is different. I was aware of Mr. Bischoff's blemish, no matter how, when he came to me, and refused him. I have engaged myself to Mr. Sperling, and how can I scuttle?" He looked up at the clock. "You'd better go." He sighed.

"If it could be managed to keep one's self-esteem without paying for it . . ."

He went and got the can of Elgetrol and started shaking it, and I headed out.

3

That was two o'clock Thursday. At two o'clock Saturday, forty-eight hours later, I was standing in the warm sunshine on a slab of white marble as big as my bedroom, flicking a bright blue towel as big as my bathroom, to chase a fly off of one of Gwenn Sperling's bare legs. Not bad for a rake's progress, even though I was under an assumed name. I was now Andrew instead of Archie. When I had told Sperling of Wolfe's suggestion that I should meet the family, not of course displaying Wolfe's blueprint, and he had objected to disclosing me to Rony, I had explained that we would use hired help for tailing and similar routine, and that I would have a try at getting Rony to like me. He bought it without haggling and invited me to spend the weekend at Stony Acres, his country place up near Chappaqua, but said I'd have to use another name because he was pretty sure his wife and son and elder daughter, Madeline, knew about Archie Goodwin. I said modestly that I doubted it, and insisted on keeping the Goodwin because it was too much of a strain to keep remembering to answer to something else, and we settled for changing Archie to Andrew. That would fit the A. G. on the bag Wolfe had given me for my birthday, which I naturally wanted to have along because it was caribou hide and people should see it.

The items in Bascom's reports about Louis Rony's visits to Bischoff's Pet Shop had cost Sperling some dough. If it hadn't been for that Wolfe would certainly have let Rony slide until I reported on my weekend, since it was a piddling little job and had no interest for him except the fee, and since he had a sneaking idea that women came on a lope from every direction when I snapped my fingers, which was foolish because it often takes more than snapping your fingers. But when I got back from my call on Sperling Thursday afternoon Wolfe had already been busy on the phone, getting Saul Panzer and Fred Durkin and Orrie Cather, and when they came to the office Friday morning for briefing Saul was assigned to a survey of Rony's past, after reading Bascom, and Fred and Orrie were given special instructions for fancy tailing. Obviously what Wolfe was doing was paying for his self-esteem—or letting Sperling pay for it. He had once told Arnold Zeck, during their third and last phone talk, that when he undertook an investigation he permitted prescription of limits only by requirements of the job, and now he was leaning backward. If Rony's Pet Shop visits really meant that he was on one of Zeck's payrolls, and if Zeck was still tacking up his KEEP OFF signs, Nero Wolfe had to make it plain that no one was roping him off. We've got our pride. So Saul and Fred and Orrie were at it.

So was I, the next morning, Saturday, driving north along the winding Westchester parkways, noticing that the trees seemed to have more leaves than they knew what to do with, keeping my temper when some dope of a snail stuck to the left lane as if he had built it, doing a little snappy passing now and then just to keep my hand in, dipping down off the parkway onto a secondary road, following it a couple of miles as directed, leaving it to turn into a graveled drive between ivy-covered stone pillars, winding through a park and assorted horticultural exhibits until I broke cover and saw the big stone mansion, stopping at what looked as if it might be the right spot, and telling a middle-aged sad-looking guy in a mohair uniform that I was the photographer they were expecting.

Sperling and I had decided that I was the son of a business associate who was concentrating on photography, and who wanted pictures of Stony Acres for a corporation portfolio, for two reasons: first, because I had to be something, and second, because I wanted some good shots of Louis Rony.

Four hours later, having met everybody and had lunch and used both cameras all over the place in as professional a manner as I could manage, I was standing at the edge of the swimming pool, chasing a fly off Gwenn's leg. We were both dripping, having just climbed out.

"Hey," she said, "the snap of that towel is worse than a fly bite—if there was a fly."

I assured her there had been.

"Well, next time show it to me first and maybe I can handle it myself. Do that dive from the high board again, will you? Where's the Leica?"

She had been a pleasant surprise. From what her father had said I had expected an intellectual treat in a plain wrapper, but the package was attractive enough to take your attention off of the contents. She was not an eye-stopper, and there was no question about her freckles, and while there was certainly nothing wrong with her face it was a little rounder than I would specify if I were ordering à la carte; but she was not in any way hard to look at, and those details which had been first disclosed when she appeared in her swimming rig were completely satisfactory. I would never have seen the fly if I had not been looking where it lit.

I did the dive again and damn near pancaked. When I was back on the marble, wiping my hair back, Madeline was there, saying, "What are you trying to do, Andy, break your back? You darned fool!"

"I'm making an impression," I told her. "Have you got a trapeze anywhere? I can hang by my toes."

"Of course you can. I know your repertory better than you think I do. Come and sit down and I'll mix you a drink."

Madeline was going to be in my way a little, in case I decided to humor Wolfe by trying to work on Gwenn. She was more spectacular than Gwenn, with her slim height and just enough curves not to call anywhere flat, her smooth dark oval face, and her big dark eyes which she liked to keep half shut so she could suddenly open them on you and let you have it. I already knew that her husband was dead, having been shot down in a B-17 over Berlin in 1943, that she thought she had seen all there was but might be persuaded to try another look, that she liked the name Andy, and that she thought there was just a chance that I might know a funny story she hadn't heard. That was why she was going to be in my way a little.

I went and sat with her on a bench in the sun, but she didn't mix me a drink because three men were gathered around the refreshment cart and one of them attended to it—James U. Sperling, Junior. He was probably a year or two older than Madeline and resembled his father hardly at all. There was nothing about his slender straightness or his nice smooth tanned skin or his wide spoiled mouth that would have led anyone to say he looked like a miner. I had never seen him before but had heard a little of him. I couldn't give you a quote, but my vague memory was that he was earnest and serious about learning to make himself useful in the corporation his father headed, and he frequently beat it to Brazil or Nevada or Arizona to see how mining was done, but he got tired easy and had to return to New York to rest, and he knew lots of people in New York willing to help him rest.

The two men with him at the refreshment cart were guests. Since our objective was confined to Rony and Gwenn I hadn't bothered with the others except to be polite, and I wouldn't be dragging them in if it wasn't that later on they called for some attention. Also it was beginning to look as if they could stand a little attention right then, on account of a situation that appeared to be developing, so the field of my interest was spreading out a little. If I ever saw a woman make a pass, Mrs. Paul Emerson, Connie to her friends and enemies, was making one at Louis Rony.

First the two men. One of them was just a super, a guy some older than me named Webster Kane. I had gathered that he was some kind of an economist who had done some kind of a job for Continental

Mines Corporation, and he acted like an old friend of the family. He had a big well-shaped head and apparently didn't own a hairbrush, didn't care what his clothes looked like, and was not swimming but was drinking. In another ten years he could pass for a senator.

I had welcomed the opportunity for a close-up of the other man because I had often heard Wolfe slice him up and feed him to the cat. At six-thirty P.M. on WPIT, five days a week, Paul Emerson, sponsored by Continental Mines Corporation, interpreted the news. About once a week Wolfe listened to him, but seldom to the end; and when, after jabbing the button on his desk that cut the circuit, Wolfe tried some new expressions and phrases for conveying his opinion of the performance and the performer, no interpreter was needed to clarify it. The basic idea was that Paul Emerson would have been more at home in Hitler's Germany or Franco's Spain. So I was glad of a chance to take a slant at him, but it didn't get me much because he confused me by looking exactly like my chemistry teacher in high school out in Ohio, who had always given me better marks than I had earned. Also it was a safe bet that he had ulcers—I mean Paul Emerson—and he was drinking plain soda with only one piece of ice. In swimming trunks he was really pitiful, and I had taken some pictures of him from the most effective angles to please Wolfe with.

It was Emerson's wife, Connie, who seemed to be heading for a situation that might possibly have a bearing on our objective as defined by Wolfe. She couldn't have had more than four or five years to dawdle away until her life began at forty, and was therefore past my deadline, but it was by no means silly of her to assume that it was still okay for her to go swimming in mixed company in broad daylight. She was one of those rare blondes that take a good tan, and had better legs and arms, judged objectively, than either Gwenn or Madeline, and even from the other side of the wide pool the blue of her eyes carried clear and strong. That's where she was at the moment, across the pool, sitting with Louis Rony, getting her breath after showing him a double knee lock that had finally put him flat, and he was no matchstick. It was a new technique for making a pass at a man, but it had obvious advantages, and anyway she had plenty of other ideas and wasn't being stingy with them. At lunch she had buttered rolls for him. Now I ask you.

I didn't get it. If Gwenn was stewing about it she was keeping it well hid, though I had noticed her casting a few quick glances. There was a chance that she was counterattacking by pretending she would rather help me take pictures than eat, and that she loved to watch me dive, but who was I to suspect a fine freckled girl of pretending? Madeline had made a couple of cracks about Connie's routine, without any sign that she really cared a damn. As for Paul Emerson, the husband, the sour look on his undistinguished map when his glance took in his wife and her playmate didn't seem to mean much, since it stayed sour no matter where he was glancing.

Louis Rony was the puzzle, though. The assumption was that he was making an all-out play for Gwenn, either because he was in love with her or because he wanted something that went with her; and if so, why the monkeyshines with the mature and beautifully tanned blonde? Was he merely trying to give Gwenn a nudge? I had of course done a survey on him, including the contrast between his square-jawed rugged phiz and the indications that the race of fat and muscle would be a tie in another couple of years, but I wasn't ready for a final vote. From my research on him, which hadn't stopped with Bascom's reports, I knew all about his record as a sensational defender of pickpockets, racketeers, pluggers, fences, and on down the line, but I was holding back on whether he was a candidate for the throne Abe Hummel had once sat on, or a Commie trying out a new formula for raising a stink, or a lieutenant, maybe even better, in one of Arnold Zeck's field divisions, or merely a misguided sucker for guys on hot spots.

However, the immediate puzzle about him was more specific. The question for the moment wasn't what did he expect to accomplish with Connie Emerson, or what kind of fuel did he have in his gas tank, but what was all the fuss about the waterproof wallet, or bag, on the inside of his swimming trunks? I had seen him give it his attention, not ostentatiously, four times altogether; and by now my curiosity had really got acute, for the fourth time, right after the knee-lock episode with Connie, he had gone so far as to pull it out for a look and stuff it back in again. My eyes were still as good as ever, and there was no doubt about what it was.

Naturally, I did not approve of it. At a public beach, or even at a private beach or pool where there is a crowd of strangers and he changes with other males in a common room, a man has a right to guard something valuable by putting it into a waterproof container and keeping it next to his hide, and he may even be a sap if he doesn't. But Rony, being a house guest like the rest of us, had changed in his own room, which wasn't far from mine on the second floor. It is not nice to be suspicious of your hosts or fellow guests, and even if you think you ought to be there must have been at least a dozen first-class hiding places in Rony's room for an object small enough to go in that thing he kept worrying about. It was an insult to everybody, including me. It was true that he kept his worry so inconspicuous that apparently no one else noticed it, but he had no right to take such a risk of hurting our feelings, and I resented it and intended to do something about it.

Madeline's fingers touched my arm. I finished a sip of my Tom Collins and turned my head.

"Yeah?"

"Yeah what?" she smiled, opening her eyes.

"You touched me."

"No, did I? Nothing."

It was evidently meant as a teaser, but I was watching Gwenn poise for a back flip, and anyway there was an interruption. Paul Emerson had wandered over and now growled down at me.

"I forgot to mention it, Goodwin, I don't want any pictures unless they have my okay—I mean for publication."

I tilted my head back. "You mean any at all, or just of you?"

"I mean of me. Please don't forget that."

"Sure. I don't blame you."

When he had made it to the edge of the pool and fallen in, presumably on purpose, Madeline spoke.

"Do you think a comparative stranger like you ought to take swipes at a famous character like him?"

"I certainly do. You shouldn't be surprised, if you know my repertory so well. What was that crack, anyhow?"

"Oh—when we go in I guess I'll have to show you something. I should control my tongue better."

On the other side Rony and Connie Emerson had got their breath back and were making a dash for the pool. Jimmy Sperling, whom I preferred to think of as Junior, called to ask if I could use a refill, and Webster Kane said he would attend to it. Gwenn stopped before me, dripping again, to say that the light would soon be right for the west terrace and we ought to put on some clothes, and didn't I agree with her?

It was one of the most congenial jobs of detecting I had had in a long while, and there wouldn't have been a cloud in sight if it hadn't been for that damn waterproof wallet or bag that Rony was so anxious about. That called for a little work, but it would have to wait.

4

Hours later, in my room on the second floor, which had three big windows, two three-quarter beds, and the kind of furniture and rugs I will never own but am perfectly willing to use as a transient without complaining, I got clean and neat for dinner. Then I retrieved my keys from where I had hid them behind a book on a shelf, took my medicine case from the caribou bag, and unlocked it. This was a totally different thing from Rony's exhibition of bad manners, since I was there on business, and the nature of my business required me to carry various unusual items in what I called my medicine case. All I took from it was a tiny, round, soft light brown object, which I placed tenderly in the little inner coin pocket inside the side pocket of my jacket. I handled it with tweezers because it was so quick to dissolve that even the moisture of my fingers might weaken it. I relocked the medicine case and returned it to the bag.

There was a knock on my door and I said come in. It opened and Madeline entered and advanced, enveloped in a thin white film of folds that started at her breasts and stopped only at her ankles. It made her face smaller and her eyes bigger.

"How do you like my dress, Archie?" she asked.

"Yep. You may not call that formal, but it certainly —" I stopped. I looked at her. "I thought you said you liked the name Andy. No?"

"I like Archie even better."

"Then I'd better change over. When did Father confide in you?"

"He didn't." She opened her eyes. "You think I think I'm sophisticated and just simply impenetrable, don't you? Maybe I am, but I wasn't always. Come along, I want to show you something." She turned and started off.

I followed her out and walked beside her along the wide hall, across a landing, and down another hall into another wing. The room she took me into, through a door that was standing open, was twice as big as mine, which I had thought was plenty big enough, and in addition to the outdoor summer smell that came in the open windows it had the fragrance of enormous vases of roses that were placed around. I would just as soon have taken a moment to glance around at details, but she took me across to a table, opened a bulky leather-bound portfolio as big as an atlas to a page where there was a marker, and pointed.

"See? When I was young and gay!"

I recognized it instantly because I had one like it at home. It was a clipping from the *Gazette* of September ninth, 1940. I have not had my picture in the paper as often as Churchill or Rocky Graziano, or even Nero Wolfe, but that time it happened that I had been lucky and shot an automatic out of a man's hand just before he pressed the trigger.

I nodded. "A born hero if I ever saw one."

She nodded back. "I was seventeen. I had a crush on you for nearly a month."

"No wonder. Have you been showing this around?"

"I have not! Damn it, you ought to be touched!"

"Hell, I am touched, but not as much as I was an hour ago. I thought you liked my nose or the hair on my chest or something, and here it was only a childhood memory."

"What if I feel it coming back?"

"Don't try to sweeten it. Anyway, now I have a problem. Who else might possibly remember this picture—and there have been a couple of others—besides you?"

She considered. "Gwenn might, but I doubt it, and I don't think anyone else would. If you have a problem, I have a question. What are you here for? Louis Rony?"

It was my turn to consider, and I let her have a poker smile while I was at it.

"That's it," she said.

"Or it isn't. What if it is?"

She came close enough to take hold of my lapels with both hands, and her eyes were certainly big. "Listen, you born hero," she said earnestly. "No matter what I might feel coming back or what I don't, you be careful where you head in on anything about my sister. She's twenty-two. When I was her age I was already pretty well messed up, and she's still as clean as a rose—my God, I don't mean a rose, you know what I mean. I agree with my dad about Louis Rony, but it all depends on how it's done. Maybe the only way not to hurt her too much is to shoot him. I don't really know what he is to her. I'm just telling you that what matters isn't Dad or Mother or me or Rony, but it's my sister, and you'd better believe me."

It was the combination of circumstances. She was so close, and the smell of roses was so strong, and she was so damned earnest after dallying around with me all afternoon, that it was really automatic. When, after a minute or two, she pushed at me, I let her go, reached for the portfolio and closed it, and took it to a tier of shelves and put it on the lowest one. When I got back to her she looked a little flushed but not too overcome to speak.

"You darned fool," she said, and had to clear her throat. "Look at my dress now!" She ran her fingers down through the folds. "We'd better go down."

As I went with her down the wide stairs to the reception hall it occurred to me that I was getting my wires crossed. I seemed to have a fair start on establishing a personal relationship, but not with the right person.

We ate on the west terrace, where the setting sun, coming over the tops of the trees beyond the lawn, was hitting the side of the house just above our heads as we sat down. By that time Mrs. Sperling was the only one who was calling me Mr. Goodwin. She had me at her right, probably to emphasize my importance as the son of a business associate of the Chairman of the Board, and I still didn't know whether she knew I was in disguise. It was her that Junior resembled, especially the wide mouth, though she had filled in a little. She seemed to have her department fairly under control, and the looks and manners of the help indicated that they had been around quite a while and intended to stay.

After dinner we loafed around the terrace until it was about dark and then went inside, all but Gwenn and Rony, who wandered off across the lawn. Webster Kane and Mrs. Sperling said they wanted to listen to a broadcast, or maybe it was video. I was invited to partake of bridge, but said I had a date with Sperling to discuss photography plans for tomorrow, which was true. He led me to a part of the house I hadn't seen yet, into a big high-ceilinged room with four thousand books around the walls, a stock ticker, and a desk with five phones on it among other things, gave me a fourth or fifth chance to refuse a cigar, invited me to sit, and asked what I wanted. His tone was not that of a host to a guest, but of a senior executive to one not yet a junior executive by a long shot. I arranged my tone to fit.

"Your daughter Madeline knows who I am. She saw a picture of me once and seems to have a good memory."

He nodded. "She has. Does it matter?"

"Not if she keeps it to herself, and I think she will, but I thought you ought to know. You can decide whether you had better mention it to her."

"I don't think so. I'll see." He was frowning, but not at me. "How is it with Rony?"

"Oh, we're on speaking terms. He's been pretty busy. The reason I asked to see you is something else. I notice there are keys for the guest-room doors, and I approve of it, but I got careless and dropped mine in the swimming pool, and I haven't got an assortment with me. When I go to bed I'll want to lock my door because I'm nervous, so if you have a master key will you kindly lend it to me?"

There was nothing slow about him. He was already smiling before I finished. Then he shook his head. "I don't think so. There are certain standards—oh, to hell with standards. But he is here as my daughter's guest, with my permission, and I think I would prefer not to open his door for you. What reason have you—"

"I was speaking of my door, not someone else's. I resent your insinuation, and I'm going to tell my father, who owns stock in the corporation, and he'll resent it too. Can I help it if I'm nervous?"

He started to smile, then thought it deserved better than that, and his head went back for a roar of laughter. I waited patiently. When he had done me justice he got up and went to the door of a big wall safe, twirled the knob back and forth, and swung the door open, pulled a drawer out and fingered its contents, and crossed to me with a tagged key in his hand.

"You can also shove your bed against the door," he suggested.

I took the key. "Yes, sir, thank you, I will," I told him and departed.

When I returned to the living room, which was about the size of a tennis court, I found that the bridge game had not got started. Gwenn and Rony had rejoined the party. With a radio going, they were dancing in a space by the doors leading to the terrace, and Jimmy Sperling was dancing with Connie Emerson. Madeline was at the piano, concentrating on trying to accompany the radio, and Paul Emerson was standing by, looking down at her flying fingers with his face sourer than ever. At the end of dinner he had taken three kinds of pills, and perhaps had picked the wrong ones. I went and asked Madeline to dance, and it took only a dozen steps to know how good she was. Still more relationship.

A little later Mrs. Sperling came in, and she was soon followed by Sperling and Webster Kane. Before long the dancing stopped, and someone mentioned bed, and it began to look as if there would be no chance to dispose of the little brown capsule I had got from my medicine case. Some of them had patronized the well-furnished bar on wheels which had been placed near a long table back of a couch, but not Rony, and I had about decided that I was out of luck when Webster Kane got enthusiastic about nightcaps and started a selling campaign. I made mine bourbon and water because that was what Rony had shown a preference for during the afternoon, and the prospect brightened when I saw Rony let Jimmy Sperling hand him one. It went as smooth as if I had written the script. Rony took a swallow and then put his glass on the table when Connie Emerson wanted both his hands to show him a rumba step. I took a swallow from mine to make it the same level as his, got the capsule from my pocket and dropped it in, made my way casually to the table, put my glass down by Rony's in order to have my hands for getting out a cigarette and lighting it, and picked the glass up again, but the wrong one—or I should say the right one. There wasn't a chance the maneuver had been observed, and it couldn't have been neater.

But there my luck ended. When Connie let him go Rony went to the table and retrieved his glass, but the damn fool didn't drink. He just held on to it. After a while I tried to prime him by sauntering over to where he was talking with Gwenn and Connie, joining in, taking healthy swallows from my glass, and even making a comment on the bourbon, but he didn't lift it for a sip. The damn camel. I wanted to ask Connie to get a knee lock on him so I could pour it down his throat. Two or three of them were saying good night and leaving, and I turned around to be polite. When I turned back again Rony had stepped to the bar to put his glass down, and when he moved away there were no glasses there but empty ones. Had he suddenly gulped it down? He hadn't. I went to put my glass down, reached across for a pretzel, and lowered my head enough to get a good whiff of the contents of the ice bucket. He had dumped it in there.

I guess I told people good night; anyway I got up to my room. Naturally I was sore at myself for having bungled it, and while I undressed I went back over it carefully. It was a cinch he hadn't seen me switch the glasses, with his back turned and no mirror he could have caught it in. Neither had Connie, for her view had been blocked by him and she only came up to his chin. I went over it again and decided no one could have seen me, but I was glad Nero Wolfe wasn't there to explain it to. In any case, I concluded in the middle of a deep yawn, I wouldn't be using Sperling's master key. Whatever reason Rony might have had for ditching the drink, he sure had ditched it, which meant he was not only undoped but also alerted . . . and therefore . . . therefore something, but what . . . therefore . . . the thought was important and it was petering out on me. . . .

I reached for my pajama top but had to stop to yawn, and that made me furious because I had no right to yawn when I had just fumbled on a simple little thing like doping a guy . . . only I didn't feel furious at all . . . I just felt awful damn sleepy. . . .

I remember saying to myself aloud through gritted teeth, *"You're doped you goddam dope and you get that door locked,"* but I don't remember locking it. I know I did, because it was locked in the morning.

5

All day Sunday was a nightmare. It rained off and on all day. I dragged myself out of bed at ten o'clock with a head as big as a barrel stuffed with wet feathers, and five hours later it was still the size of a keg and the inside was still swampy. Gwenn was keeping after me to take interiors with flashbulbs, and I had to deliver. Strong black coffee didn't seem to help, and food was my worst enemy. Sperling thought I had a hangover, and he certainly didn't smile when I returned the master key and refused to report events if any. Madeline thought there was something funny about it, but the word funny has different meanings at different times. There was one thing, when I got roped in for bridge I seemed to be clairvoyant and there was no stopping me. Jimmy suspected I was a shark but tried to conceal it. About the worst was when Webster Kane decided I was in exactly the right condition to start a course in economics and devoted an hour to the first lesson.

I was certainly in no shape to make any headway in simple fractions, let alone economics or establishing a relationship with a girl like Gwenn. Or Madeline either. Sometime during the afternoon Madeline got me alone and started to open me up for a look at my intentions and plans—or rather, Wolfe's—regarding her sister, and I did my best to keep from snarling under the strain. She was willing to reciprocate, and I collected a few items about the family and guests without really caring a damn. The only one who was dead set against Rony was Sperling himself. Mrs. Sperling and Jimmy, the brother, had liked him at first, then had switched more or less to Sperling's viewpoint, and later, about a month ago, had switched again and taken the attitude that it was up to Gwenn. That was when Rony had been allowed to darken the door again. As for the guests, Connie Emerson had apparently decided to solve the problem by getting Rony's mind off of Gwenn and onto someone else, namely her; Emerson seemed to be neither more nor less sour on Rony than on most of his other fellow creatures; and Webster Kane was judicious. Kane's attitude, of some importance because of his position as a friend of the family, was that he didn't care for Rony personally but that a mere suspicion didn't condemn him. He had had a hot argument with Sperling about it.

Some of the stuff Madeline told me might have been useful in trying to figure who doped Rony's drink if I had been in any condition to use it, but I wasn't. I would have made myself scarce long before the day was done but for one thing. I intended to get even, or at least make a stab at it.

As for the doping, I had entered a plea of not guilty, held the trial, and acquitted myself. The possibility that I had taken my own dope was ruled out; I had made that switch clean. And Rony had not seen the switch or been told of it; I was standing pat on that. Therefore Rony's drink had been doped by someone else, and he had either known it or suspected it. It would have been interesting to know who had done it, but there were too many nominations. Webster Kane had been mixing, helped by Connie and Madeline, and Jimmy had delivered Rony's drink to him. Not only that, after Rony had put it down on the table I had by no means had my eyes fixed on it while I was making my way across. So while Rony might have a name for the supplier of the dose I had guzzled, to me he was just X.

That, however, was not what had me hanging on. To hell with X, at least for the present. What had me setting my jaw and bidding four spades, or trotting around after Gwenn with two cameras and my pockets bulging with flashbulbs, when I should have been home in bed, was a picture I would never forget: Louis Rony pouring into a bucket the drink I had doped for him, while I stood and gulped the last drop of the drink someone else had doped for him. He would pay for that or I would never look Nero Wolfe in the face again.

Circumstances seemed favorable. I collected the information cautiously and without jostling. Rony had come by train Friday evening and been met at the station by Gwenn, and had to return to town this evening, Sunday; and no one was driving in. Paul and Connie Emerson were house guests at Stony Acres for a week; Webster Kane was there for an indefinite period, preparing some economic something for the corporation; Mom and the girls were there for the summer; and Sperling Senior and Junior would certainly not go to town Sunday evening. But I would, waiting until late to miss the worst of the traffic, and surely Rony would prefer a comfortable roomy car to a crowded train.

I didn't ask him. Instead, I made the suggestion, casually, to Gwenn. Later I made it pointedly to Madeline, and she agreed to drop a word in if the occasion offered. Then I got into the library alone with Sperling, suggested it to him even more pointedly, asked him which phone I could use for a New York call, and told him the call was not for him to hear. He was a little difficult about it, which I admit he had a right to be, but by that time I could make whole sentences again and I managed to sell him. He left and closed the door behind him, and I got Saul Panzer at his home in Brooklyn and talked to him all of twenty minutes. With my head still soggy, I had to go over it twice to be sure not to leave any gaps.

That was around six o'clock, which meant I had four more hours to suffer, since I had picked ten for the time of departure and was now committed to it, but it wasn't so bad. A little later the clouds began to sail around and you could tell them apart, and the sun even took a look at us just before it dropped over the edge; and what was more important, I risked a couple of nibbles at a chicken sandwich and before I was through the sandwich was too, and also a piece of cherry pie and a glass of milk. Mrs. Sperling patted me on the back and Madeline said that now she would be able to get some sleep.

It was six minutes past ten when I slid behind the wheel of the convertible, asked Rony if he had remembered his toothbrush, and rolled along the plaza into the curve of the drive.

"What's this," he asked, "a forty-eight?"

"No," I said, "forty-nine."

He let his head go back to the cushion and shut his eyes.

There were enough openings among the clouds to show some stars but no moon. We wound along the drive, reached the stone pillars, and eased out onto the public road. It was narrow, with an asphalt surface that wouldn't have been hurt by a little dressing, and for the first mile we had it to ourselves, which suited me fine. Just beyond a sharp turn the shoulder widened at a spot where there was an old shed at the edge of thick woods, and there at the roadside, headed the way we were going, a car was parked. I was going slow on account of the turn, and a woman darted out and blinked a flashlight, and I braked to a stop. As I did so the woman called, "Got a jack, mister?" and a man's voice came, "My jack's broke, you got one?"

I twisted in the seat to back off the road onto the grass. Rony muttered at me, "What the hell," and I muttered back, "Brotherhood of man." As the man and woman came toward us I got out and told Rony, "Sorry, but I guess you'll have to move; the jack's under the seat." The woman, saying something about what nice people we were, was on his side and opened the door for him, and he climbed out. He went out backwards, facing me, and just as he was clear something slammed against the side of my head and I sank to the ground, but the grass was thick and soft. I stayed down and listened. It was only a few seconds before I heard my name.

"Okay, Archie."

I got to my feet, reached in the car to turn off the engine and lights, and circled around the hood to the other side, away from the road. Louis Rony was stretched out flat on his back. I didn't waste time checking on him, knowing that Ruth Brady could give lectures on the scientific use of a persuader, and anyhow she was kneeling at his head with her flashlight.

"Sorry to break into your Sunday evening, Ruth darling."

"Nuts to you, Archie my pet. Don't stand talking. I don't like this, out here in the wilderness."

"Neither do I. Don't let him possum."

"Don't worry. I've got a blade of grass up his nose."

"Good. If he wiggles tap him again." I turned to Saul Panzer, who had his shirt sleeves rolled up. "How are the wife and children?"

"Wonderful."

"Give 'em my love. You'd better be busy the other side of the car, in case of traffic."

He moved as instructed and I went to my knees beside Ruth. I expected to find it on him, since it wouldn't have been sensible for him to take such pains with it when he went swimming and then carelessly pack it in his bag, which had been brought down by one of the help. And I did find it on him. It was not in a waterproof container but in a cellophane envelope, in the innermost compartment of his alligator-skin wallet. I knew that must be it, because nothing else on him was out of the ordinary, and because its nature was such that I knelt there and goggled, with Ruth's flashlight focused on it.

"The surprise is wasted on me," she said scornfully. "I'm on. It's yours and you had to get it back. Comrade!"

"Shut up." I was a little annoyed. I removed it from the cellophane cover and inspected it some more, but there was nothing tricky about it. It was merely what it was, a membership card in the American Communist party, Number 128-394, and the name on it was William Reynolds. What annoyed me was that it was so darned pat. Our client had insisted that Rony was a Commie, and the minute I do a little personal research on him, here's his membership card! Of course the name meant nothing. I didn't like it. It's an anti-climax to have to tell a client he was dead right in the first place.

"What do they call you, Bill or Willie?" Ruth asked.

"Hold this," I told her, and gave her the card. I got the key and opened up the car trunk, hauled out the big suitcase, and got the big camera and some bulbs. Saul came to help. Ruth was making comments which we ignored. I took three pictures of that card, once held in Saul's hand, once propped up on the suitcase, and once leaning against Rony's ear. Then I slipped it back in the cellophane cover and replaced it in the wallet, and put the wallet where I found it, in Rony's breast pocket.

One operation remained, but it took less time because I had more experience at taking wax impressions of keys than at photography. The wax was in the medicine case, and the keys, eight of them, were in Rony's fold. There was no need to label the impressions, since I didn't know which key was for what anyway. I took all eight, not wanting to skimp.

"He can't last much longer," Ruth announced.

"He don't need to." I shoved a roll of bills at Saul, who had put the suitcase back in the trunk. "This came out of his wallet. I don't know how much it is and don't care, but I don't want it on me. Buy Ruth a string of pearls or give it to the Red Cross. You'd better get going, huh?"

They lost no time. Saul and I understand each other so well that all he said was, "Phone in?" and I said, "Yeah." The next minute they were off. As soon as their car was around the next bend I circled to the other side of the convertible, next the road, stretched out on the grass, and started groaning. When nothing happened I quit after a while. Just as my weight was bringing the wet in the ground through the grass and on through my clothes, and I was about to shift, a noise came from Rony's side and I let out a groan. I got onto my knees, muttered an expressive word or two, groaned again, reached for the handle of the door and pulled myself to my feet, reached inside and turned on the lights, and saw Rony sitting on the grass inspecting his wallet.

"Hell, you're alive," I muttered.

He said nothing.

"The bastards," I muttered.

He said nothing. It took him two more minutes to decide to try to stand up.

I admit that an hour and fifty minutes later, when I drove away from the curb in front of his apartment on Thirty-seventh Street after letting him out, I was totally in the dark about his opinion of me. He hadn't said more than fifty words all the way, leaving it to me to decide whether we should stop at a State Police barracks to report our misfortune, which I did, knowing that Saul and Ruth were safely out of the county; but I couldn't expect the guy to be very talkative when he was busy recovering after an expert operation by Ruth Brady. I couldn't make up my mind whether he had been sitting beside me in silent sympathy with a fellow sufferer or had merely decided that the time for dealing with me would have to come later, after his brain had got back to something like normal.

The clock on the dash said 1:12 as I turned into the garage on Eleventh Avenue. Taking the caribou bag, but leaving the other stuff in the trunk, I didn't feel too bad as I rounded the corner into Thirty-fifth Street and headed for our stoop. I was a lot better prepared to face Wolfe than I had been all day, and my head was now clear and comfortable. The weekend hadn't been a washout after all, except that I was coming home hungry, and as I mounted the stoop I was looking forward to a session in the kitchen, knowing what to expect in the refrigerator kept stocked by Wolfe and Fritz Brenner.

I inserted the key and turned the knob, but the door would open only two inches. That surprised me, since when I am out and expected home it is not customary for Fritz or Wolfe to put on the chain bolt except on special occasions. I pushed the button, and in a moment the stoop light went on and Fritz's voice came through the crack.

"That you, Archie?"

That was odd too, since through the one-way glass

panel he had a good view of me. But I humored him and told him it really was me, and he let me in. After I crossed the threshold he shut the door and replaced the bolt, and then I had a third surprise. It was past Wolfe's bedtime, but there he was in the door to the office, glowering at me.

I told him good evening. "Quite a reception I get," I added. "Why the barricade? Someone been trying to swipe an orchid?" I turned to Fritz. "I'm so damned hungry I could even eat your cooking." I started for the kitchen, but Wolfe's voice stopped me.

"Come in here," he commanded. "Fritz, will you bring in a tray?"

Another oddity. I followed him into the office. As I was soon to learn, he had news that he would have waited up all night to tell me, but something I had said had pushed it aside for the moment. No concern at all, not even life or death, could be permitted to shove itself ahead of food. As he lowered himself into the chair behind his desk he demanded, "Why are you so hungry? Doesn't Mr. Sperling feed his guests?"

"Sure." I sat. "There's nothing wrong with the grub, but they put something in the drinks that takes your appetite. It's a long story. Want to hear it tonight?"

"No." He looked at the clock. "But I must. Go ahead."

I obliged. I was still getting the characters introduced when Fritz came with the tray, and I bit into a sturgeon sandwich and went on. I could tell from Wolfe's expression that for some reason anything and everything would be welcome, and I let him have it all. By the time I finished it was after two o'clock, the tray had been cleaned up except for a little milk in the pitcher, and Wolfe knew all that I knew, leaving out a few little personal details.

I emptied the pitcher into the glass. "So I guess Sperling's hunch was good and he really is a Commie. With a picture of the card and the assortment I got of Rony, I should think you could get that lined up by that character who has appeared as Mr. Jones on our expense list now and then. He may not actually be Uncle Joe's nephew, but he seems to be at least a deputy in the Union Square Politburo. Can't you get him to research it?"

Fritz had brought another tray, with beer, and Wolfe poured the last of the second bottle.

"I could, yes." He drank and put the glass down. "But it would be a waste of Mr. Sperling's money. Even if that is Mr. Rony's card and he is a party member, as he well may be, I suspect that it is merely a masquerade." He wiped his lips. "I have no complaint of your performance, Archie, which was in character, and I should know your character; and I can't say you transgressed your instructions, since you had a free hand, but you might have phoned before assuming the risks of banditry."

"Really." I was sarcastic. "Excuse me, but since when have you invited constant contact on a little job like tripping up a would-be bridegroom?"

"I haven't. But you were aware that another factor had entered, or at least been admitted as conjecture. It is no longer conjecture. You didn't phone me, but someone else did. A man—a voice you are acquainted with. So am I."

"You mean Arnold Zeck?"

"No name was pronounced. But it was that voice. As you know, it is unmistakable."

"What did he have to say?"

"Neither was Mr. Rony's name pronounced, nor Mr. Sperling's. But he left no room for dubiety. In effect I was told to cease forthwith any inquiry into the activities or interests of Mr. Rony or suffer penalties."

"What did you have to say?"

"I—demurred." Wolfe tried to pour beer, found the bottle was empty, and set it down. "His tone was more peremptory than it was the last time I heard it, and I didn't fully conceal my resentment. I stated my position in fairly strong terms. He ended with an ultimatum. He gave me twenty-four hours to recall you from your week end."

"He knew I was up there?"

"Yes."

"I'll be damned." I let out a whistle. "This Rony boy is really something. A party member *and* one of Mr. Z.'s little helpers—which isn't such a surprising combination, at that. And not only have I laid hands on him, but Saul and Ruth have too. Goddam it! I'll have to—when did this phone call come?"

"Yesterday afternoon—" Wolfe glanced up at the clock. "Saturday, at ten minutes past six."

"Then his ultimatum expired eight hours ago and we're still breathing. Even so, it wouldn't have hurt to get time out for changing our signals. Why didn't you phone me and I could—"

"Shut up!"

I lifted the brows. "Why?"

"Because even if we are poltroons cowering in a corner, we might have the grace not to talk like it! I reproach you for not phoning. You reproach me for not phoning. It is only common prudence to keep the door bolted, but there is no possible—"

That may not have been his last syllable, but if he got one more in I didn't hear it. I have heard a lot of different noises here and there, and possibly one or two as loud as the one that interrupted Wolfe and made me jump out of my chair halfway across the room, but nothing much like it. To reproduce it you could take a hundred cops, scatter them along the block you live in, and have them start unanimously shooting windows with forty-fives.

Then complete silence.

Wolfe said something.

I grabbed a gun from a drawer, ran to the hall, flipped the switch for the stoop light, removed the chain bolt, opened the door, and stepped out. Across the street to the left two windows went up, and voices came and heads poked out, but the street was deserted. Then I saw that I wasn't standing on the stone of the stoop but on a piece of glass, and if I didn't like that piece there were plenty of others. They were all over the stoop, the steps, the areaway, and the sidewalk. I looked straight up, and another piece came flying down, missed me by a good inch, and crashed and tinkled at my feet. I backed across the sill, shut the door, and turned to face Wolfe, who was standing in the hall looking bewildered.

"He took it out on the orchids," I stated. "You stay here. I'll go up and look."

As I went up the stairs three at a time I heard the sound of the elevator. He must have moved fast. Fritz was behind me but couldn't keep up. The top landing, which was walled with concrete tile and plastered, was intact. I flipped the light switch and opened the door to the first plant room, the warm room, but I stopped after one step in because there was no light. I stood for five seconds, waiting for my eyes to adjust, and by then Wolfe and Fritz were behind me.

"Let me get by," Wolfe growled like a dog ready to spring.

"No." I pushed back against him. "You'll scalp yourself or cut your throat. Wait here till I get a light."

He bellowed past my shoulder. "Theodore! *Theodore!*"

A voice came from the dim starlit ruins. "Yes, sir! What happened?"

"Are you all right?"

"No, sir! What—"

"Are you hurt?"

"No, I'm not hurt, but what happened?"

I saw movement in the direction of the corner where Theodore's room was, and a sound came of glass falling and breaking.

"You got a light?" I called.

"No, the doggone lights are all—"

"Then stay still, damn it, while I get a light."

"Stand still!" Wolfe roared.

I beat it down to the office. By the time I got back up again there were noises from windows across the street, and also from down below. We ignored them. The sight disclosed by the flashlights was enough to make us ignore anything. Of a thousand panes of glass and ten thousand orchid plants some were in fact still whole, as we learned later, but it certainly didn't look like it that first survey. Even with the lights, moving around through that jungle of jagged glass hanging down and protruding from plants and benches and underfoot wasn't really fun, but Wolfe had to see and so did Theodore, who was okay physically but got so damn mad I thought he was going to choke.

Finally Wolfe got to where a dozen Odontoglossum harryanum, his current pride and joy, were kept. He moved the light back and forth over the gashed and fallen stems and leaves and clusters, with fragments of glass everywhere, turned, and said quietly, "We might as well go downstairs."

"The sun will be up in two hours," Theodore said through his teeth.

"I know. We need men."

When we got to the office we phoned Lewis Hewitt and G. M. Hoag for help before we called the police. Anyway, by that time a prowl car had come.

6

Six hours later I pushed my chair back from the dining table, stretched all the way, and allowed myself a good thorough yawn without any apology, feeling that I had earned it. Ordinarily I have my breakfast in the kitchen with Fritz, and Wolfe has his in his room, but that day wasn't exactly ordinary.

A gang of fourteen men, not counting Theodore, was up on the roof cleaning up and salvaging, and an army of glaziers was due at noon. Andy Krasicki had come in from Long Island and was in charge. The street was roped off because of the danger from falling glass. The cops were still nosing around out in front and across the street, and presumably in other quarters too, but none was left in our house except Captain Murdoch, who, with Wolfe, was seated at the table I was just leaving, eating griddlecakes and honey.

They knew all about it, back to a certain point. The people who lived in the house directly across the street were away for the summer. On its roof they had found a hundred and ninety-two shells from an SM and a tommy gun, and they still had scientists up there collecting clues to support the theory that that was where the assault had come from, in case the lawyer for the defense should claim that the shells had been dropped by pigeons. Not that there was yet any call for a lawyer for the defense, since there were no defendants. So far there was no word as to how they had got to the roof of the unoccupied house. All they knew was that persons unknown had somehow got to that roof and from it, at 2:24 A.M., had shot hell out of our plant rooms, and had made a getaway through a passage into Thirty-sixth Street, and I could have told them that much without ever leaving our premises.

I admit we weren't much help. Wolfe didn't even mention the name of Sperling or Rony, let alone anything beginning with Z. He refused to offer a specific guess at the identity of the perpetrators, and it wasn't too hard to get them to accept that as the best to be had, since it was quite probable that there were several inhabitants of the metropolitan area who would love to make holes not only in Wolfe's plant rooms but in Wolfe himself. Even so, they insisted that some must be more likely to own tommy guns and more willing to use them in such a direct manner, but Wolfe said that was irrelevant because the gunners had almost certainly been hired on a piece-work basis.

I left the breakfast table as soon as I was through because there were a lot of phone calls to make—to slat manufacturers, hardware stores, painters, supply houses, and others. I was at it when Captain Murdoch left and Wolfe took the elevator to the roof, and still at it when Wolfe came down again, trudged into the office, got himself lowered into his chair, leaned back, and heaved a deep sigh.

I glanced at him. "You'd better go up and take a

nap. And I'll tell you something. I can be just as stubborn as you can, and courage and valor and spunk are very fine things and I'm all for them, but I'm also a fairly good bookkeeper. If this keeps up, as I suppose it will, the balance sheet will be a lulu. I have met Gwenn socially and therefore might be expected to grit my teeth and stick; but you haven't, and all you need to do is return his retainer. What I want to say is that if you do I promise never to ride you about it. Never. Want me to get the Bible?"

"No." His eyes were half closed. "Is everything arranged for the repairs and replacements?"

"As well as it can be now."

"Then call that place and speak to the elder daughter."

I was startled. "Why her? What reason have you—"

"Pfui. You thought you concealed the direction your interest took—your personal interest—but you didn't. I know you too well. Call her and learn if all the family is there—all except the son, who probably doesn't matter. If they are, tell her we'll be there in two hours and want to see them."

"We?"

"Yes. You and I."

I got at the phone. He was not really smashing a precedent. It was true that he had an unbreakable rule not to stir from his office to see anyone on business, but what had happened that night had taken this out of the category of business and listed it under struggle for survival.

One of the help answered, and I gave my name and asked for Miss Madeline Sperling. Her husband's name had been Pendleton, but she had tossed it in the discard. My idea was to keep to essentials, but she had to make it a conversation. Rony had called Gwenn only half an hour ago and told her about the holdup, and of course Madeline wanted it all over again from me. I had to oblige. She thought she was worried about my head, and I had to assure her there were no bad cracks in it from the bandit's blow. When I finally got her onto the subject at hand, though, and she knew from the way I put it that this was strictly business and deserved attention, she snapped nicely into it and made it straight and simple. I hung up and turned to Wolfe.

"All set. They're there, and she'll see that they stay until we come. We're invited for lunch."

"Including her sister?"

"All of 'em."

He glanced at the clock, which said 11:23. "We should make it by one-thirty."

"Yeah, easy. I think I know where I can borrow an armored car. The route goes within five miles of where a certain man has a palace on a hill."

He made a face. "Get the sedan."

"Okay, if you'll crouch on the floor or let me put you in the trunk. It's you he's interested in, not me. By the way, what about Fred and Orrie? I've phoned Saul and warned him that there are other elements involved besides the law boys, and I should think Fred and Orrie might take a day off. After you have a talk with the family, whatever you're going to say, you can have them pick it up again if that's the program, which I hope to God it isn't."

He made that concession. I couldn't get Fred or Orrie, but they would certainly call in soon and word was left with Fritz to tell them to lay off until further notice. Then Wolfe had to go up to the roof for another look while I went to the garage for the car, so it was nearly noon when we got rolling. Wolfe, in the back seat as always, because that gave him a better chance to come out alive when we crashed, had a firm grip on the strap with his right hand, but that was only routine and didn't mean he was any shakier than usual when risking his neck in a thing on wheels. However, I noticed in the mirror that he didn't shut his eyes once the whole trip, although he hadn't been in bed for thirty hours now.

The day was cloudy and windy, not one of June's best samples, though no rain fell. When we were approaching Stony Acres and reached the spot on the secondary road where Rony and I had been assaulted by highwaymen, I stopped to show Wolfe the terrain, and told him Saul had reported that the take from

Rony had been three hundred and twelve bucks, and was awaiting instructions for disposal.

Wolfe wasn't interested in the terrain. "Are we nearly there?"

"Yes, sir. A mile and a half."

"Go ahead."

When we rolled up to the front entrance of the mansion, we were honored. It was not the sad-looking guy in a mohair uniform who appeared and came to us, but James U. Sperling himself. He was not smiling. He spoke through the open car window.

"What does this mean?"

He couldn't be blamed for not knowing that Wolfe would never stay in a vehicle any longer than he had to, since their acquaintance was brief. Before replying, Wolfe pushed the door open and manipulated himself out onto the gravel.

Meanwhile Sperling was going on. "I tried to get you on the phone, but by the time I got the number you had left. What are you trying to do? You know damn well I don't want this."

Wolfe met his eye. "You looked me up, Mr. Sperling. You must know that I am not hairbrained. I assure you that I can justify this move, but I can do so only by proceeding with it. When I have explained matters to you and your family, we'll see if you can find any alternative to approval. I'll stake my reputation that you can't."

Sperling wanted to argue it then and there, but Wolfe stood pat, and seeing that he had to choose between letting us come on in and ordering us off the place, the Chairman of the Board preferred the former. He and Wolfe headed for the door. Since no help had shown up, I took the car around the house to a graveled plaza in the rear, screened by shrubbery, left it there, and made for the nearest entrance, which was the west terrace. As I was crossing it a door opened and there was Madeline. I told her hello.

She inspected me with her head cocked to one side and the big dark eyes half open. "You don't look so battered."

"No? I am. Internal injuries. But not from the hold-up. From—" I waved a hand. "You ought to know."

"I'm disappointed in you." Her eyes went open. "Why didn't you shoot them?"

"My mind was elsewhere. You ought to know that too. We can compare notes on that some other time. Thank you very much for stalling it until it was too late for your father to head us off. Also thank you for taking my word for it that this is the best we can do for Gwenn. How many names have I got here now and where do they fit?"

"Oh, you're Archie everywhere. I explained that much to Webster and Paul and Connie too, because they'll eat lunch with us and it would have been too complicated, and anyway with Nero Wolfe here—they're not halfwits. Incidentally, you've made lunch late; we usually have it at one, so come on. How's your appetite?"

I told her I'd rather show her than tell her, and we went in.

Lunch was served in the big dining room. Wolfe and I were the only ones with neckties on, though the day was too chilly for extremes like shorts. Sperling had a striped jacket over a light blue silk shirt open at the neck. Jimmy and Paul Emerson were sporting dingy old coat sweaters, one brown and one navy. Webster Kane varied it with a wool shirt with loud red and yellow checks. Mrs. Sperling was in a pink rayon dress and a fluffy pink sweater, unbuttoned; Connie Emerson in a dotted blue thing that looked like a dressing gown but maybe I didn't know; Gwenn in a tan shirt and slacks; and Madeline in a soft but smooth wool dress of browns and blacks that looked like a PSI fabric.

So it was anything but a formal gathering, but neither was it free and easy. They ate all right, but they all seemed to have trouble deciding what would be a good thing to talk about. Wolfe, who can't stand a strained atmosphere at meals, tried this and that with one and then another, but the only line that got anywhere at all was a friendly argument with Webster Kane about the mechanism of money and a book by some Englishman which nobody else had ever heard of, except maybe Sperling, who may have known it by heart but wasn't interested.

When that was over and we were on our feet again, there was no loitering around. The Emersons, with Paul as sour as ever and Connie not up to form in her dressing gown if she will excuse me, went in the direction of the living room, and Webster Kane said he had work to do and went the other way. The destination of the rest of us had apparently been arranged. With Sperling in the lead, we marched along halls and across rooms to arrive at the library, the room with books and a stock ticker where I had wangled the master key and had later phoned Saul Panzer. Wolfe's eyes, of course, immediately swept the scene to appraise the chairs, which Sperling and Jimmy began herding into a group; and, knowing he had had a hard night, I took pity on him, grabbed the best and biggest one, and put it in the position I knew he would like. He gave me a nod of appreciation as he got into it, leaned back and closed his eyes, and sighed.

The others got seated, except Sperling, who stood and demanded, "All right, justify this. You said you could."

7

Wolfe stayed motionless for seconds. He raised his hands to press his fingertips against his eyes, and again was motionless. Finally he let his hands fall to the chair arms, opened the eyes, and directed them at Gwenn.

"You look intelligent, Miss Sperling."

"We're all intelligent," Sperling snapped. "Get on."

Wolfe looked at him. "It's going to be long-winded,

but I can't help it. You must have it all. If you try prodding me you'll only lengthen it. Since you head a large enterprise, sir, and therefore are commander-in-chief of a huge army, surely you know when to bullyrag and when to listen. Will you do me a favor? Sit down. Talking to people who are standing makes my neck stiff."

"I want to say something," Gwenn declared.

Wolfe nodded at her. "Say it."

She swallowed. "I just want to be sure you know that I know what you're here for. You sent that man"—she flashed a glance at me which gave me a fair idea of how my personal relationship with her stood as of now—"to snoop on Louis Rony, a friend of mine, and that's what this is about." She swallowed again. "I'll listen because my family—my mother and sister asked me to, but I think you're a cheap filthy little worm, and if I had to earn a living the way you do I'd rather starve!"

It was all right, but it would have been better if she had ad libbed it instead of sticking to a script that she had obviously prepared in advance. Calling Wolfe little, which she wouldn't have done if she had worded it while looking at him, weakened it.

Wolfe grunted. "If you had to earn a living the way I do, Miss Sperling, you probably *would* starve. Thank you for being willing to listen, no matter why." He glanced around. "Does anyone else have an irrepressible comment?"

"Get on," said Sperling, who was seated.

"Very well, sir. If at first I seem to wander, bear with me. I want to tell you about a man. I know his name but prefer not to pronounce it, so shall call him X. I assure you he is no figment; I only wish he were. I have little concrete knowledge of the immense properties he owns, though I do know that one of them is a high and commanding hill not a hundred miles from here on which, some years ago, he built a large and luxurious mansion. He has varied and extensive sources of income. All of them are illegal and some of them are morally repulsive. Narcotics, smuggling, industrial and commercial rackets, gambling, waterfront blackguardism, professional larceny, blackmailing, political malfeasance—that by no means exhausts his curriculum, but it sufficiently indicates his character. He has, up to now, triumphantly kept himself invulnerable by having the perspicacity to see that a criminal practicing on a large scale over a wide area and a long period of time can get impunity only by maintaining a gap between his person and his crimes which cannot be bridged; and by having unexcelled talent, a remorseless purpose, and a will that cannot be dented or deflected."

Sperling jerked impatiently in his chair. Wolfe looked at him as a sixth-grade teacher looks at a restless boy, moved his eyes for a roundup of the whole audience, and went on.

"If you think I am describing an extraordinary man, I am indeed. How, for instance, does he maintain the gap? There are two ways to catch a criminal: one, connect him with the crime itself; or two, prove that he knowingly took a share of the spoils. Neither is feasible with X. Take for illustration a typical crime—anything from a triviality like pocket picking or bag snatching up to a major raid on the public treasury. The criminal or gang of criminals nearly always takes full responsibility for the operation itself, but in facing the problem of disposal of the loot, which always appears, and of protection against discovery and prosecution, which is seldom entirely absent, he cannot avoid dealing with others. He may need a fence, a lawyer, a witness for an alibi, a channel to police or political influence—no matter what; he will almost inevitably need someone or something. He goes to one he knows, or knows about, one named A. A, finding a little difficulty, consults B. We are already, observe, somewhat removed from the crime, and B now takes us still further away by enlisting the help of C. C, having trouble with a stubborn knot in the thread, communicates with D. Here we near the terminal. D knows X and how to get to him.

"In and around New York there are many thousands of crimes each month, from mean little thefts to the highest reaches of fraud and thuggery. In a majority of them the difficulties of the criminals are met, or are not met, either by the criminals themselves or by A or B or C. But a large number of them get up to D, and if they reach D they go to X. I don't know how many D's there are, but certainly not many, for they are selected by X after a long and hard scrutiny and the application of severe tests, since he knows that a D once accepted by him must be backed with a fierce loyalty at almost any cost. I would guess that there are very few of them and, even so, I would also guess that if a D were impelled, no matter how, to resort to treachery, he would find that that too had been foreseen and provision had been made."

Wolfe turned a palm up. "You see where X is. Few criminals, or A's or B's or C's, even know he exists. Those few do not know his name. If a fraction of them have guessed his name, it remains a guess. Estimates of the total annual dollar volume involved in criminal operations in the metropolitan area vary from three hundred million to half a billion. X has been in this business more than twenty years now, and the share that finds its way tortuously to him must be considerable, after deducting his payments to appointed and elected persons and their staffs. A million a year? Half that? I don't know. I do know that he doesn't pay for everything he gets. Some years ago a man not far from the top of the New York Police Department did many favors for X, but I doubt if he was ever paid a cent. Blackmailing is one of X's favorite fields, and that man was susceptible."

"Inspector Drake," Jimmy blurted.

Wolfe shook his head. "I am not giving names, and anyway I said not far from the top." His eyes went from right to left and back again. "I am obliged for your forbearance; these details are necessary. I have told you that I know X's name, but I have never seen him. I first got some knowledge of him eleven years ago, when a police officer came to me for an opinion regarding a murder he was working on. I undertook a little inquiry through curiosity, a luxury I no longer indulge in, and found myself on a trail leading onto ground where the footing was treacherous for a private investigator. Since I had no client and was not committed, I reported what I had found to the police officer and dropped it. I then knew there was such a man as X, and something of his activities and methods, but not his name.

"During the following eight years I saw hints here and there that X was active, but I was busy with my own affairs, which did not happen to come into contact with his. Then, early in 1946, while I was engaged on a job for a client, I had a phone call. A voice I had never heard—hard, cold, precise, and finicky with its grammar—advised me to limit my efforts on behalf of my client. I replied that my efforts would be limited only by the requirements of the job I had undertaken to do. The voice insisted, and we talked some, but only to an impasse. The next day I finished the job to my client's satisfaction, and that ended it."

Wolfe closed his fingers into fists and opened them again. "But for my own satisfaction I felt that I needed some information. The character of the job, and a remark the voice had made during our talk, raised the question whether the voice could have been that of X himself. Not wishing to involve the men I often hire to help me, and certainly not Mr. Goodwin, I got men from an agency in another city. Within a month I had all the information I needed for my satisfaction, including of course X's name, and I dismissed the men and destroyed their reports. I hoped that X's affairs and mine would not again touch, but they did. Months later, a little more than a year ago, I was investigating a murder, this time for a client—you may remember it. A man named Orchard poisoned while appearing on a radio program?"

All but Sperling nodded, and Mrs. Sperling said she had been listening to the program the day it happened. Wolfe went on.

"I was in the middle of that investigation when the same voice called me on the phone and told me to drop it. He was not so talkative that second time, perhaps because I informed him that I knew his name, which was of course childish of me. I ignored his fiat. It soon transpired that Mr. Orchard and a woman who had also been killed had both been professional blackmailers, using a method which clearly implied a large organization, ingeniously contrived and ably conducted.

I managed to expose the murderer, who had been blackmailed by them. The day after the murderer was sentenced another phone call came from X. He had the cheek to congratulate me on keeping my investigation within the limits he had prescribed! I told him that his prescription had been ignored. What had happened was that I had caught the murderer, which was my job, without stretching the investigation to an attack on X himself, which had been unnecessary and no part of my commitment."

Sperling had been finding it impossible to get properly settled in his chair. Now he broke training and demanded,

"Damn it, can't you cut this short?"

"Not and earn my fee," Wolfe snapped. He resumed.

"That was in May of last year—thirteen months ago. In the interval I have not heard from X, because I haven't happened to do anything with which he had reason to interfere. That good fortune ended—as I suppose it was bound to do soon or late, since we are both associated with crime—day before yesterday, Saturday, at six-ten P.M. He phoned again. He was more peremptory than formerly, and gave me an ultimatum with a time limit. I responded to his tone as a man of my temperament naturally would—I am congenitally tart and thorny—and I rejected his ultimatum. I do not pretend that I was unconcerned. When Mr. Goodwin returned from his weekend here, after midnight on Sunday, yesterday, and gave me his report, I told him of the phone call and we discussed the situation at length."

Wolfe looked around. "Do any of you happen to know that there are plant rooms on the roof of my house, in which I keep thousands of orchids, all of them good and some of them new and rare and extremely beautiful?"

Yes, they all did, again all but Sperling.

Wolfe nodded. "I won't try to introduce suspense. Mr. Goodwin and I were in my office talking, between two and three o'clock this morning, when we heard an outlandish noise. Men hired by X had mounted to the roof of a building across the street, armed with sub-machine guns, and fired hundreds of rounds at my plant rooms, with what effect you can guess. I shall not describe it. Thirty men are there now, salvaging and repairing. That my gardener was not killed was fortuitous. The cost of repairs and replacements will be around forty thousand dollars, and some of the damaged or destroyed plants are irreplaceable. The gunmen have not been found and probably never will be, and what if they are? It was incorrect to say they were hired by X. They were hired by a D or C or B—most likely a C. Assuredly X is not on speaking terms with anyone as close to crime as a gunman, and I doubt if a D is. In any—"

"You say," Sperling put in, "this just happened? Last night?"

"Yes, sir. I mentioned the approximate amount of the damage because you'll have to pay it. It will be on my bill."

Sperling made a noise. "It may be on your bill, but I won't have to pay it. Why should I?"

"Because you'll owe it. It is an expense incurred on the job you gave me. My plant rooms were destroyed because I ignored X's ultimatum, and his demand was that I recall Mr. Goodwin from here and stop my inquiry into the activities and character of Louis Rony. You wanted me to prove that Mr. Rony is a Communist. I can't do that, but I can prove that he is one of X's men, either a C or a D, and is therefore a dangerous professional criminal."

The quickest reaction was from Madeline. Before Wolfe had finished she said, "My God!" and got up, crossed impolitely in front of people to Gwenn, and put her hand on her sister's shoulder. Then Mrs. Sperling was up too, but she just stood a second and sat down again. Jimmy, who had been frowning at Wolfe, shifted the frown to his father.

The Chairman of the Board sat a moment gazing at Wolfe, then gazed a longer moment at his younger daughter, and then arose and went to her and said, "He says he can prove it, Gwenn."

I am not lightning, but I had caught on quite a while

back that Wolfe's real target was Gwenn, so it was her I was interested in. When Wolfe had started in, the line of her pretty lips and the stubbornness in her eyes had made it plain that she simply didn't intend to believe a word he said, but as he went on telling about a mysterious X who couldn't possibly be her Louis she had relaxed a little, and was even beginning to think that maybe it was an interesting story when suddenly Rony's name popped in, and then the shot straight at her. When she felt Madeline's hand on her shoulder she put her own hand up to place it on top of her sister's, and said in a low voice, "It's all right, Mad." Then she spoke louder to Wolfe.

"It's a lot of bunk!"

When Sperling stood in front of her, Wolfe and I couldn't see her. Wolfe stated to Sperling's back, "I've barely started, you know. I've merely given you the background. Now I must explain the situation."

Gwenn was on her feet at once, saying firmly, "You won't need me for that. I know what the situation is well enough."

They all started talking. Madeline had hold of Gwenn's arm. Mrs. Sperling was out of her depth but was flapping. Jimmy was being completely ignored but kept trying. Wolfe allowed them a couple of minutes and then cut in sharply.

"Confound it, are you a bunch of ninnies?"

Sperling wheeled on him. "You shouldn't have done it like this! You should have told me! You should—"

"Nonsense! Utter nonsense. For months you have been telling your daughter that Mr. Rony is a Communist, and she has quite properly challenged you to prove it. If you had tried to tell her this she would have countered with the same challenge, and where would you have been? I am better armed. Will you please get out of the way so I can see her?—Thank you.—Miss Sperling, you were not afraid to challenge your father to show you proof. But now you want to walk out. So you're afraid to challenge me? I don't blame you."

"I'm not afraid of anything!"

"Then sit down and listen. All of you. Please?"

They got back to their chairs. Gwenn wasn't so sure now that all she needed was a simple and steadfast refusal to believe a word. Her lower lip was being held tight by her teeth, and her eyes were no longer straight and stubborn at Wolfe. She even let me have a questioning, unsure glance, as if I might contribute something that would possibly help.

Wolfe focused on her. "I didn't skimp on the background, Miss Sperling, because without it you can't decide intelligently, and, though your father is my client, the decision rests with you. The question that must be answered is this: am I to proceed to assemble proof or not? If I—"

"You said you had proof!"

"No, I didn't. I said I could prove it, and I can—and if I must I will. I would vastly prefer not to. One way out would be for me simply to quit—to return the retainer your father has paid me, shoulder the expense of my outlay on this job and restoration of my damaged property, and let X know that I have scuttled. That would unquestionably be the sensible and practical thing to do, and I do not brag that I'm not up to it. It is a weakness I share with too many of my fellow men, that my self-conceit will not listen to reason. Having undertaken to do a job offered to me by your father in good faith, and with no excuse for withdrawal that my vanity will accept, I do not intend to quit.

"Another way out would be for you to assume that I am not a liar; or that if I am one, at least I am incapable of such squalid trickery as the invention of this rigmarole in order to earn a fee by preventing you from marrying a man who has your affection and is worthy of it. If you make either of those assumptions, it follows that Mr. Rony is a blackguard, and since you are plainly not a fool you will have done with him. But—"

"You said you could prove it!"

Wolfe nodded. "So I can. If my vanity won't let me scuttle, and if you reject both those assumptions, that's what I'll have to do. Now you see why I gave you so full a sketch of X. It will be impossible to brand Mr.

Rony without bringing X in, and even if that were feasible X would get in anyway. Proof of that already exists, on the roof of my house. You may come home with me and take a look at it—by the way, I have failed to mention another possibility."

Wolfe looked at our client. "You, sir, could of course pay my bill to date and discharge me. In that event I presume your daughter would consider my indictment of Mr. Rony as unproven as yours, and she would proceed—to do what? I can't say; you know her better than I do. Do you want to send me home?"

Sperling was slumped in his chair, his elbow resting on its arm and his chin propped on his knuckles, with his gaze now on Gwenn and now on Wolfe. "Not now," he said quietly. "Only—a question—how much of that was straight fact?"

"Every word."

"What is X's name?"

"That will have to wait. If we are forced into this, and you still want me to work for you, you will of course have to have it."

"All right, go ahead."

Wolfe went back to Gwenn. "One difficulty in an attempt to expose X, which is what this would amount to, will be the impossibility of knowing when we are rubbing against him. I am acquainted, more or less, with some three thousand people living or working in New York, and there aren't more than ten of them of whom I could say with certainty that they are in no way involved in X's activities. None may be; any may be. If that sounds extreme, Miss Sperling, remember that he has been devising and spreading his nets all your lifetime, and that his talents are great.

"So I can't match him in ubiquity, no matter how many millions your father contributes to the enterprise, but I must match his inaccessibility, and I shall. I shall move to a base of operations which will be known only to Mr. Goodwin and perhaps two others; for it is not a fantasy of trepidation, but a painful fact, that when he perceives my objective, as he soon will, he will start all his machinery after me. He has told me on the telephone how much he admires me, and I was flattered, but now I'll have to pay for it. He will know it is a mortal encounter, and he does not underrate me—I only wish he did."

Wolfe lifted his shoulders and let them down again. "I'm not whimpering—or perhaps I am. I shall expect to win, but there's no telling what the cost will be. It may take a year, or five years, or ten." He gestured impatiently. "Not for finishing your Mr. Rony; that will be the merest detail. It won't be long until you'll have to talk with him through the grill in the visitors' room, if you still want to see him. But X will never let it stop there, though he might want me to think he would. Once started, I'll have to go on to the end. So the cost in time can't be estimated.

"Neither can the cost in money. I certainly haven't got enough, nothing like it, and I won't be earning any, so your father will have to foot the bill, and he will have to commit himself in advance. If I stake my comfort, my freedom, and my life, he may properly be expected to stake his fortune. Whatever his resources may be—"

Wolfe interrupted himself. "Bah!" he said scornfully. "You deserve complete candor. As I said, Mr. Rony is a mere trifle; he'll be disposed of in no time, once I am established where I can be undisturbed. But I hope I have given you a clear idea of what X is like. He will know I can't go on without money and, when he finds he can't get at me, will try to stop the source of supply. He will try many expedients before he resorts to violence, for he is a man of sense and knows that murder should always be the last on the list, and of course the murder of a man in your father's position would be excessively dangerous; but if he thought it necessary he would risk it. I don't—"

"You can leave that out," Sperling cut in. "If she wants to consider the cost in money she can, but I'll not have her saving my life. That's up to me."

Wolfe looked at him. "A while ago you told me to go ahead. What about it now? Do you want to pay me off?"

"No. You spoke about your vanity, but I've got more up than vanity. I'm not quitting and I don't intend to."

"Listen, Jim—" his wife began, but to cut her off he didn't even have to speak. He only looked at her.

"In that case," Wolfe told Gwenn, "there are only two alternatives. I won't drop it, and your father won't discharge me, so the decision rests with you, as I said it would. You may have proof if you insist on it. Do you?"

"You said," Madeline exploded at me, "it would be the best you could do for her!"

"I still say it," I fired back. "You'd better come down and look at the plant rooms too!"

Gwenn sat gazing at Wolfe, not stubbornly—more as if she were trying to see through him to the other side.

"I have spoken," Wolfe told her, "of what the proof, if you insist on it, will cost me and your father and family. I suppose I should mention what it will cost another person: Mr. Rony. It will get him a long term in jail. Perhaps that would enter into your decision. If you have any suspicion that it would be necessary to contrive a frame-up, reject it. He is pure scoundrel. I wouldn't go to the extreme of calling him a cheap filthy little worm, but he is in fact a shabby creature. Your sister thinks I'm putting it brutally, but how else can I put it? Should I hint that he may be not quite worthy of you? I don't know that, for I don't know you. But I do know that I have told you the truth about him, and I'll prove it if you say I must."

Gwenn left her chair. Her eyes left Wolfe for the first time since her unsure glance at me. She looked around at her family.

"I'll let you know before bedtime," she said firmly, and walked out of the room.

8

More than four hours later, at nine o'clock in the evening, Wolfe yawned so wide I thought something was going to give.

We were in the room where I had slept Saturday night, if it can be called sleep when a dose of dope has knocked you out. Immediately after Gwenn had ended the session in the library by beating it, Wolfe had asked where he could go to take a nap, and Mrs. Sperling had suggested that room. When I steered him there he went straight to one of the three-quarter beds and tested it, pulled the coverlet off, removed his coat and vest and shoes, lay down, and in three minutes was breathing clear to China. I undressed the other bed to get a blanket to put over him, quit trying to fight temptation, and followed his example.

When we were called to dinner at seven o'clock I was conscripted for courier duty, to tell Mrs. Sperling that under the circumstances Mr. Wolfe and I would prefer either to have a sandwich upstairs or go without, and it was a pleasure to see how relieved she was. But even in the middle of that crisis she didn't let her household suffer shame, and instead of a sandwich we got jellied consommé, olives and cucumber rings, hot roast beef, three vegetables, lettuce and tomato salad, cold pudding with nuts in it, and plenty of coffee. It was nothing to put in your scrapbook, but was more than adequate, and except for the jellied consommé, which he hates, and the salad dressing, which he made a face at, Wolfe handled his share without comment.

I wouldn't have been surprised if he had had me take him home as soon as the library party was over, but neither was I surprised that he was staying. The show that he had put on for them hadn't been a show at all. He had meant every word of it, and I had meant it along with him. That being so, it was no wonder that he wanted the answer as soon as it was available, and besides, he would be needed if Gwenn had questions to ask or conditions to offer. Not only that, if Gwenn said nothing doing I don't think he would have gone home at all. There would have been a lot of arranging to do with Sperling, and when we finally got away from Stony Acres we wouldn't have been headed for Thirty-fifth Street but for a foxhole.

At nine o'clock, after admiring Wolfe's yawn, I looked around for an excuse to loosen up my muscles, saw the coffee tray, which had been left behind when the rest of the dinner remains had been called for, and decided that would do. I got it and took it downstairs. When I delivered it to the kitchen there was no one around and, feeling in need of a little social contact, I did a casual reconnoiter. I tried the library first. The door to it was open and Sperling was there, at his desk, looking over some papers. When I entered he honored me with a glance but no words.

After I had stood a moment I informed him, "We're upstairs hanging on."

"I know it," he said without looking up.

He seemed to think that completed the conversation, so I retired. The living room was uninhabited, so when I stepped out to the west terrace no one was to be seen or heard. The game room, which was down a flight, was dark, and the lights I turned on disclosed no fellow beings. So I went back upstairs and reported to Wolfe.

"The joint is deserted, except for Sperling, and I think he's going over his will. You scared 'em so that they all scrammed."

"What time is it?"

"Nine twenty-two."

"She said before bedtime. Call Fritz."

We had talked with Fritz only an hour ago, but what the hell, it was on the house, so I went to the instrument on the table between the beds and got him. There was nothing new. Andy Krasicki was up on the roof with five men, still working, and had reported that enough glass and slats were in place for the morning's weather, whatever it might be. Theodore was still far from cheerful, but had had a good appetite for dinner and so on.

I hung up and relayed the report to Wolfe, and added, "It strikes me that all that fixing up may be a waste of our client's money. If Gwenn decides we've got to prove it and we make a dive for a foxhole, what do glass and slats matter? It'll be years before you see the place again, if you ever do. Incidentally, I noticed you gave yourself a chance to call it off, and also Sperling, but not me. You merely said that your base of operations will be known only to Mr. Goodwin, taking Mr. Goodwin for granted. What if he decides he's not as vain as you are?"

Wolfe, who had put down a book by Laura Hobson to listen to my end of the talk with Fritz, and had picked it up again, scowled at me.

"You're twice as vain as I am," he said gruffly.

"Yeah, but it may work different. I may be so vain I won't want me to take such a risk. I may not want to deprive others of what I've got to be vain about."

"Pfui. Do I know you?"

"Yes, sir. As well as I know you."

"Then don't try shaking a bogy at me. How the devil could I contemplate such a plan without you?" He returned to the book.

I knew he thought he was handing me a compliment which should make me beam with pleasure, so I went and flopped on the bed to beam. I didn't like any part of it, and I knew Wolfe didn't either. I had a silly damn feeling that my whole future depended on the verdict of a fine freckled girl, and while I had nothing against fine girls, freckled or unfreckled, that was going too far. But I wasn't blaming Wolfe, for I didn't see how he could have done any better. I had brought a couple of fresh magazines up from the living room, but I never got to look at them, because I was still on the bed trying to decide whether I should hunt up Madeline to see if she couldn't do something that would help on the verdict, when the phone buzzed. I rolled over to reach for it.

It was one of the help saying there was a call for Mr. Goodwin. I thanked her and then heard a voice I knew.

"Hello, Archie?"

"Right. Me."

"This is a friend."

"So say you. Let me guess. The phones here are complicated. I'm in a bedroom with Mr. Wolfe. If I pick up the receiver I get an outside line, but on the other hand your incoming call was answered downstairs."

"I see. Well, I'm sitting here looking at an Indian holding down papers. I went out for a walk, but there was too much of a crowd, so I decided to ride and here I am. I'm sorry you can't keep that date."

"So am I. But I might be able to make it if you'll sit tight. Okay?"

"Okay."

I hung up, got to my feet, and told Wolfe, "Saul started to go somewhere, found he had a tail on him, shook it off, and went to the office to report. He's there now. Any suggestions?"

Wolfe closed the book on a finger to mark the place. "Who was following him?"

"I doubt if he knows, but he didn't say. You heard what I told him about the phone."

Wolfe nodded and considered a moment. "How far will you have to go?"

"Oh, I guess I can stand it, even in the dark. Chappaqua is seven minutes and Mount Kisco ten. Any special instructions?"

He had none, except that since Saul was in the office he might as well stick there until he heard from us again, so I shoved off.

I left the house by the west terrace because that was the shortest route to the place behind the shrubbery where I had parked the car, and found a sign of life. Paul and Connie Emerson were in the living room looking at television, and Webster Kane was on the terrace, apparently just walking back and forth. I exchanged greetings with them on the fly and proceeded.

It was a dark night, with no stars on account of the clouds, but the wind was down. As I drove to Chappaqua I let my mind drift into a useless habit, speculating on who Saul's tail had been—state or city employees, or an A, B, C, or D. After I got to a booth in a drugstore and called Saul at the office and had a talk with him, it was still nothing but a guess. All Saul knew was that it had been a stranger and that it hadn't been too easy to shake him. Since it was Saul Panzer, I knew I didn't have to check any on the shaking part, and since he had no news to report except that he had acquired a tail, I told him to make himself comfortable in one of the spare rooms if he got sleepy, treated myself to a lemon coke, and went back to the car and drove back to Stony Acres.

Madeline had joined the pair in the living room, or maybe I should just put it that she was there when I entered. When she came to intercept me the big dark eyes were wide open, but not for any effect they might have on me. Her mind was obviously too occupied with something else for dallying.

"Where have you been?" she asked.

I told her to Chappaqua to make a phone call. She took my arm and eased me along through the door into the reception hall, and there faced me to ask, "Have you seen Gwenn?"

"No. Why, where is she?"

"I don't know. But I think—"

She stopped. I filled in. "I supposed she was off in a corner making up her mind."

"You didn't go out to meet her?"

"Now I ask you," I objected. "I'm not even a worm, I just work for one. Why should she be meeting me?"

"I suppose not." Madeline hesitated. "After dinner she told Dad she would let him know as soon as she could, and went up to her room. I went in and wanted to talk to her, but she chased me out, and I went to Mother's room. Later I went back to Gwenn's room and she let me talk some, and then she said she was going outdoors. I went downstairs with her. She went out the back way. I went back up to Mother, and when I came down again and found you had gone out I thought maybe you had met her."

"Nope." I shrugged. "She may have had trouble finding the answer in the house and went outdoors for it. After all, she said before bedtime and it's not eleven yet. Give her time. Meanwhile you ought to relax. How about a game of pool?"

She ignored the invitation. "You don't know Gwenn," she stated.

"Not very well, no."

"She has a good level head, but she's stubborn as a mule. She's a little like Dad. If he had kept off she might have had enough of Louis long ago. But now—I'm scared. I suppose your Nero Wolfe did the best he could, but he left a hole. Dad hired him to find out something about Louis that would keep Gwenn from marrying him. Is that right?"

"Right."

"And the way Nero Wolfe put it, one of four things had to happen. Either he had to quit the job, or Dad had to fire him, or Gwenn had to believe what he said about Louis and drop him, or he had to keep on and get proof. But he left out something else that could happen. What if Gwenn went away with Louis and married him? That would fix it too, wouldn't it? Would Dad want Wolfe to go on, to keep after Louis if he was Gwenn's husband? Gwenn wouldn't think so." Madeline's fingers gripped my arm. "I'm scared! I think she went to meet him!"

"I'll be damned. Did she take a bag?"

"She wouldn't. She'd know I'd try to stop her, and Dad too—all of us. If your Nero Wolfe is so damn smart, why didn't he think of this?"

"He has blind spots, and people running off to get married is one of them. But I should have—my God, am I thick. How long ago did she leave?"

"It must have been an hour—about an hour."

"Did she take a car?"

Madeline shook her head. "I listened for it. No."

"Then she must have—" I stopped to frown and

think. "If that wasn't it, if she just went out to have more air while she decided, or possibly to meet him here somewhere and have a talk, where would she go? Has she got a favorite spot?"

"She has several." Madeline was frowning back at me. "An old apple tree in the back field, and a laurel thicket down by the brook, and a—"

"Do you know where there's a flashlight?"

"Yes, we keep—"

"Get it."

She went. In a moment she was back, and we left by the front door. She seemed to think the old apple tree was the best bet, so we circled the house halfway, crossed the lawn, found a path through a shrubbery border, and went through a gate into a pasture. Madeline called her sister's name but no answer came, and when we got to the old apple tree there was no one there. We returned to the vicinity of the house the other way, around back of the barn and kennels and other buildings, with a halt at the barn to see if Gwenn had got romantic and saddled a horse to go to meet her man, but the horses were all there. The brook was in the other direction, in the landscape toward the public road, and we headed that way. Occasionally Madeline called Gwenn's name, but not loud enough to carry to the house. We both had flashlights. I used mine only when I needed it, and by that time our eyes had got adjusted. We stuck to the drive until we reached the bridge over the brook and then Madeline turned sharp to the left. I admit she had me beat at cross-country going in the dark. The bushes and lower limbs had formed the habit of reaching out for me from the sides, and while Madeline hardly used her light at all, I shot mine right or left now and then, as well as to the front.

We were about twenty paces from the drive when I flashed my light to the left and caught a glimpse of an object on the ground by a bush that stopped me. The one glimpse was enough to show me what it was—there was no doubt about that—but not who it was. Madeline, ahead of me, was calling Gwenn's name. I stood. Then she called to me, "You coming?" and I called back that I was and started forward. I was opening my mouth to tell her that I was taking time out and would be with her in a minute, when she called Gwenn's name again, and an answer came faintly through the trees in the night. It was Gwenn's voice.

"Yes, Mad, I'm here!"

So I had to postpone a closer inspection of the object behind the bush. Madeline had let out a little cry of relief and was tearing ahead, and I followed. I got tangled in a thicket before I knew it and had to fight my way out, and nearly slid into the brook; then I was in the clear again, headed toward voices, and soon my light picked them up at the far side of an open space. I crossed to them.

"What's all the furor?" Gwenn was asking her sister. "Good Lord, I came outdoors on a summer night, so what? That's been known to happen before, hasn't it? You even brought a detective along!"

"This isn't just a summer night," Madeline said shortly, "and you know darned well it isn't. How did I know—anyway, you haven't even got a jacket on."

"I know I haven't. What time is it?"

I aimed the light at my wrist and told her. "Five past eleven."

"Then he didn't come on that train, either."

"Who didn't?" Madeline asked.

"Who do you suppose?" Gwenn was pent up. "That dangerous criminal! Oh, I suppose he is. All right, he is. But I wasn't going to cross him off without telling him first, and not on the phone or in a letter, either. I phoned him to come here."

"Sure," Madeline said, not like a loving sister. "So you could make him tell you who X is and make him reform."

"Not me," Gwenn declared. "Reforming is your department. I was simply going to tell him we're through—and good-by. I merely preferred to do it that way, before telling Dad and the rest of you. He was coming up on the nine-twenty-three and taxi from the station and meet me here. I thought he had missed it—and now I guess he didn't get the next one either—but there's a—what time is it?"

I told her. "Nine minutes after eleven."

"There's a train at eleven-thirty-two, and I'll wait for that and then quit. I don't usually wait around for a man for two hours, but this is different. You admit that, don't you, Mad?"

"If you could use a suggestion from a detective," I offered, "I think you ought to phone him again and find out what happened. Why don't you girls go and do that, and I'll wait here in case he shows up. I promise not to say a word to him except that you'll soon be back. Get a jacket, too."

That appealed to them. The only part that didn't appeal to me was that they might wave flashlights around on their way to the drive, but they went in another direction, a shortcut by way of the rose garden. I waited until they were well started and then headed toward the drive, used the light to spot the object on the ground by the bush, and went to it.

First, was he dead? He was. Second, what killed him? The answer to that wasn't as conclusive, but there weren't many alternatives. Third, how long ago had he died? I had a guess for that one, with some experience to go by. Fourth, what was in his pockets? That took more care and time on account of complications. For instance, when I had frisked him at the roadside Sunday night, after Ruth Brady had prepared him for me, I had used a fair amount of caution, but now fair wasn't good enough. I gave his leather wallet a good rub with my handkerchief, inside and out, put prints from both of his hands all over it but kept them haphazard, and returned it to his pocket. It contained a good assortment of bills, so he must have cashed a check since I had cleaned him. I wanted very much to repeat the performance on the Communist party membership card and its cellophane holder, but couldn't because it wasn't there. Naturally that irritated me, and I felt all the seams and linings to make sure. It wasn't on him.

My mind was completely on getting the job done right and in time, before the girls returned, but when I finally gave up on the membership card I felt my stomach suddenly go tight, and I stood up and backed off. It will happen that way sometimes, no matter how thick and hard you think your shell is, when you least expect it. I turned to face the other way, made my chest big, and took some deep breaths. If that doesn't work the only thing to do is lie down. But I didn't have to, and anyhow I would have had to pop right up again, for in between two breaths I heard voices. Then I saw that I had left the flashlight turned on, there on the ground. I got it and turned it off, and made my way back to the clearing beyond the thicket in the dark, trying not to sound like a charging moose.

I was at my post, a patient sentinel, when the girls appeared and crossed the open space to me, with Madeline asking as they approached, "Did he come?"

"Not a sound of him," I told them, preferring the truth when it will serve the purpose. "Then you didn't get him?"

"I got a phone-answering service." That was Gwenn. "They said he would be back after midnight and wanted me to leave a message. I'm going to stay here a little while, in case he came on the eleven-thirty-two, and then quit. Do you think something happened to him?"

"Certainly something happened to him, if he stood you up, but God knows what. Time will tell." The three of us were making a little triangle. "You won't need me, and if he comes you won't want me. I'm going in to Mr. Wolfe. His nerves are on edge with the suspense, and I want to ease his mind. I won't go around the house shouting it, but I want to tell him he'll be going home soon."

They didn't care for that much but had to admit it was reasonable, and I got away. I took the shortcut as they directed, got lost in the woods twice but finally made it to the open, skirted the rose garden and crossed the lawn, and entered the house by the front door. In the room upstairs Wolfe was still reading the book. As I closed the door behind me he started to scorch me with an indignant look for being gone so long, but when he saw my face, which he knows better than I do, he abandoned it.

"Well?" he asked mildly.

"Not well at all," I declared. "Somebody has killed Louis Rony, I think by driving a car over him, but that will take more looking. It's behind a bush about twenty yards from the driveway, at a point about two-thirds of the distance from the house to the public road. It's a rotten break in every way, because Gwenn had decided to toss him out."

Wolfe was growling. "Who found it?"

"I did."

"Who knows about it?"

"No one. Now you."

Wolfe got up, fast. "Where's my hat?" He looked around. "Oh, downstairs. Where are Mr. and Mrs. Sperling? We'll tell them there is nothing more for us to do here and we're going home—but not in a flurry—merely that it's late and we can go now—come on!"

"Flurry hell. You know damn well we're stuck."

He stood and glared at me. When that didn't seem to be improving the situation any he let himself go back onto the chair, felt the book under his fanny, got up and grabbed it—and for a second I thought he was going to throw it at something, maybe even me. For him to throw a book, loving them as he did, would have been a real novelty. He controlled himself in time, tossed the book onto a handy table, got seated again, and rasped at me, "Confound it, sit down! Must I stretch my neck off?"

I didn't blame him a particle. I would have been having a tantrum myself if I hadn't been too busy.

9

"The first thing," I said, "is this: have I seen it or not? If I have, there's the phone, and any arrangements to be made before company comes will have to be snappy. If I haven't, take your time. It's behind the bush on the side away from the drive and might not be noticed for a week, except for dogs. So?"

"I don't know enough about it," Wolfe said peevishly. "What were you doing there?"

I told him. That first question was too urgent, for me personally, to fill in with details such as stopping at the barn to count the horses, but I didn't skip any points that mattered, like Madeline's reason for being upset over Gwenn's trip outdoors, or like my handling of the fingerprint problem on the wallet. I gave it to him compact and fast but left out no essentials. When I finished he had only three questions:

"Have you had the thought, however vaguely, with or without evidence to inspire it, that Miss Sperling took you past that spot intentionally?"

"No."

"Can footprints be identified in the vicinity of the body?"

"I'm not sure, but I doubt it."

"Can your course be traced, no matter how, as you went from the thicket to the body and back again?"

"Same answer. Davy Crockett might do it. I didn't have him in mind at the time, anyhow it was dark."

Wolfe grunted. "We're away from home. We can't risk it. Get them all up here—the Sperlings. Go for the young women yourself, or the young one may not come. Just get them; leave the news for me. Get the young women first, and the others when you're back in the house. I don't want Mr. Sperling up here ahead of them."

I went, and wasted no time. It was only a simple little chore, compared with other occasions when he had sent me from the office to get people, and this time my heart was in my work. Evidently the answer to the question whether I had seen the body was to be yes, and in that case the sooner the phone got used the better. Wolfe would do his part, that was all right, but actually it was up to me, since I was old enough to vote and knew how to dial a number. On the long list of things that cops don't like, up near the top is acting as if finding a corpse is a purely private matter.

It was simple with the girls. I told Gwenn that Wolfe had just received information which made it certain that Rony would not show up, and he wanted to see her at once to tell her about it, and of course there was no argument. Back at the house, the others were just as simple. Jimmy was downstairs playing ping-pong with Connie, and Madeline went and got him. Mr. and Mrs. Sperling were in the living room with Webster Kane and Paul Emerson, and I told them that Wolfe would like to speak with them for a minute. Just Sperlings.

There weren't enough chairs for all of us in the bedroom, so for once Wolfe had to start a conversation with most of his audience standing, whether he liked it or not. Sperling was obviously completely fed up with his long wait, a full seven hours now, for an important decision about his affairs to be made by someone else, even his own daughter, and he wanted to start in after Gwenn, but Wolfe stopped him quick. He fired a question at them.

"This afternoon we thought we were discussing a serious matter. Didn't we?"

They agreed.

He nodded. "We were. Now it is either more serious or less, I don't know which. It's a question of Mr. Rony alive or Mr. Rony dead. For he is now dead."

There's a theory that it's a swell stunt to announce a man's death to a group of people when you think one of them may have killed him, and watch their faces. In practice I've never seen it get anybody to first base, let alone on around, not even Nero Wolfe, but it's still attractive as a theory, and therefore I was trying to watch all of them at once, and doubtless Wolfe was too.

They all made noises, some of them using words, but nobody screamed or fainted or clutched for support. The prevailing expression was plain bewilderment, all authentic as far as I could tell, but as I say, no matter how popular a theory may be, it's still a theory.

Gwenn demanded, "You mean Louis?"

Wolfe nodded. "Yes, Miss Sperling, Louis Rony is dead. Mr. Goodwin found his body about an hour ago, when he was out with your sister looking for you. It is on this property, behind a bush not far from where they found you. It seems—"

"Then—then he did come!"

I doubt if it was as heartless as it looks. I would not have called Gwenn heartless. In the traffic jam in her head caused by the shock, it just happened that that little detail got loose first. I saw Madeline dart a sharp glance at her. The others were finding their tongues for questions. Wolfe pushed a palm at them.

"If you please. There is no time—"

"What killed him?" Sperling demanded.

"I was about to tell you. The indications are that a car ran over him, and the body was dragged from the drive for concealment behind the bush, but of course it requires further examination. It hadn't been there long when it was found, not more than two hours. The police must be notified without delay. I thought, Mr. Sperling, you might prefer to do that yourself. It would look better."

Gwenn was starting to tremble. Madeline took her arm and led her to a bed and pushed her onto it, with Jimmy trying to help. Mrs. Sperling was stupefied.

"Are you saying—" Sperling halted. He was either incredulous or doing very well. "Do you mean he was murdered?"

"I don't know. Murder requires premeditation. If after inquiry the police decide it was murder they'll still have to prove it. That, of course, will start the routine hunt for motive, means, opportunity—I don't know whether you're familiar with it, but if not, I'm afraid you soon will be. Whom are you going to notify, the county authorities or the State Police? You have a choice. But you shouldn't postpone it. You will—"

Mrs. Sperling spoke for the first time. "But this is—this will be terrible! Here on our place! Why can't you take it away—away somewhere for miles—and leave it somewhere—"

No one paid any attention to her. Sperling asked Wolfe, "Do you know what he was doing here?"

"I know what brought him. Your daughter phoned him to come."

Sperling jerked to the bed. "Did you do that, Gwenn?"

There was no reply from Gwenn. Madeline furnished it. "Yes, Dad, she did. She decided to drop him and wanted to tell him first."

"I hope," Wolfe said, "that your wife's suggestion needs no comment, for a dozen reasons. He took a cab here from the station—"

"My wife's suggestions seldom need comment. There is no way of keeping the police out of it? I know a doctor—"

"None. Dismiss it."

"You're an expert. Will they regard it as murder?"

"An expert requires facts to be expert about. I haven't got enough. If you want a guess, I think they will."

"Shouldn't I have a lawyer here?"

"That will have to come later. You'll probably need one or more." Wolfe wiggled a finger. "It can't be delayed longer, sir. Mr. Goodwin and I are under an obligation, both as citizens and as men holding licenses as private detectives."

"You're under obligation to me too. I'm your client."

"We know that. We haven't ignored it. It was eleven o'clock when Mr. Goodwin found a corpse with marks of violence, and it was his legal duty to inform the authorities immediately. It is now well after midnight. We felt we owed you a chance to get your mind clear. Now I'm afraid I must insist."

"Damn it, I want to think!"

"Call the police and think while they're on the way."

"No!" Sperling yanked a chair around and sat on its edge, close to Wolfe, facing him. "Look here. I hired you on a confidential matter, and I have a right to expect you to keep it confidential. There is no reason why it should be disclosed, and I certainly don't want it to be. It was a privileged—"

"No, sir." Wolfe was crisp. "I am not a member of

the bar, and communications to detectives, no matter what you're paying them, are not privileged."

"But you—"

"No, please. You think if I repeat the conversation I had with you and your family this afternoon it will give the impression that all of you, except one, had good reason to wish Mr. Rony dead, and you're quite right. That will make it next to impossible for them to regard his death as something short of murder, and, no matter what your position in this community may be, you and your family will be in a devil of a fix. I'm sorry, but I can't help it. I have withheld information from the police many times, but only when it concerned a case I was myself engaged on and I felt I could make better use of it if I didn't share it. Another—"

"Damn it, you're engaged on this case!"

"I am not. The job you hired me for is ended, and I'm glad of it. You remember how I defined the objective? It has been reached—though not, I confess, by my—"

"Then I hire you for another job now. To investigate Rony's death."

Wolfe frowned at him. "You'd better not. I advise against it."

"You're hired."

Wolfe shook his head. "You're in a panic and you're being impetuous. If Mr. Rony was murdered, and if I undertake to look into it, I'll get the murderer. It's conceivable that you'll regret you ever saw me."

"But you're hired."

Wolfe shrugged. "I know. Your immediate problem is to keep me from repeating that conversation to the police, and, being pugnacious and self-assured, you solve your problems as they come. But you can't hire me today and fire me tomorrow. You know what I would do if you tried that."

"I know. You won't be fired. You're hired." Sperling arose. "I'll phone the police."

"Wait a minute!" Wolfe was exasperated. "Confound it, are you a dunce? Don't you know how ticklish this is? There were seven of us in that conversation—"

"We'll attend to that after I've phoned."

"No, we won't. I'll attend to it now." Wolfe's eyes darted around. "All of you, please. Miss Sperling?"

Gwenn was face down on the bed and Madeline was seated on the edge.

"Do you have to bark at her now?" Madeline demanded.

"I'll try not to bark. But I do have to speak to her—all of you."

Gwenn was sitting up. "I'm all right," she said. "I heard every word. Dad hired you again, to—oh, my God." She hadn't been crying, which was a blessing since it would have demoralized Wolfe, but she looked fairly ragged. "Go ahead," she said.

"You know," Wolfe told them curtly, "what the situation is. I must first have a straight answer to this: have any of you repeated the conversation we had in the library, or any part of it, to anyone?"

They all said no.

"This is important. You're sure?"

"Connie was—" Jimmy had to clear his throat. "Connie was asking questions. She was curious." He looked unhappy.

"What did you tell her?"

"Oh, just—nothing much."

"Damn it, how much?" Sperling demanded.

"Not anything, Dad, really. I guess I mentioned Louis—but nothing about X and all that crap."

"You should have had more sense." Sperling looked at Wolfe. "Shall I get her?"

Wolfe shook his head. "By no means. We'll have to risk it. That was all? None of you has reported that conversation?"

They said no again.

"Very well. The police will ask questions. They will be especially interested in my presence here—and Mr. Goodwin's. I shall tell them that Mr. Sperling suspected that Mr. Rony, who was courting his daughter, was a Communist, and that—"

"No!" Sperling objected. "You will not! That's—"

"Nonsense." Wolfe was disgusted. "If they check in New York at all, and they surely will, they'll learn that you hired Mr. Bascom, and what for, and then what? No; that much they must have. I shall tell them of your suspicion, and that you engaged me to confirm it or remove it. You were merely taking a natural and proper precaution. I had no sooner started on the job, by sending Mr. Goodwin up here and putting three men to work, than an assault was made on my plant rooms in the middle of the night and great damage was done. I thought it probable that Mr. Rony and his comrades were responsible for the outrage; that they feared I would be able to expose and discredit him, and were trying to intimidate me.

"So today—yesterday now—I came here to discuss the matter with Mr. Sperling. He gathered the family for it because it was a family affair, and we assembled in the library. He then learned that what I was after was reimbursement; I wanted him to pay for the damage to my plant rooms. The whole time was devoted to an argument between Mr. Sperling and me on that point alone. No one else said anything whatever—at least nothing memorable. You stayed because you were there and there was no good reason to get up and go. That was all."

Wolfe's eyes moved to take them in. "Well?"

"It'll do," Sperling agreed.

Madeline was concentrating hard. She had a question. "What did you stay here all evening for?"

"A good question, Miss Sperling, but my conduct can be left to me. I refused to leave here without the money or a firm commitment on it."

"What about Gwenn's phoning Louis to come up here?"

Wolfe looked at Gwenn. "What did you tell him?"

"This is awful," Gwenn whispered. She was gazing at Wolfe as if she couldn't believe he was there. She repeated aloud, "This is awful!"

Wolfe nodded. "No one will contradict you on that. Do you remember what you said to him?"

"Of course I do. I just told him I had to see him, and he said he had some appointments and the first train he could make was the one that leaves Grand

Central at eight-twenty. It gets to Chappaqua at nine-twenty-three."

"You told him nothing of what had happened?"

"No, I—I didn't intend to. I was just going to tell him I had decided to call it off."

"Then that's what you'll tell the police." Wolfe returned to Madeline. "You have an orderly mind, Miss Sperling, and you want to get this all neatly arranged. It can't be done that way; there's too much of it. The one vital point, for all of you, is that the conversation in the library consisted exclusively of our argument about paying for the damage to my plant rooms. Except for that, you will all adhere strictly to fact. If you try anything else you're sunk. You probably are anyway, if a strong suspicion is aroused that one of you deliberately murdered Mr. Rony, and if one of the questioners happens to be a first-rate man, but that's unlikely and we'll have to chance it."

"I've always been a very poor liar," Mrs. Sperling said forlornly.

"Damn it!" Sperling said, not offensively. "Go up and go to bed!"

"An excellent idea," Wolfe assented. "Do that, madam." He turned to Sperling. "Now, if you will—"

The Chairman of the Board went to the telephone.

10

At eleven o'clock the next morning, Tuesday, Cleveland Archer, District Attorney of Westchester County, said to James U. Sperling, "This is a very regrettable affair. Very."

It would probably have been not Archer himself, but one of his assistants, sitting there talking like that, but for the extent of Stony Acres, the number of rooms in the house, and the size of Sperling's tax bill. That was only natural. Wolfe and I had had a couple of previous contacts with Cleveland Archer, most recently when we had gone to the Pitcairn place near Katonah to get a replacement for Theodore when his mother was sick. Archer was a little plump and had a round red face, and he could tell a constituent from a tourist at ten miles, but he wasn't a bad guy.

"Very regrettable," he said.

None of the occupants of the house had been kept up all night, not even me, who had found the body. The State cops had arrived first, followed soon by a pair of county dicks from White Plains, and, after some rounds of questions without being too rude, they had told everyone to go to bed—that is, everyone but me. I was singled out not only because I had found the body, which was just a good excuse, but because the man who singled me would have liked to do unto me as I would have liked to do unto him. He was Lieutenant Con Noonan of the State Police, and he would never forget how I had helped Wolfe make a monkey out of him in the Pitcairn affair. Add to that the fact that he was fitted out at birth for a career as a guard at a slave-labor camp and somehow got delivered to the wrong country, and you can imagine his attitude when he came and saw Wolfe and me there. He was bitterly disappointed when he learned that Wolfe was on Sperling's payroll and therefore he would have to pretend he knew how to be polite. He was big and tall and in love with his uniform, and he thought he was handsome. At two o'clock one of the county boys, who was really in charge, because the body had not been found on a public highway, told me to go to bed.

I slept five hours, got up and dressed, went downstairs, and had breakfast with Sperling, Jimmy, and Paul Emerson. Emerson looked as sour as ever, but claimed he felt wonderful because of an unusual experience. He said he couldn't remember when he had had a good night's sleep, on account of insomnia, but that last night he had gone off the minute his head hit the pillow, and he had slept like a log. Apparently, he concluded, what he needed was the stimulant of a homicide at bedtime, but he didn't see how he could magage that often enough to help much. Jimmy tried halfheartedly to help along with a bum joke, Sperling wasn't interested, and I was busy eating in order to get through and take Wolfe's breakfast tray up to him.

From the bedroom I phoned Fritz and learned that Andy and the others were back at work on the roof and everything was under control. I told him I couldn't say when we'd be home, and I told Saul to stay on call but to go out for air if he wanted some. I figured that he and Ruth were in the clear, since with Rony gone no one could identify the bandits but me. I also told Saul of the fatal accident that had happened to a friend of the Sperling family, and he felt as Archer did later, that it was very regrettable.

When Wolfe had cleaned the tray I took it back downstairs and had a look around. Madeline was having strawberries and toast and coffee on the west terrace, with a jacket over her shoulders on account of the morning breeze. She didn't look as if homicides stimulated her the way they did Paul Emerson, to sounder sleep. I had wondered how her eyes would be, wide open or half shut, when her mind was too occupied to keep them to a program, and the answer seemed to be wide open, even though the lids were heavy and the whites not too clear.

Madeline told me that things had been happening while I was upstairs. District Attorney Archer and Ben Dykes, head of the county detectives, had arrived and were in the library with Sperling. An Assistant District Attorney was having a talk with Gwenn up in her room. Mrs. Sperling was staying in bed with a bad headache. Jimmy had gone to the garage for a car to drive to Mount Kisco on a personal errand, and had been told nothing doing because the scientific inspection of the Sperlings' five vehicles had not been completed. Paul and Connie Emerson had decided that house guests must be a nuisance in the circumstances, and that they should leave, but Ben Dykes earnestly requested them to stay; and anyhow their car too, with the others in the garage, was not available. A New

York newspaper reporter had got as far as the house by climbing a fence and coming through the woods to the lawn, and had been bounced by a State cop.

It looked as if it wouldn't be merely a quick hello and good-by, in spite of the size of the house and grounds, with all the fancy trees and bushes and three thousand roses. I left Madeline to her third cup of coffee on the terrace and strolled to the plaza behind the shrubbery where I had left the sedan. It was still there, and so were two scientists, making themselves familiar with it. I stood and watched them a while without getting as much as a glance from them, and then moved on. Moseying around, it seemed to me that something was missing. How had all the law arrived, on foot or horseback? It needed investigation. I circled the house and struck out down the front drive. In the bright June morning sun the landscape certainly wasn't the same as it had been the night before when I had taken that walk with Madeline. The drive was perfectly smooth, whereas last night it had kept having warts where my feet landed.

As I neared the bridge over the brook I got my question answered. Fifteen paces this side of the brook a car was parked in the middle of the drive, and another car was standing on the bridge. More scientists were at work on the drive, concentrated at its edge, in the space between the two cars. So they had found something there last night that they wanted to preserve for daylight inspection, and no cars had been allowed to pass, including the DA's. I thoroughly approved. Always willing to learn, I approached and watched the operations with deep interest. One who was presumably not a scientist but an executive, since he was just standing looking, inquired, "You doing research?"

"No sir," I told him. "I smelled blood, and my grandfather was a cannibal."

"Oh, a gag man. You're not needed. Beat it."

Not feeling like arguing, I stood and watched. In about ten minutes, not less, he reminded me. "I said beat it."

"Yeah, I know. I didn't think you were serious, because I have a friend who is a lawyer, and that would be silly." I tilted my head back and sniffed twice. "Chicken blood. From a White Wyandotte rooster with catarrh. I'm a detective."

I had an impulse to go take a look at the bush where I had found Rony, which looked much closer to the drive than it had seemed last night, but decided that might start a real quarrel, and I didn't want to make enemies. The executive was glaring at me. I grinned at him as a friend and headed back up the drive.

As I mounted the three steps to the wide front terrace a State employee in uniform stepped toward me.

"Your name Goodwin?"

I admitted it.

He jerked his head sideways. "You're wanted inside."

I entered and crossed the vestibule to the reception hall. Madeline, passing through, saw me and stopped.

"Your boss wants you."

"The worm. Where, upstairs?"

"No, the library. They sent for him and they want you too."

I went to the library.

Wolfe did not have the best chair this time, probably because it had already been taken by Cleveland Archer when he got there. But the one he had would do, and on a little table at his elbow was a tray with a glass and two bottles of beer. Sperling was standing, but after I had pulled up a chair and joined them he sat down too. Archer, who had a table in front of him with some papers on it, was good enough to remember that he had met me before, since of course there was always a chance that I might buy a plot in Westchester and establish a voting residence there.

Wolfe said Archer had some questions to ask me.

Archer, not at all belligerent, nodded at me. "Yes, I've got to be sure the record is straight. Sunday night you and Rony were waylaid on Hotchkiss Road."

It didn't sound like a question, but I was anxious to cooperate, so I said that was right.

"It's a coincidence, you see," Archer explained. "Sunday night he got blackjacked and robbed, and Monday night he got run over and killed. A sort of epidemic of violence. It makes me want to ask, was there any connection?"

"If you're asking me, none that I know of."

"Maybe not. But there were circumstances—I won't say suspicious, but peculiar. You gave a false name and address when you reported it at the State Police barracks."

"I gave the name Goodwin."

"Don't quibble," Wolfe muttered, pouring beer.

"I suppose you know," I told Archer, "that I was sent up here by Mr. Wolfe, who employs me, and that Mr. Sperling and I arranged what my name and occupation would be to his family and guests. Rony was present while I was reporting at the barracks, and I didn't think I ought to confuse him by changing names on him when he was still dim."

"Dim?"

"As you said, he had just been blackjacked. His head was not clear."

Archer nodded. "Even so, giving a false name and address to the police should be avoided whenever possible. You were held up by a man and a woman."

"That's right."

"You reported the number of the license on their car, but it's no good."

"That doesn't surprise me."

"No. Nor me. Did you recognize either the man or the woman?"

I shook my head. "Aren't you wasting your time, Mr. Archer?" I pointed at the papers on the table. "You must have it all there."

"I have, certainly. But now that the man who was with you has been killed, that might sharpen your memory. You're in the detective business, and you've been around a lot and seen lots of people. Haven't you remembered that you had seen that man or woman before?"

"No, sir. After all, this is—okay. No, sir."

"Why did you and Rony refuse to let the police take your wallets to get fingerprints?"

"Because it was late and we wanted to get home,

and anyway it looked to me as if they were just living up to routine and didn't really mean it."

Archer glanced at a paper. "They took around three hundred dollars from Rony, and over two hundred from you. Is that right?"

"For Rony, so he said. For me, right."

"He was wearing valuable jewelry—stickpin, cuff-links, and a ring. It wasn't taken. There was luggage in the car, including two valuable cameras. It wasn't touched. Didn't that strike you as peculiar?"

I turned a hand over. "Now listen, Mr. Archer. You know damn well they have their prejudices. Some of them take everything that's loose, even your belt or suspenders. These babies happened to prefer cash, and they got over five Cs. The only thing that struck me worth mentioning was something on the side of my head."

"It left no mark on you."

"Nor on Rony either. I guess they had had practice."

"Did you go to a doctor?"

"No sir. I didn't know that Westchester required a doctor's certificate in a holdup case. It must be a very progressive county. I'll remember it next time."

"You don't have to be sarcastic, Goodwin."

"No, sir." I grinned at him. "Nor do you have to be so goddam sympathetic with a guy who got a bat on the head on a public road in your jurisdiction. Thank you just the same."

"All right." He flipped a hand to brush it off. "Why did you feel so bad you couldn't eat anything all day Sunday?"

I admit that surprised me. Wolfe had mentioned the possibility that there would be a first-rate man among the questioners, and while this sudden question was no proof of brilliancy it certainly showed that someone had been good and thorough.

"The boys have been getting around," I said admiringly. "I didn't know any of the servants here had it in for me—maybe they used the third degree. Or could one of my fellow guests have spilled it?" I leaned forward and spoke in a low voice. "I had nine drinks and they were all doped."

"Don't clown," Wolfe muttered, putting down an empty glass.

"What then?" I demanded. "Can I tell him it must have been something I ate with my host sitting here?"

"You didn't have nine drinks," Archer said. "You had two or three."

"Okay," I surrendered. "Then it must have been the country air. All I know is, I had a headache and my stomach kept warning me not to make any shipments. Now ask me if I went to a doctor. I ought to tell you, Mr. Archer, that I think I may get sore, and if I get sore I'll start making wisecracks, and if I do that you'll get sore. What good will that do us?"

The District Attorney laughed. His laughing routine was quite different from Sperling's, being closer to a giggle than a roar, but it suited him all right. No one joined him, and after a moment he looked around apologetically and spoke to James U. Sperling.

"I hope you don't think I'm taking this lightly. This is a very regrettable affair. Very."

"It certainly is," Sperling agreed.

Archer nodded, puckering his mouth. "Very regrettable. There's no reason why I shouldn't be entirely frank with you, Mr. Sperling—and in Mr. Wolfe's presence, since you have retained him in your interest. It is not the policy of my office to go out of its way to make trouble for men of your standing. That's only common sense. We have considered your suggestion that Rony was killed elsewhere, in a road accident, and the body brought here and concealed on your property, but we can't—that is, it couldn't have happened that way. He got off the train at Chappaqua at nine-twenty-three, and the taxi driver brought him to the entrance to your grounds, and saw him start walking up the driveway. Not only that, there is clear evidence that he was killed, run over by a car, on your drive at a point about thirty feet this side of the bridge crossing the brook. That evidence is still being accumulated, but there is already enough to leave no room for doubt. Do you want me to send for a man to give you the details?"

"No," Sperling said.

"You're welcome to them at any time. The evidence indicates that the car was going east, away from the house, toward the entrance, but that is not conclusive. Inspection of the cars belonging here has not been completed. It is possible that it was some other car—any car—which came in from the road, but you will understand why that theory is the least acceptable. It seems improbable, but we haven't rejected it, and frankly, we see no reason for rejecting it unless we have to."

Archer puckered his lips again, evidently considering words that were ready to come, and decided to let them through. "My office cannot afford to be offhand about sudden and violent death, even if it wanted to. In this case we have to answer not only to our own consciences, and to the people of this county whose servants we are, but also to—may I say, to other interests. There have already been inquiries from the New York City authorities, and an offer of co-operation. They mean it well and we welcome it, but I mention it to show that the interest in Rony's death is not confined to my jurisdiction, and that of course increases my responsibility. I hope—do I make my meaning clear?"

"Perfectly," Sperling assented.

"Then you will see that nothing can be casually overlooked—not that it should be or would be, in any event. Anyhow, it can't be. As you know, we have questioned everyone here fairly rigorously—including all of your domestic staff—and we have got not the slightest clue to what happened. No one knows anything about it at all, with the single exception of your younger daughter, who admits—I should say states—that she asked Rony to come here on that train and meet her at a certain spot on this property. No one—"

Wolfe grunted. "Miss Sperling didn't ask him to come on that train. She asked him to come. It was his convenience that determined the train."

"My mistake," Archer conceded. "Anyhow, it was her summons that brought him. He came on that train. It was on time. He got into the taxi at once, and the driving time from the railroad station to the entrance to these grounds is six or seven minutes, therefore he arrived at half past nine—perhaps a minute or so later. He may have headed straight for the place of his rendezvous, or he may have loitered on the drive—we don't know."

Archer fingered among the papers before him, looked at one, and sat up again. "If he loitered your daughter may have been at the place of the rendezvous at the time he was killed. She intended to get there at nine-thirty but was delayed by a conversation with her sister and was a little late—she thinks about ten minutes, possibly fifteen. Her sister, who saw her leave the house, corroborates that. If Rony loitered—"

"Isn't this rather elaborate?" Sperling put in.

Archer nodded. "These things usually are. If Rony loitered on the drive, and if your daughter was at the place of rendezvous at the time he was killed, why didn't she hear the car that killed him? She says she heard no car. That has been thoroughly tested. It is slightly downhill along the drive clear to the entrance. From the place of rendezvous, beyond that thicket, the sound of a car going down the drive is extremely faint. Even with a car going up the drive you have to listen for it, and last night there was some wind from the northeast. So Rony might have been killed while your daughter was there waiting for him, and she might have heard nothing."

"Then damn it, why so much talk about it?"

Archer was patient. "Because that's all there is to talk about. Except for your daughter's statement, nothing whatever has been contributed by anyone. No one saw or heard anything. Mr. Goodwin's contribution is entirely negative. He left here at ten minutes to ten—" Archer looked at me. "I understand that time is definite?"

"Yes, sir. When I get in the car I have a habit of checking the dash clock with my wrist watch. It was nine-fifty."

Archer returned to Sperling. "He left at nine-fifty to drive to Chappaqua to make a phone call, and noticed nothing along the drive. He returned thirty or thirty-five minutes later, and again noticed nothing—so his contribution is entirely negative. By the way, your daughter didn't hear his car either—or doesn't remember hearing it."

Sperling was frowning. "I still would like to know why all the concentration on my daughter."

"I don't concentrate on her," Archer objected. "Circumstances do."

"What circumstances?"

"She was a close friend of Rony's. She says that she had not engaged to marry him, but she—uh, saw a great deal of him. Her association with him had been the subject of—uh, much family discussion. It was that that led to your engaging the services of Nero Wolfe, and he doesn't concern himself with trivialities. It was that that brought him up here yesterday, and his—"

"It was not. He wanted me to pay for the damage to his plant rooms."

"But because he thought it was connected with your employment of him. His aversion to leaving his place for anything at all is well known. There was a long family conference—"

"Not a conference. He did all the talking. He insisted that I must pay the damages."

Archer nodded. "You all agree on that. By the way, how did it come out? Are you paying?"

"Is that relevant?" Wolfe inquired.

"Perhaps not," Archer conceded. "Only, since you have been engaged to investigate this other matter—I'll withdraw the question if it's impertinent."

"Not at all," Sperling declared. "I'm paying the damage, but not because I'm obliged to. There's no evidence that it had any connection with me or my affairs."

"Then it's none of my business," Archer further conceded. "But the fact remains that something happened yesterday to cause your daughter to decide to summon Rony and tell him she was through with him. She says that it was simply that the trouble her friendship with him was causing was at last too much for her, and she made up her mind to end it. That may well be. I can't even say that I'm skeptical about it. But it is extremely unfortunate, *extremely*, that she reached that decision the very day that Rony was to die a violent death, under circumstances which no one can explain and for which no one can be held accountable."

Archer leaned forward and spoke from his heart. "Listen, Mr. Sperling. You know quite well I don't want to make trouble for you. But I have a duty and a responsibility, and, besides that, I'm not functioning in a vacuum. Far from it! I can't say how many people know about the situation here regarding your daughter and Rony, but certainly some do. There are three guests here in the house right now, and one of them is a prominent broadcaster. Whatever I do or don't do, people are going to believe that that situation and Rony's death are connected, and therefore if I tried to ignore it I would be hooted out of the county. I've got to go the limit on this homicide, and I'm going to. I've got to find out who killed Rony and why. If it was an accident no one will be better pleased than me, but I've got to know who was responsible. It's going to be unpleasant—" Archer stopped because the door had swung open. Our heads turned to see the intruder. It was Ben Dykes, the head of the county detectives, and behind him was the specimen who had been born in the wrong country, Lieutenant Con Noonan of the State Police. I didn't like the look on Noonan's face, but then I never do.

"Yes, Ben?" Archer demanded impatiently. No wonder he was irritated, having been interrupted in the middle of his big speech.

"Something you ought to know," Dykes said, approaching.

"What is it?"

"Maybe you'd rather have it privately."

"Why? We have nothing to conceal from Mr. Sperling, and Wolfe's working for him. What is it?"

Dykes shrugged. "They've finished on the cars and got the one that killed him. It's the one they did last, the one that's parked out back. Nero Wolfe's."

"No question about it!" Noonan crowed.

11

I had a funny mixed feeling. I was surprised, I was even flabbergasted, that is true. But it is also that the surprise was canceled out by its exact opposite; that I had been expecting this all along. They say that the conscious mind is the upper tenth and everything else is down below. I don't know how they got their percentages, but if they're correct I suppose nine-tenths of me had been doing the expecting, and it broke through into the upper layer when Ben Dykes put it into words.

Wolfe darted a glance at me. I lifted my brows and shook my head. He nodded and lifted his glass for the last of his beer.

"That makes it different," said Sperling, not grief-stricken. "That seems to settle it."

"Look, Mr. Archer," Lieutenant Noonan offered. "It's only a hit-and-run now, and you're a busy man and so is Dykes. This Goodwin thinks he's tough. Why don't I just take him down to the barracks?"

Archer, skipping him, asked Dykes, "How good is it? Enough to bank on?"

"Plenty," Dykes declared. "It all has to go to the laboratory, but there's blood on the under side of the fender, and a button with a piece of his jacket wedged between the axle and the spring, and other things. It's good all right."

Archer looked at me. "Well?"

I smiled at him. "I couldn't put it any better than you did, Mr. Archer. My contribution is entirely negative. If that car killed Rony I was somewhere else at the time. I wish I could be more help, but that's the best I can do."

"I'll take him to the barracks," Noonan offered again.

Again he was ignored. Archer turned to Wolfe. "You own the car, don't you? Have you got anything to say?"

"Only that I don't know how to drive, and that if Mr. Goodwin is taken to a barracks, as this puppy suggests, I shall go with him."

The DA came back to me. "Why don't you come clean with it? We can wind it up in ten minutes and get out of here."

"I'm sorry," I said courteously. "If I tried to fake it at a minute's notice I might bitch it up and you'd catch me in a lie."

"You won't tell us how it happened?"

"No I won't. I can't."

Archer stood up and spoke to Sperling. "Is there another room I can take him to? I have to be in court at two o'clock and I'd like to finish this if possible."

"You can stay here," Sperling said, leaving his chair, eager to co-operate. He looked at Wolfe. "I see you've finished your beer. If you'll come—"

Wolfe put his hands on the chair arms, got himself erect, took three steps, and was facing Archer. "As you say, I own the car. If Mr. Goodwin is taken away without first notifying me, and without a warrant, this affair will be even more regrettable than it is now. I don't blame you for wanting to talk with him; you don't know him as well as I do; but I owe it to you to say that you will be wasting valuable time."

He marched to the door, with Sperling at his heels, and was gone.

Dykes asked, "Will you want me?"

"I might," Archer said. "Sit down."

Dykes moved to the chair Wolfe had vacated, sat, took out a notebook and pencil, inspected the pencil point, and settled back. Meanwhile Noonan walked across and deposited himself in the chair Sperling had used. He hadn't been invited and he hadn't asked if he was wanted. Naturally I was pleased, since if he had acted otherwise I would have had to take the trouble to change my opinion of him.

Archer, his lips puckered, was giving me a good look.

He spoke. "I don't understand you, Goodwin. I don't know why you don't see that your position is impossible."

"That's easy," I told him. "For exactly the same reason that you don't."

"That I don't see it's impossible? But I do."

"Like hell you do. If you did you'd be on your way by now, leaving me to Ben Dykes or one of your assistants. You've got a busy schedule ahead of you, but here you still are. May I make a statement?"

"By all means. That's just what I want you to do."

"Fine." I clasped my hands behind my head. "There's no use going over what I did and when. I've already told it three times and it's on the record. But with this news, that it was Mr. Wolfe's car that killed him, you don't have to bother any more with what anybody was doing, even me, eight o'clock or nine or ten. You know exactly when he was killed. It couldn't have been before nine-thirty, because that's when he got out of the cab at the entrance. It couldn't have been after nine-fifty, because that's when I got in the car to drive to Chappaqua. Actually, it's even narrower, say between nine-thirty-two and nine-forty-six—only fourteen minutes. During that time I was up in the bedroom with Mr. Wolfe. Where were the others? Because of course it's all in the family now, since our car was used. Someone here did it, and during that fourteen minutes. You'll want to know where the key to the ignition was. In the car. I don't remove it when I'm parking on the private grounds of a friend or a client. I did remove it, however, when I got back from Chappaqua, since it might be there all night. I didn't know how long it would take Sperling to decide to let go of forty grand. You will also want to know if the engine was warm when I got in and started it. I don't know. It starts like a dream, warm or cold. Also it is June. Also, if all it had done was roll down the drive and kill Rony, and turn around at the entrance and come back again, and there wasn't time for much more than that, it wouldn't have got warmed up to speak of."

I considered a moment. "That's the crop."

"You can eat that timetable," Noonan said in his

normal voice, which you ought to hear. "Try again, bud. He wasn't killed in that fifteen minutes. He was killed at nine-fifty-two, when you went down the drive on your way to Chappaqua. Do your statement over."

I turned my head to get his eyes. "Oh, you here?"

Archer said to Dykes, "Ask him some questions, Ben."

I had known Ben Dykes sort of off and on for quite a while, and as far as I knew, he was neither friend nor enemy. Most of the enforcers of the law, both in and out of uniform, in the suburban districts, have got an inferiority complex about New York detectives, either public or private, but Dykes was an exception. He had been a Westchester dick for more than twenty years, and all he cared about was doing his work well enough to hang onto his job, steering clear of mudholes, and staying as honest as he could.

He kept after me, with Archer cutting in a few times, for over an hour. In the middle of it a colleague brought sandwiches and coffee in to us, and we went ahead between bites. Dykes did as well as he could, and he was an old hand at it, but even if he had been one of the best, which he wasn't, there was only one direction he could get at me from, and from there he always found me looking straight at him. He was committed to one simple concrete fact: that going down the drive on my way to Chappaqua I had killed Rony, and I matched it with the simple concrete fact that I hadn't. That didn't allow much leeway for a fancy grilling, and the only thing that prolonged it to over an hour was their earnest drive to wrap it up quick and cart it away from Stony Acres.

Archer looked at his wrist watch for the tenth time. A glance at mine showed me 1:20.

"The only thing to do," he said, "is get a warrant. Ben, you'd better phone—no, one of the men can ride down with me and bring it back."

"I'll go," Noonan offered.

"We've got plenty of men," Dykes said pointedly, "since it looks like we're through here."

Archer had got up. "You leave us no other course,

Goodwin," he told me. "If you try to leave the county before the warrant comes you'll be stopped."

"I've got his car key," Dykes said.

"This is so damned unnecessary!" Archer complained, exasperated. He sat down again and leaned forward at me. "For God's sake, haven't I made it plain enough? There's no possibility of jeopardy for a major crime, and very little of any jeopardy at all. It was night. You didn't see him until you were on top of him. When you got out and went to him he was dead. You were rattled, and you had an urgent confidential phone call to make. You didn't want to leave his body there in the middle of the drive, so you dragged it across the grass to a bush. You drove to Chappaqua, made the phone call, and drove back here. You entered the house, intending to phone a report of the accident, and were met by Miss Sperling, who was concerned about the absence of her sister. You went out with her to look for the sister, and you found her. Naturally you didn't want to tell her, abruptly and brutally, of Rony's death. Within a short time you went to the house and told Wolfe about it, and he told Sperling, and Sperling notified the police. You were understandably reluctant to admit that it was your car that had killed him, and you could not bring yourself to do so until the course of the investigation showed you that it was unavoidable. Then, to me, to the highest law officer of the county, you stated the facts—all of them."

Archer stretched another inch forward. "If those facts are set down in a statement, and you sign it, what will happen? You can't even be charged with leaving the scene of an accident, because you didn't—you're here and haven't left here. I'm the District Attorney. It will be up to me to decide if any charge shall be lodged against you, and if so what charge. What do you think I'll decide? Considering all the circumstances, which you're as familiar with as I am, what would any man of sense decide? Whom have you injured, except one man by an unavoidable accident?"

Archer turned to the table, found a pad of paper, got a pen from his pocket, and offered them to me.

"Here. Write it down and sign it, and let's get it over with. You'll never regret it, Goodwin, you have my word for that."

I smiled at him. "Now I *am* sorry, Mr. Archer, I really am."

"Don't be sorry! Just write it down and sign it."

I shook my head. "I guess you'll have to get the warrant, but you'd better count ten. I'm glad you weren't peddling a vacuum cleaner or you'd have sold me. But I won't buy signing such a statement. If all it had to have in it was what you said—hitting him and dragging him off the road, and going on to make the phone call, and coming back and helping Miss Sperling hunt her sister, and getting the cops notified but not mentioning the fact that it was me that ran over him—if that was all there was to it I might possibly oblige you, in spite of the fact that it wouldn't be true, just to save trouble all around. But one detail that you didn't include would be too much for me."

"What? What are you talking about?"

"The car. I'm in the detective business. I'm supposed to know things. I'm certainly supposed to know that if you run over a man and squash him the way Rony was squashed, the car will have so much evidence on it that a blindfolded Boy Scout could get enough to cinch it. Yet I drove the car back here and parked it, and played innocent all night and all morning, so Ben Dykes could walk in on us at noon and announce aha, it was Nero Wolfe's car! That I will not buy. It would get me a horse laugh from the Battery to Spuyten Duyvil. I would never live it down. And speaking of a warrant, I don't think any judge or jury would buy it either."

"We could make it—"

"You couldn't make it anything but what it is. I'll tell you another thing. I don't believe Ben Dykes has bought it, and I doubt very much if you have. Ben may not like me much, I don't know, but he knows damn well I'm not a sap. He went after me as well as he could because you told him to and you're the boss. As for you, I can't say, except that I don't blame you a bit for not liking to start fires under people like the

Sperlings. If nothing else, they hire only the best lawyers. As for this bird in uniform named Noonan, you may be a church member and I'd better keep within bounds."

"You see what he's like, sir," Noonan said under restraint. "I told you he thinks he's tough. If you had let me take him to the barracks—"

"Shut up!" Archer squeaked.

It may not be fair to call it a squeak, but it was close to it. He was harassed and I felt sorry for him. In addition to everything else, he was going to be late at court, as he realized when he took another look at his watch. He ignored me and spoke to Dykes.

"I've got to go, Ben. Take care of these papers. If anyone wants to leave the place you can't hold them, the way it stands now, but ask them not to leave the jurisdiction."

"What about Wolfe and Goodwin?"

"I said anyone. We can't hold them without a warrant, and that will have to wait. But the car stays where it is. Immobilize it and keep a guard on it. Have you tried it for prints?"

"No, sir, I thought—"

"Do so. Thoroughly. Keep a man at the car and one at the entrance, and you stay. You might have another try at the servants, especially the assistant gardener. Tell Mr. Sperling that I'll be back some time between five and six—it depends on when court adjourns. Tell him I would appreciate it if they can all find it convenient to be here."

He trotted out without even glancing at me, which I thought was uncalled for.

I grinned at Ben Dykes, strolled insolently out of the room, and went in search of Wolfe, to do a little mild bragging. I found him out at the greenhouse, inspecting some concrete benches with automatic watering.

12

A couple of hours later Wolfe and I were up in the bedroom. He had found that the biggest chair there, while it would do for a short stretch, was no good for a serious distance, and therefore he was on the bed with his book, flat on his back, though he hated to read lying down. His bright yellow shirt was still bright but badly wrinkled, worse than it ever was at home, since he changed every day; and both his yellow socks showed the beginnings of holes at the big toes, which was no wonder, considering that they hadn't been changed either and were taking the push of more than an eighth of a ton for the second day.

I had finally got around to the magazines I had brought upstairs the previous evening. There was a knock at the door and I said come in.

It was the Chairman of the Board. He closed the door and approached. I said hello. Wolfe let his book down to rest on his belly but otherwise stayed put.

"You look comfortable," Sperling said like a host.

Wolfe grunted. I said something gracious.

Sperling moved a chair around to a different angle and sat.

"So you talked yourself out of it?" he asked.

"I doubt if I rate a credit line," I said modestly. "The picture was out of focus, that's all. It would have needed too much retouching, and all I did was point that out."

He nodded. "I understand from Dykes that the District Attorney offered to guarantee immunity if you would sign a statement."

"Not quite. He didn't offer to put it in writing. Not

that I think he would have crossed me, but I liked the immunity I already had. As I heard a guy say once, virtue is never left to stand alone."

"Where did you get that?" Wolfe demanded from his pillows. "That's Confucius."

I shrugged. "It must have been him I heard say it."

Our host gave me up and turned to Wolfe. "The District Attorney will be back between five and six. He left word that he would like all of us to be here. What does that mean?"

"Apparently," Wolfe said dryly, "it means that he feels compelled to annoy you some more, much as he would prefer not to. By the way, I wouldn't underrate Mr. Archer. Don't let the defects of his personality mislead you."

"They haven't. But what evidence has he got that this was anything but an accident?"

"I don't know, beyond what he hinted to you. Possibly none. Even if he accepts it as an accident, he needs to find out who was driving the car. Being a man in your position, Mr. Sperling, a man of wealth and note, bestows many advantages and privileges, but it also bestows handicaps. Mr. Archer knows he cannot afford to have it whispered that he winked at this affair because you are such a man. The poor devil."

"I understand that," Sperling was controlling himself admirably, considering that he had stated before witnesses that he would pay for the damage to the plant rooms. "But what about you? You have spent three hours this afternoon questioning my family and guests and servants. You have no intention of running for office, have you?"

"Good heavens, no." From Wolfe's tone you might have thought he had been asked if he intended to take up basketball. "But you have hired me to investigate Mr. Rony's death. I was trying to earn my fee. I admit it doesn't look much like it at this moment, but I had a hard night Sunday, and I'm waiting to learn what line Mr. Archer is going to take. What time is it, Archie?"

"Quarter past four."

"Then he should be here in an hour or so."

Sperling stood up. "Things are piling up at my office," he said, just stating a fact, and strode out of the room.

"On him a crown looks good," I remarked.

"It doesn't chafe him," Wolfe agreed, and went back to his book.

After a while it began to irritate me to see the toes of the yellow socks sticking up with holes started, so I tossed the magazines on a table, wandered out of the room, on downstairs, and outdoors. Sounds came from the direction of the swimming pool, and I went that way. The wind was no longer even a breeze, the sun was warm and friendly, and for anyone who likes grass and flowers and trees better than sidewalks and buildings it would have been a treat.

Connie Emerson and Madeline were in the pool. Paul Emerson, in a cotton shirt and slacks, not too clean, was standing on the marble at the edge, scowling at this. Gwenn, in a dress dark in color but summery in weight, was in a chair under an umbrella, her head leaning back and her eyes closed.

Madeline interrupted an expert crawl to call to me, "Come on in!"

"No trunks!" I called back.

Gwenn, hearing, swiveled her head to give me a long straight look, had nothing to say, turned her head back as before, and shut her eyes.

"You not getting wet?" I asked Emerson.

"I got cramps Saturday," he said in an irritated tone, as if I should have had sense enough to know that. "How does it stand now?"

"What? The cramp situation?"

"The Rony situation."

"Oh. He's still dead."

"That's surprising." The eminent broadcaster flicked a glance at me, but liked the sunlight on the water better. "I bet he rises from the grave. I hear it was your car."

"Mr. Wolfe's car, yeah. So they say."

"Yet here you are without a guardian, no handcuffs. What are they doing, giving you a medal?"

"I'm waiting and hoping. Why, do you think I deserve one?"

Emerson tightened his lips and relaxed them again, a habit he had. "Depends on whether you did it on purpose or not. If it was accidental I don't think you ought to get more than honorable mention. How does it stand? Would it help any if I put in a word for you?"

"I don't—excuse me, I'm being paged."

I stooped to grab the hand Madeline was putting up at me, braced myself, straightened, bringing her out of the water onto the marble and on up to her feet.

"My, you're big and strong," she said, standing and dripping. "Congratulations!"

"Just for that? Gee, if I wanted to I could pull Elsa Maxwell—"

"No, not that. For keeping out of jail. How did you do it?"

I waved a hand. "I've got something on the DA."

"No, really? Come and sit while I let the sun dry me, and tell me about it."

She went and stretched out on the grassy slope, and I sat beside her. She had been doing some fast swimming but wasn't out of breath, and her breast, with nothing but the essentials covered, rose and fell in easy smooth rhythm. Even with her eyes closed for the sun she seemed to know where I was looking, for she said complacently, "I expand three inches. If that's not your type I'll smoke more and get it down. Is it true that you were driving the car when it ran over Louis?"

"Nope. Not guilty."

"Then who was?"

"I don't know yet. Ask me tomorrow and keep on asking me. Call my secretary and make appointments so you can keep on asking me. She expands four inches."

"Who, your secretary?"

"Yes, ma'am."

"Bring her up here. We'll do a pentathlon and the winner gets you. What would you advise me to do?"

Her eyes, opened from force of habit, blinked in the sun and went shut again. I asked, "You mean to train for the pentathlon?"

"Certainly not. I won't have to. I mean when the District Attorney comes to ask more questions. You know he's coming?"

"Yeah, I heard about it."

"All right, what shall I do? Shall I tell him that I may have a suspicion that I might have an idea about someone using your car?"

"You might take a notion that you might try it. Shall we make it up together? Who shall we pick on?"

"I don't want to pick on anybody. That's the trouble. Why should anyone pay a penalty for accidentally killing Louis Rony?"

"Maybe they shouldn't." I patted her round brown soft firm shoulder to see if it was dry yet. "There I'm right with you, ma'am. But the hell of it—"

"Why do you keep on calling me ma'am?"

"To make you want me to call you something else. Watch and see if it don't work. It always does. The hell of it is that both the DA and Nero Wolfe insist on knowing, and the sooner they find out the sooner we can go on to other things like pentathlons. Knowing how good you are at dare-base, I suppose you do have an idea about someone using my car. What gave it to you?"

She sat up, said, "I guess my front's dry," turned over onto a fresh spot, and stretched out again, face down. The temptation to pat was now stronger than before, but I resisted it.

"What gave it to you?" I asked as if it didn't matter much.

No reply. In a moment her voice came, muffled. "I ought to think it over some more."

"Yeah, that never does any harm, but you haven't got much time. The DA may be here any minute. Also you asked my advice, and I'd be in better shape to make it good if I knew something about your idea. Go ahead and describe it."

She turned her head enough to let her eyes, now shielded from the sun, take me in at an angle. "You could be clever if you worked at it," she said. "It's fun to watch you going after something. Say I saw or heard something last night and now I tell you about it. Within thirty seconds, for as you say there isn't much time, you would have to go in to wash your hands, and as soon as you're in the house you run upstairs and tell Nero Wolfe. He gets busy immediately, and probably by the time the District Attorney gets here the answer is all ready for him—or if it doesn't go as fast as that, when they do get the answer it will be Nero Wolfe that started it, and so the bill he sends my father can be bigger than it could have been otherwise. I don't know how much money Dad has spent on me in my twenty-six years, but it's been plenty, and now for the first time in my life I can save him some. Isn't that wonderful? If you had a widowed middle-aged daughter whose chest expanded three inches, wouldn't you want her to act as I am acting?"

"No, ma'am," I said emphatically.

"Of course you would. Call me something else, like darling or little cabbage. Here we are, locked in a tussle, you trying to make money for your boss and me trying to save money for my father, and yet we're—"

She sat up abruptly. "Is that a car coming? Yes, it is." She was on her feet. "Here he comes, and I've got to do my hair!" She streaked for the house.

13

I walked into the bedroom and announced to Wolfe, "The law has arrived. Shall I arrange to have the meeting held up here?"

"No," he said testily. "What time is it?"

"Eighteen minutes to six."

He grunted. "I'd have a devil of a time getting anywhere on this from the office, with these people here for the summer. You'd have to do it all, and you don't seem to take to this place very well. You gulp down drinks that have been drugged, plan and execute hold-ups, and leave my car where it can be used to kill people."

"Yep," I agreed cheerfully. "I'm no longer what I used to be. If I were you I'd fire me. Am I fired?"

"No. But if I'm to spend another night here, and possibly more, you'll have to go home and get me some shirts and socks and other things." He was gazing gloomily at his toes. "Have you seen those holes?"

"I have. Our car's immobilized, but I can borrow one. If you want to keep up with developments you'd better shake a leg. The elder daughter thinks she saw or heard something last night that gave her an idea about someone using your car, and she's making up her mind whether to tell the DA about it. I tried to get her to tell me, but she was afraid I might pass it on to you. Still another proof I've seen my best days. At least you can be there when she spills it, if you'll get off that bed and put your shoes on."

He pushed himself up, swung his legs around, and grunted as he reached for his shoes. He had them on and was tying a lace when there was a knock at the door, and before I uttered an invitation it swung open. Jimmy Sperling appeared, said, "Dad wants you in the library," and was gone, without closing the door. Apparently his visits to mines had had a bad effect on his manners.

Wolfe took his time about getting his shirttail in and putting on his tie and vest and jacket. We went along the hall to the stairs, and down, and took the complicated route to the library without seeing a soul, and I supposed they had already assembled for the meeting, but they hadn't. When we entered there were only three people there: the District Attorney, the Chairman of the Board, and Webster Kane. Again Archer had copped the best chair and Wolfe had to take a second choice. I was surprised to see Webster Kane and not to see Ben Dykes, and pleased not to see Madeline. Maybe there would still be time for me to finagle a priority on her idea.

Wolfe spoke to Archer. "I congratulate you, sir, on

your good judgment. I knew that Mr. Goodwin was incapable of such a shenanigan, but you didn't. You had to use your brain, and you did so."

Archer nodded. "Thanks. I tried to." He looked around. "I had a bad afternoon in court, and I'm tired. I shouldn't be here, but I said I'd come. I'm turning this matter over to Mr. Gurran, one of my assistants, who is a much better investigator than I am. He was tied up today and couldn't come with me, but he would like to come and talk with all of you tomorrow morning. Meanwhile—"

"May I say something?" Sperling put in.

"Certainly. I wish you would."

Sperling spoke easily, with no tension in his voice or manner. "I'd like to tell you exactly what happened. When Dykes came in this morning and said he had evidence that it was Wolfe's car, I thought that settled it. I believe I said so. Naturally I thought it was Goodwin, knowing that he had driven to Chappaqua last evening. Then when I learned that you weren't satisfied that it was Goodwin, I was no longer myself satisfied, because I knew you would have welcomed that solution if it had been acceptable. I put my mind on the problem as it stood then, with the time limit narrowed as it was, and I remembered something. The best way to tell you about it is to read you a statement."

Sperling's hand went to his inside breast pocket and came out with a folded paper. "This is a statement," he said, unfolding it, "dated today and signed by Mr. Kane. Webster Kane."

Archer was frowning. "By Kane?"

"Yes. It reads as follows:

"On Monday evening, June 20, 1949, a little before half past nine, I entered the library and saw on Mr. Sperling's desk some letters which I knew he wanted mailed. I had heard him say so. I knew he was upset about some personal matter and supposed he had forgotten about them. I decided to go to Mount Kisco and mail them in the post office so they would make the early morning train. I left the house by way of the west terrace, intending to go to the garage for a car, but remembered that Nero Wolfe's car was parked near by, much closer than the garage, and decided to take it instead.

"The key was in the car. I started the engine and went down the drive. It was the last few minutes of dusk, not yet completely dark, and, knowing the drive well, I didn't switch the lights on. The drive is a little downhill, and I was probably going between twenty and twenty-five miles an hour. As I was approaching the bridge over the brook I was suddenly aware of an object in the drive, on the left side, immediately in front of the car. There wasn't time for me to realize, in the dim light, that it was a man. One instant I saw there was an object, and the next instant the car had hit it. I jammed my foot on the brake, but not with great urgency, because at that instant there was no flash of realization that I had hit a man. But I had the car stopped within a few feet. I jumped out and ran to the rear, and saw it was Louis Rony. He was lying about five feet back of the car, and he was dead. The middle of him had been completely crushed by the wheels of the car.

"I could offer a long extenuation of what I did then, but it will serve just as well to put it into one sentence and simply say that I lost my head. I won't try to describe how I felt, but will tell what I did. When I had made certain that he was dead, I dragged the body off the drive and across the grass to a shrub about fifty feet away, and left it on the north side of the shrub, the side away from the drive. Then I went back to the car, drove across the bridge and on to the entrance, turned around, drove back up to the house, parked the car where I had found it, and got out.

"I did not enter the house. I paced up and down the terrace, trying to decide what to do, collecting my nerves enough to go in and tell what had happened. While I was there on the terrace Goodwin came out of the house, crossed the terrace, and went in the direction of the place where the car was parked. I heard him start the engine and drive away. I didn't know where he was going. I thought he might be going to New York and the car might not return. Anyway, his going away in the car seemed somehow to make up my mind for me. I went into the house and up to my room, and tried to compose my mind by working on an economic report I was preparing for Mr. Sperling.

"This afternoon Mr. Sperling told me that he had noticed that the letters on his desk, ready for mailing, were gone. I told him that I had taken them up to my room, which I had, intending to have them taken to Chappaqua early this morning, but that the blocking of the road by the police, and their guarding of all the cars, had made it impossible. But his bringing up the matter of the letters changed the whole aspect of the situation for me, I don't know why. I at once told him, of my own free will, all of the facts herein stated. When he told me that the District Attorney would be here later this afternoon, I told him that I would set down those facts in a written signed statement, and I have now done so. This is the statement."

Sperling looked up. "Signed by Webster Kane," he said. He stretched forward to hand the paper to the District Attorney. "Witnessed by me. If you want it more detailed I don't think he'll have any objection. Here he is—you can ask him."

Archer took it and ran his eye over it. In a moment he looked up and, with his head to one side, gazed at Kane. Kane met the gaze.

Archer tapped the paper with a finger. "You wrote and signed this, did you, Mr. Kane?"

"I did," Kane said clearly and firmly but without bragging.

"Well—you're a little late with it, aren't you?"

"I certainly am." Kane did not look happy, but he was bearing up. The fact that he let his hair do as it pleased was of some advantage to him, for it made it seem less unlikely that the man with the head and face of a young statesman—that is, young for a statesman—would make such a fool of himself. He hesitated and then went on, "I am keenly aware that my conduct was indefensible. I can't even explain it in terms that make sense to me now. Apparently I'm not as good in a crisis as I would like to think I am."

"But this wasn't much of a crisis, was it? An unavoidable accident? It happens to lots of people."

"I suppose it does—but I had killed a man. It seemed like a hell of a crisis to me." Kane gestured. "Anyhow, you see what it did to me. It threw me completely off balance."

"Not completely." Archer glanced at the paper. "Your mind was working well enough so that when Goodwin went to the car and drove away, down that same drive, only fifteen minutes after the accident, you thought there was a good chance that it would be blamed on him. Didn't you?"

Kane nodded. "I put that in the statement deliberately, even though I knew it could be construed like that. I can only say that if that thought was in my mind I wasn't conscious of it. How did I put it?"

Archer looked at the paper. "Like this: 'His going away in the car seemed somehow to make up my mind for me. I went into the house and up to my room,' and so on."

"That's right." Kane looked and sounded very earnest. "I was simply trying to be thoroughly honest about it, after behavior of which I was ashamed. If I had in me the kind of calculation you have described I didn't know it."

"I see." Archer looked at the paper, folded it, and sat holding it. "How well did you know Rony?"

"Oh—not intimately. I had seen him frequently the past few months, mostly at the Sperling home in New York or here."

"Were you on good terms with him?"

"No."

It was a blunt uncompromising no. Archer snapped, "Why not?"

"I didn't like what I knew of the way he practiced his profession. I didn't like him personally—I just didn't like him. I knew that Mr. Sperling suspected him of being a Communist, and while I had no evidence or knowledge of my own, I thought that the suspicion might easily be well founded."

"Did you know that Miss Gwenn Sperling was quite friendly with him?"

"Certainly. That was the only reason he was allowed to be here."

"You didn't approve of that friendship?"

"I did not, no, sir—not that my approval or disapproval mattered any. Not only am I an employee of Mr. Sperling's corporation, but for more than four years I have had the pleasure and honor of being a friend—a friend of the family, if I may say that?"

He looked at Sperling. Sperling nodded to indicate that he might say that.

Kane went on. "I have deep respect and affection for all of them, including Miss Gwenn Sperling, and I thought Rony wasn't fit to be around her. May I ask a question?"

"Certainly."

"I don't know why you're asking about my personal opinion of Rony unless it's because you suspect me of killing him, not by accident, but intentionally. Is that it?"

"I wouldn't say I suspect that, Mr. Kane. But this statement disposes of the matter with finality, and before I accept it as it stands—" Archer puckered his lips. "Why do you resent my questions?"

"I do not," Kane said emphatically. "I'm in no position to resent questions, especially not from you. But it—"

"I do," Sperling blurted. He had been restraining himself. "What are you trying to do, Archer, make some mud if you can't find any? You said this morning it wasn't the policy of your office to go out of the way to make trouble for men of my standing. When did you change your policy?"

Archer laughed. It was even closer to a giggle than it had been in the morning, but it lasted longer and it sounded as if he was enjoying it more.

"You're entirely justified," he told Sperling. "I'm tired and I was going on merely through habit. I also said this morning that if it was an accident no one would be better pleased than me but I had to know who was responsible. Well, this certainly should satisfy me on that." He put the folded paper in his pocket. "No, I don't want to make mud. God knows enough gets made without me helping." He got to his feet. "Will you call at my office in White Plains tomorrow morning, Mr. Kane—say around eleven o'clock? If I'm not there ask for Mr. Gurran."

"I'll be there," Kane promised.

"What for?" Sperling demanded.

"For a formality." Archer nodded. "That's all, a formality. I'll commit myself to that now. I can't see that any good purpose would be served by a charge and a prosecution. I'll phone Gurran this evening and ask him to look up the motor vehicle statutes regarding an accident occurring on private property. It's possible there will have to be a fine or suspension of driving license, but under all the circumstances I would prefer to see it wiped off."

He extended a hand to Sperling. "No hard feelings, I hope?"

Sperling said not. Archer shook with Kane, with Wolfe, and even with me. He told us all that he hoped that the next time he saw us it would be on a more cheerful occasion. He departed.

Wolfe was sitting with his head tilted to one side, as if it needed too much energy to keep it straight, and his eyes were shut. Kane and Sperling and I were standing, having been polite enough to arise to tell Archer good-by, unlike Wolfe.

Kane spoke to Sperling. "Thank God that's over. If you don't need me any more I'll go and see if I can get some work done. I'd rather not show up at dinner. Of course they'll have to know about it, but I'd prefer not to face them until tomorrow."

"Go ahead," Sperling agreed. "I'll stop by your room later."

Kane started off. Wolfe opened his eyes, muttered, "Wait a minute," he straightened his head.

Kane halted and asked, "Do you mean me?"

"If you don't mind." Wolfe's tone wasn't as civil as his words. "Can your work wait a little?"

"It can if it has to. Why?"

"I'd like to have a little talk with you."

Kane sent a glance at Sperling, but it didn't reach its

destination because the Chairman of the Board had taken another piece of paper from his pocket and was looking at it. This one was unfolded, oblong, and pink in color. As Kane stood hesitating, Sperling stepped to Wolfe and extended his hand with the paper in it.

"You earned it," he said. "I'm glad I hired you."

Wolfe took the paper, lowered his eyes to it, and looked up. "Indeed," he said. "Fifty thousand dollars."

Sperling nodded, as I nod to a bootblack when I tip him a dime. "Added to five makes fifty-five. If it doesn't cover your damage and expenses and fee, send me a bill."

"Thank you, I'll do that. Of course I can't tell what expenses are still to come. I may—"

"Expenses of what?"

"Of my investigation of Mr. Rony's death. I may—"

"What is there to investigate?"

"I don't know." Wolfe put the check in his pocket. "I may be easily satisfied. I'd like to ask Mr. Kane a few questions."

"What for? Why should you?"

"Why shouldn't I?" Wolfe was bland. "Surely I'm entitled to as many as Mr. Archer. Does he object to answering a dozen questions? Do you, Mr. Kane?"

"Certainly not."

"Good. I'll make it brief, but I do wish you'd sit down."

Kane sat, but on the edge of the chair. Sperling did not concede that much. He stood with his hands in his pockets, looking down at Wolfe with no admiration.

"First," Wolfe asked, "how did you determine that Mr. Rony was dead?"

"My God, you should have seen him!"

"But I didn't; and you couldn't have seen him any too well, since it was nearly dark. Did you put your hand inside and feel his heart?"

Kane shook his head. I wasn't surprised he didn't nod, since I had learned for myself that Rony's upper torso had been in no condition for that test, with his clothes all mixed up with his ribs. That was how I had described it to Wolfe.

"I didn't have to," Kane said. "He was all smashed."

"Could you see how badly he was smashed, in the dark?"

"I could feel it. Anyhow it wasn't pitch dark—I could see some."

"I suppose you could see a bone, since bones are white. I understand that a humerus—the bone of the upper arm—had torn through the flesh and the clothing and was extruding several inches. Which arm was it?"

That was a pure lie. He understood no such thing, and it wasn't true.

"My God, I don't know," Kane protested. "I wasn't making notes of things like that."

"I suppose not," Wolfe admitted. "But you saw, or felt, the bone sticking out?"

"I—perhaps I did—I don't know."

Wolfe gave that up. "When you dragged him across to the shrub, what did you take hold of? What part of him?"

"I don't remember."

"Nonsense. You didn't drag him a yard or two, it was fifty feet or more. You couldn't possibly forget. Did you take him by the feet? The head? The coat collar? An arm?"

"I don't remember."

"I don't see how you could help remembering. Perhaps this will bring it back to you: when you got him behind the shrub was his head pointing toward the house or away from the house?"

Kane was frowning. "I should remember that."

"You should indeed."

"But I don't." Kane shook his head. "I simply don't remember."

"I see." Wolfe leaned back. "That's all, Mr. Kane." He flipped a hand. "Go and get on with your work."

Kane was on his feet before Wolfe had finished. "I did the best I could," he said apologetically. "As I said, I don't seem to measure up very well in a crisis. I must have been so rattled I didn't know what I was doing." He glanced at Sperling, got no instructions one way or another, glanced again at Wolfe, sidled between two chairs, headed for the door, and was gone.

When the door closed behind him Sperling looked down at Wolfe and demanded, "What good did that do?"

Wolfe grunted. "None at all. It did harm. It made it impossible for me, when I return home, to forget all this and set about restoring my plants." He slanted his head back to get Sperling's face. "He must owe you a great deal—or he would hate to lose his job. How did you get him to sign that statement?"

"I didn't get him to. As it says, he wrote and signed it of his own free will."

"Pfui. I know what it says. But why should I believe that when I don't believe anything in it?"

"You're not serious." Sperling smiled like an angel. "Kane is one of this country's leading economists. Would a man of his reputation and standing sign such a statement if it weren't true?"

"Whether he would or not, he did," Wolfe was getting peevish. "With enough incentive, of course he would; and you have a good supply. You were lucky he was around, since he was ideal for the purpose." Wolfe waved a hand, finishing with Mr. Kane. "You handled it well; that statement is admirably drafted. But I wonder if you fully realize the position you've put me in?"

"Of course I do." Sperling was sympathetic. "You engaged to do a job and you did it well. Your performance here yesterday afternoon was without a flaw. It persuaded my daughter to drop Rony, and that was all I wanted. The accident of his death doesn't detract from the excellence of your job."

"I know it doesn't," Wolfe agreed, "but that job was finished. The trouble is, you hired me for another job, to investigate Mr. Rony's death. I now—"

"That one is finished too."

"Oh, no. By no means. You've hoodwinked Mr. Archer by getting Mr. Kane to sign that statement, but you haven't gulled me." Wolfe shook his head and sighed. "I only wish you had."

Sperling gazed at him a moment, moved to the chair Archer had used, sat, leaned forward, and demanded,

"Listen, Wolfe, who do you think you are, Saint George?"

"I do not." Wolfe repudiated it indignantly. "No matter who killed a wretch like Mr. Rony, and whether by accident or design, I would be quite willing to let that false statement be the last word. But I have committed myself. I have lied to the police. That's nothing, I do it constantly. I warned you last night that I withhold information from the police only when it concerns a case I'm engaged on; and that commits me to stay with the case until I am satisfied that it's solved. I said you couldn't hire me one day and fire me the next, and you agreed. Now you think you can. Now you think you can drop me because I can no longer get you in a pickle by giving Mr. Archer a true account of the conversation in this room yesterday afternoon, and you're right. If I went to him now and confessed, now that he has that statement, he would reproach me politely and forget about it. I wish I could forget about it too, but I can't. It's my self-conceit again. You have diddled me; and I will not be diddled."

"I've paid you fifty-five thousand dollars."

"So you have. And no more?"

"No more. For what?"

"For finishing the job. I'm going to find out who killed Mr. Rony, and I'm going to prove it." Wolfe aimed a finger at him. "If I fail, Mr. Sperling—" He let the finger down and shrugged. "I won't. I won't fail. See if I do."

Suddenly, without the slightest preliminary, Sperling got mad. In a flash his eyes changed, his color changed —he was a different man. Up from the chair, on his feet, he spoke through his teeth.

"Get out! Get out of here!"

Evidently there was only one thing to do, get out. It was nothing much to me, since I had had somewhat similar experiences before, but for Wolfe, who had practically always been in his own office when a conference reached the point of breaking off relations, it was a novelty to be told to get out. He did well, I thought. He neither emphasized dignity nor abandoned it, but moved as if he had taken a notion to go to the bathroom but was in no terrible hurry. I let him precede me, which was only proper.

However, Sperling was a many-sided man. His flare-up couldn't possibly have fizzled out as quick as that, but as I hopped ahead of Wolfe to open the door his voice came.

"I won't stop payment on that check!"

14

The package arrived a little before noon on Wednesday.

We hadn't got back to normal, since there was still a small army busy up in the plant rooms, but in many respects things had settled down. Wolfe had on a clean shirt and socks, meals were regular and up to standard, the street was cleared of broken glass, and we had caught up on sleep. Nothing much had yet been done toward making good on Wolfe's promise to finish the Rony job, but we had only been home fourteen hours and nine of them had been spent in bed.

Then the package came. Wolfe, having been up in the plant room since breakfast, was in the office with me, checking invoices and shipping memos of everything from osmundine fiber to steel sash putty. When I went to the front door to answer the bell, and a boy handed me a package about the size of a small suitcase and a receipt to sign, I left the package in the hall because I supposed it was just another item for the operations upstairs, and I was busy. But after I returned to the office it struck me as queer that there was no shipper's name on it, so I went back to the hall for another look. There was no mark of any kind on the heavy wrapping paper but Wolfe's name and address. It was tied securely with thick cord. I lifted it and guessed six pounds. I pressed it against my ear and held my breath for thirty seconds, and heard nothing.

Nuts, I thought, and cut the cord with my knife and slashed the paper. Inside was a fiber carton with the flaps taped down. I got cautious again and severed the flaps from the sides by cutting all the way around, and lifted one corner for a peek. All I saw was newspaper. I inserted the knife point and tore a piece of it off, and what I saw then made me raise my brows. Removing the flaps and the newspaper, and seeing more of the same, I got the carton up under my arm, marched into the office with it, and asked Wolfe, "Do you mind if I unpack this on your desk? I don't want to make a mess in the hall?"

Ignoring his protest, I put the package down on his desk and started taking out stacks of twenty-dollar bills. They were used bills, not a new one among them as well as I could tell from the edges, and they were banded in bundles of fifty, which meant a thousand bucks to a bundle.

"What the devil is this?" Wolfe demanded.

"Money," I told him. "Don't touch it, it may be a trap. It may be covered with germs." I was arranging the bundles ten to a pile, and there were five piles. "That's a coincidence," I remarked. "Of course we'll have to check the bundles, but if they're labeled right it's exactly fifty grand. That's interesting."

"Archie." Wolfe was glowering. "What fatuous flummery is this? I told you to deposit that check, not cash it." He pointed. "Wrap that up and take it to the bank."

"Yes, sir. But before I do—" I went to the safe and got the bank book, opened it to the current page, and displayed it to him. "As you see, the check was deposited. This isn't flummery, it's merely a coincidence. You heard the doorbell and saw me go to answer it. A boy handed me this package and gave me a receipt to sign—General Messenger Service, Twenty-eight West Forty-seventh Street. I thought it might be a clock bomb and opened it in the hall, away from you. There is nothing on the package or in it to show who sent it. The only clue is the newspaper the carton was lined with—from the second section of the *New York Times*. Who do we know that reads the *Times* and has fifty thousand bucks for a practical joke?" I gestured. "Answer that and we've got him."

Wolfe was still glowering, but at the pile of dough, not at me. He reached for one of the bundles, flipped through it, and put it back. "Put it in the safe. The package too."

"Shouldn't we count it first? What if one of the bundles is short a twenty?"

There was no reply. He was leaning back in his chair, pushing his lips out and in, and out and in again. I followed instructions, first returning the stuff to the carton to save space, and then went to the hall for the wrapping paper and cord and put them in the safe also.

I sat at my desk, waited until Wolfe's lips were quiet again, and asked coldly, "How about a raise? I could use twenty bucks a week more. So far this case has brought us one hundred and five thousand, three hundred and twelve dollars. Deduct expenses and the damage—"

"Where did the three hundred and twelve come from?"

"From Rony's wallet. Saul's holding it. I told you."

"You know, of course, who sent that package."

"Not exactly. D, C, B, or A, but which? It wouldn't come straight from X, would it?"

"Straight? No." Wolfe shook his head. "I like money, but I don't like that. I only wish you could answer a question."

"I've answered millions. Try me."

"I've already tried you on this one. Who drugged that drink Saturday evening—the one intended for Mr. Rony which you drank?"

"Yeah. That's *the* question. I myself asked it all day yesterday, off and on, and again this morning, and I don't know."

Wolfe sighed. "That, of course, is what constrains us. That's what forces us to assume that it was not an accident, but murder. But for that I might be able to persuade myself to call it closed, in spite of my deception of Mr. Archer." He sighed again. "As it is, we must either validate the assumption or refute it, and heaven knows how I'm going to manage it. The telephone upstairs has been restored. I wanted to test it, and thought I might as well do so with a call to Mr. Lowenfeld of the police laboratory. He was obliging but didn't help much. He said that if a car is going slightly downhill at twenty-five miles an hour, and its left front hits a man who is standing erect, and its wheels pass over him, it is probable that the impact will leave dents or other visible marks on the front of the car, but not certain. I told him that the problem was to determine whether the man was upright or recumbent when the car hit him, and he said the absence of marks on the front of the car would be suggestive but not conclusive. He also asked why I was still interested in Louis Rony's death. If policemen were women they couldn't be more gossipy. By evening the story will be around that I'm about ready to expose that reptile Paul Emerson as a murderer. I only wish it were true." Wolfe glanced up at the clock. "By the way, I also phoned Doctor Vollmer, and he should be here soon."

So I was wrong in supposing that nothing had been done toward making good on his promise. "Your trip to the country did you good," I declared. "You're full of energy. Did you notice that the *Gazette* printed Kane's statement in full?"

"Yes. And I noticed a defect that escaped me when Mr. Sperling read it. His taking my car, the car of a fellow guest whom he had barely met, was handled too casually. Reading it, it's a false note. I told Mr. Sperling it was well drafted, but that part wasn't. A better explanation could have been devised and put in a brief sentence. I could have—"

The phone ringing stopped him. I reached for my instrument and told the transmitter, "Nero Wolfe's office."

"May I speak to Mr. Wolfe, please?"

There was a faint tingle toward the bottom of my spine. The voice hadn't changed a particle in thirteen months.

"Your name, please?" I asked, hoping my voice was the same too.

"Tell him a personal matter."

I covered the transmitter with a palm and told Wolfe, "X."

He frowned. "What?"

"You heard me. X."

He reached for his phone. Getting no sign to do otherwise, I stayed on.

"Nero Wolfe speaking."

"How do you do, Mr. Wolfe. Goodwin told you who I am? Or my voice does?"

"I know the voice."

"Yes, it's easily recognized, isn't it? You ignored the advice I gave you Saturday. You also ignored the demonstration you received Sunday night. May I say that that didn't surprise me?"

"You may say anything."

"It didn't. I hope there will never be occasion for a more pointed demonstration. It's a more interesting world with you in it. Have you opened the package you received a little while ago?"

"Yes."

"I don't need to explain why I decided to reimburse you for the damage to your property. Do I?"

"Yes."

"Oh, come. Surely not. Not you. If the amount you received exceeds the damage, no matter. I intended that it should. The District Attorney has decided that Rony's death is fully and satisfactorily explained by Kane's statement, and no charge will be made. You have already indicated that you do not concur in that decision by your inquiry to the New York police laboratory, and anyway of course you wouldn't. Not you. Rony was an able young man with a future, and he deserves to have his death investigated by the best brain in New York. Yours. I don't live in New York, as you know. Goodby and good luck."

The connection went. Wolfe cradled his receiver. I did likewise.

"Jesus," I said softly. I whistled. "Now there's a client for you. Money by messenger, snappy phone calls, hopes he'll never have to demonstrate by croaking you, keep the change, best brain in New York, go to it, click. As I think I said once before, he's an abrupt bastard."

Wolfe was sitting with his eyes closed to slits. I asked him, "How do I enter it? Under X, or Z for Zeck?"

"Archie."

"Yes, sir."

"I told you once to forget that you know that man's name, and I meant it. The reason is simply that I don't want to hear his name because he is the only man on earth that I'm afraid of. I'm not afraid he'll hurt me; I'm afraid of what he may someday force me to do to keep him from hurting me. You heard what I told Mr. Sperling."

"Okay. But I'm the bookkeeper. What do I put it under, X?"

"Don't put it. First, go through it. As you do so you might as well count it, but the point is to see if there is anything there besides money. Leave ten thousand dollars in the safe. I'll need it soon, tomorrow probably, for something that can't appear in our records. For your information only, it will be for Mr. Jones. Take the remainder to a suburban bank, say somewhere in New Jersey, and put it in a safe deposit box which you will rent under an assumed name. If you need a reference, Mr. Parker will do. After what happened Saturday night—we'll be prepared for contingencies. If we ever meet him head on and have to cut off from here and from everyone we know, we'll need supplies. I hope I never touch it. I hope it's still there when I die, and if so it's yours."

"Thank you very much. I'll be around eighty then and I'll need it."

"You're welcome. Now for this afternoon. First, what about the pictures you took up there?"

"Six o'clock. That was the best they could do."

"And the keys?"

"You said after lunch. They'll be ready at one-thirty."

"Good. Saul will be here at two?"

"Yes, sir."

"Have Fred and Orrie here this evening after dinner. I don't think you'll need them this afternoon; you and Saul can manage. This is what we want. There must—"

But that was postponed by the arrival of Doc Vollmer. Doc's home and office were on our street, toward Tenth Avenue, and over the years we had used his services for everything from stitching up Dora Chapin's head to signing a certificate that Wolfe was batty. When he called he always went to one of the smaller yellow chairs because of his short legs, sat, took off his spectacles and looked at them, put them on again, and asked, "Want some pills?"

Today he added, "I'm afraid I'm in a hurry."

"You always are," Wolfe said, in the tone he uses only to the few people he really likes. "Have you read about the Rony case?"

"Of course. Since you're involved in it—or were."

"I still am. The body is at the morgue in White Plains. Will you go there? You'll have to go to the District Attorney's office first to get yourself accredited. Tell them I sent you, and that I have been engaged by one of Mr. Rony's associates. If they want more than that they can phone me, and I'll try to satisfy them. You want to examine the body—not an autopsy, merely superficially, to determine whether he died instantly or was left to suffer a prolonged agony. What I really want you to inspect is his head, to see if there is any indication that he was knocked out by a blow before the car ran over him. I know the chance of finding anything conclusive is remote, but I wish you'd try, and there'll be no grumbling about your charge for the trip."

Vollmer blinked. "It would have to be done this afternoon?"

"Yes, sir."

"Have you any idea what weapon might have been used?"

"No, sir."

"According to the papers he had no family, no relatives at all. Perhaps I should know whom I'm representing—one of his professional associates?"

"I'll answer that if they ask it. You're representing me."

"I see. Anything to be mysterious." Vollmer stood up. "If one of my patients dies while I'm gone—" He left it hanging and trotted out, making me move fast to get to the front door in time to open it for him. His habit of leaving like that, as soon as he had all he really needed, was one of the reasons Wolfe liked him.

I returned to the office.

Wolfe leaned back. "We have only ten minutes until lunch. Now this afternoon, for you and Saul . . ."

15

The locksmith soaked me $8.80 for eleven keys. That was about double the market, but I didn't bother to squawk because I knew why: he was still collecting for a kind of a lie he had told a homicide dick six years ago at my suggestion. I think he figured that he and I were fellow crooks and therefore should divvy.

Even with keys it might have taken a little maneuvering if Louis Rony had lived in an apartment house with a doorman and elevator man, but as it was there was nothing to it. The address on East Thirty-seventh Street was an old five-story building that had been done over in good style, and in the downstairs vestibule was a row of mailboxes, push buttons, and perforated circles for reception on the speaking tube. Rony's name was at the right end, which meant the top floor. The first key I tried was the right one, and Saul and I entered, went to the self-service elevator, and pushed the button marked 5. It was the best kind of setup for an able young man with a future like Rony, who had probably had visitors of all kinds at all hours.

Upstairs it was the second key I tried that worked. Feeling that I was the host, in a way, I held the door open for Saul to precede me and then followed him in. We were at the center of a hall, not wide and not very long. Turning right, toward the street front, we stepped into a fairly large room with modern furniture that matched, bright-colored rugs that had been cleaned not long ago, splashy colored pictures on the walls, a good supply of books, and a fireplace.

"Pretty nice," Saul remarked, sending his eyes around. One difference between Saul and me is that I sometimes have to look twice at a thing to be sure I'll never lose it, but once will always do for him.

"Yeah," I agreed, putting my briefcase on a chair. "I understand the tenant has given it up, so maybe you could rent it." I got the rubber gloves from the briefcase and handed him a pair. He started putting them on.

"It's too bad," he said, "you didn't keep that membership card Sunday night when you had your hands on it. It would have saved trouble. That's what we want, is it?"

"It's our favorite," I began on the second glove. "We would buy anything that looks interesting, but we'd love a souvenir of the American Communist party. The best bet is a safe of some kind, but we won't hop around." I motioned to the left. "You take that side."

It's a pleasure to work with Saul because I can concentrate completely on my part and pay no attention to him. We both like a searching job, when it's not the kind where you have to turn couches upside down or use a magnifying glass, because when you're through you've got a plain final answer, yes or no. For that room, on which we spent a good hour, it was no. Not only was there no membership certificate, there was nothing at all that was worth taking home to Wolfe. The only thing resembling a safe was a locked bond box, which one of the keys fitted, in a drawer of the desk, and all that it contained was a bottle of fine liqueur Scotch, McCrae's, half full. Apparently that was the one item he didn't care to share with the cleaning woman. We left the most tedious part, flipping through the books, to the last, and did it together. There was nothing in any of them but pages.

"This bird trusted nobody," Saul complained.

In our next objective, the bedroom, which was about half the size of the front room, Saul darted a glance around and said, "Thank God, no books."

I agreed heartily. "We ought to always bring a boy along for it. Flipping through books is a hell of a way to earn a living for grownups."

The bedroom didn't take as long, but it produced as little. The further we went the more convinced I got that Rony had either never had a secret of any kind, or had had so many dangerous ones that no cut and dried precautions would do, and in view of what had happened to the plant rooms the choice was easy. By the time we finished with the kitchenette, which was about the size of Wolfe's elevator, and the bathroom, which was much larger and spick-and-span, the bottle of Scotch locked in the bond box, hidden from the cleaning woman, struck me as pathetic—the one secret innocent enough to let into his home.

Thinking that that notion showed how broad-minded I was, having that kind of a feeling even for a grade A bastard like Rony, I thought I should tell Saul about it. The gloves were back in the briefcase and the briefcase under my arm, and we were in the hall, headed for the door, ready to leave. I never got the notion fully explained to Saul on account of an interruption. I was just reaching for the doorknob, using my handkerchief, when the sound of the elevator came, stopping at that floor, and then its door opening. There was no question as to which apartment someone was headed for because there was only one to a floor. There were steps outside, and the sound of a key being inserted in the lock, but by the time it was turned and the door opened Saul and I were in the bathroom, with its door closed to leave no crack, but unlatched.

A voice said, not too loud, "Anybody here?" It was Jimmy Sperling.

Another voice said, lower but with no sign of a tremble in it, "Are you sure this is it?" It was Jimmy's mother.

"Of course it is," Jimmy said rudely. It was the rudeness of a guy scared absolutely stiff. "It's the fifth floor. Come on, we can't just stand here."

Steps went to the front, to the living room. I whispered to Saul to tell him who they were, and added, "If they came after something they're welcome to anything they find."

I opened the door to a half-inch crack, and we stood and listened. They were talking and, judging from other sounds, they weren't anything like as methodical and efficient as Saul and I had been. One of them dropped a drawer on the floor, and a little later something else hit that sounded more like a picture. Still later it must have been a book, and that was too much for me. If Saul and I hadn't been so thorough it might have been worth while to wait it out, on the chance that they might find what they were after and we could ask them to show us before they left; but to stand there and let them waste their time going through those books when we had just flipped every one of them—it was too damn silly. So I opened the bathroom door, walked down the hall into the living room, and greeted them.

"Hello there!"

Some day I'll learn. I thought I had Jimmy pretty well tagged. I have a rule never to travel around on homicide business without a shoulder holster, but my opinion of Jimmy was such that I didn't bother to transfer the gun to my pocket or hand. However, I have read about mothers protecting their young, and have also run across it now and then, and I might at least have been more alert. Not that a gun in my hand would have helped any unless I had been willing to slam it against her skull. Happening to be near the arch when I entered, she had only a couple of yards to come, just what she needed to get momentum.

She came at me like a hurricane, her hands straight for my face, screeching at the top of her voice, "Run run run!"

It didn't make any sense, but a woman in that condition never does. Even if I had been alone, and she had been able to keep me busy enough long enough for her son to make a getaway, what of it? Since I was neither a killer nor a cop, my only threat was the discovery that Jimmy was there, and since I had already seen him she couldn't peel that off of me no matter how long her fingernails were. However, she tried, and her first wild rush got her in so close that she actually reached my face. Feeling the stinging little streak of one of her nails, I stiff-armed her out of range, and would merely have kept her off that way if it hadn't been for Jimmy, who had been at the other side of the room when I entered. Instead of dashing in to support Mom's attack, he was standing there by the table pointing a gun. At the sight of the gun, Saul, following me in, had stopped just inside the arch to think it over, and I didn't blame him, for Jimmy's right hand, which held the gun, was anything but steady, which meant there was no way of telling what might happen next.

I lunged at Mom, and before she knew it she was hugged tight against me. She couldn't even wriggle, though she tried. With my chin dug into her shoulder, I spoke to Jimmy.

"I can snap her in two, and don't think I won't. Do you want to hear her spine crack? Drop it. Just open your fingers and let it fall."

"Run run run!" Mom was screeching as well as she could with me squeezing the breath out of her.

"Here we go," I said. "It'll hurt but it won't last long."

Saul walked over and tapped Jimmy's wrist underneath, and the gun fell to the floor. Saul picked it up and backed off. Jimmy started for me. When the distance was right I threw his mother at him. Then she was in his arms instead of mine, and for the first time she saw Saul. The damn fool actually hadn't known I wasn't alone until then.

"Go look at your face," Saul told me.

I went to the bathroom and looked in the mirror, and was sorry I had let her off so easy. It started just below my left eye and went straight down a good three inches.

I dabbed cold water on it, looked for a styptic and found none, and took a damp towel back to the living room with me. Jimmy and Mom were at bay over by the table, and Saul, with Jimmy's gun, was at ease near the arch.

I complained, "What for?" I demanded. "All I said was hello. Why the scratching and shooting?"

"He didn't shoot," Mrs. Sperling said indignantly.

I waved it aside. "Well, you sure scratched. Now we've got a problem. We can search your son all right, that's easy, but how are we going to search you?"

"Try searching me," Jimmy said. His voice was mean and his face was mean. I had tagged him as the one member of the family who didn't count one way or another, but now I wasn't so sure.

"Nuts," I told him. "You're sore because you didn't have the guts to shoot, which shows how thick you are. Sit down on that couch, both of you." I used the damp towel on my face. They didn't move. "Will I have to come and sit you?"

Mom pulled at his arm and they went to the couch, sidewise, and sat. Saul dropped the gun in his pocket and took a chair.

"You startled us, Andy," Mom said. "That was all. I was so startled I didn't recognize you."

It was a nice little touch that no man would ever have thought of. She was putting us back on our original basis, when I had been merely a welcome guest at her home.

I refused to revert. "My name's Archie now, remember? And you've fixed me so that no one will recognize me. You certainly react strong to being startled." I moved a chair and sat. "How did you get in here?"

"Why, with a key!"

"Where did you get it?"

"Why, we—we had one—"

"How did *you* get in?" Jimmy demanded.

I shook my head at him. "That won't get you anywhere. I suppose you know that your father fired Mr. Wolfe. We now have another client, one of Rony's associates. Do you want to make a point of this? Like calling a cop? I thought not. Where did you get the key?"

"None of your damn business!"

"I just told you," Mom said reproachfully, "we had one."

Having quit using logic on women the day I graduated from high school, I skipped that. "We have a choice," I informed them. "I can phone the precinct and get a pair of city detectives here, a male and a female, to go over you and see what you came after, which would take time and make a stink, or you can tell us—by the way, I believe you haven't met my friend and colleague, Mr. Saul Panzer. That's him on the chair. Also by the way, don't you ever go to the movies? Why don't you wear gloves? You've left ten thousand prints all over the place. Or you can tell us where you got the key and what you came for—only it will have to be good. One reason you might prefer us is that we don't really have to search you, because you were still looking, so you haven't found it."

They looked at each other.

"May I make a suggestion?" Saul inquired.

"Yes indeed."

"Maybe they'd rather have us phone Mr. Sperling, to ask—"

"No!" Mom cried.

"Much obliged," I thanked Saul. "You remind me of Mr. Wolfe." I returned to them. "Now it will have to be even better. Where did you get the key?"

"From Rony," Jimmy muttered sullenly.

"When did he give it to you?"

"A long while ago. I've had it—"

"That's a swell start," I said encouragingly. "He had something here, or you thought he had, which you wanted so much that you two came here to get it the first possible chance after he died, but he gave you a key long ago so you could drop in for it someday while he was at his office. Mr. Panzer and I don't care for that. Try another one."

They exchanged glances.

"Why don't you try this?" I suggested. "That you borrowed it from your younger sister, and—"

"You sonofabitch," Jimmy growled, rising and taking a step. "No, I didn't shoot, but by God—"

"You shouldn't get nasty, Andy," Mom protested.

"Then give us something better." I had drawn my feet back for leverage in case Jimmy kept coming, but he didn't. "Whatever it is, remember we can always check it with Mr. Sperling."

"No you can't!"

"Why not?"

"Because he knows nothing about it! I'm just going to tell you the truth! We persuaded the janitor to lend us a key."

"How much did it take to persuade him?"

"I offered—I gave him a hundred dollars. He'll be downstairs in the hall when we go out, to see that we don't take anything."

"You got a bargain," I declared, "unless he intends to frisk you. Don't you think we ought to meet him, Saul?"

"Yes."

"Then get him. Bring him up here."

Saul went. As the three of us sat and waited Mom suddenly asked, "Does your face hurt, Andy?"

I thought of three replies, all good, but settled for a fourth because it was shortest.

"Yes," I said.

When the outside door opened again I stood up, thinking that the janitor's arrival would make it two to two, even not counting Mom, and he might be an athlete. But as soon as I saw him I sat down again. He was a welterweight, his expansion would have been not more than half of Madeline's, and his eyes refused to lift higher than a man's knees.

"His name's Tom Fenner," Saul informed me. "I had to take hold of him."

I eyed him. He eyed my ankles. "Look," I told him, "this can be short and simple. I represent an associate of Mr. Rony. As far as I know these people have done no harm here, and I'll see that they don't. I don't like to get people into trouble if I don't have to. Just show me the hundred bucks they gave you."

"Jeez, I never saw a hundred bucks," Fenner

squeaked. "Why would they give me a hundred bucks?"

"To get a key to this apartment. Come on, let's see it."

"They never got a key from me. I'm in charge here. I'm responsible."

"Quit lying," Jimmy snapped.

"Here's the key," Mom said, displaying it. "You see, that proves it!"

"Give it here," Fenner took a step. "Let me take a look at it."

I reached for his arm and swiveled him. "Why drag it out? No matter how brave and strong you are, three of us could probably hold you while the lady goes through your pockets. Save time and energy, Mac. Maybe they planted it on you when you weren't looking."

He was so stubborn and game that his eyes got nearly as high as my knees before he surrendered. Then they dropped again, and his hand went into his pants pocket and emerged with a tight little roll between his fingers. I took it and unrolled it enough to see a fifty, two twenties, and a ten, and offered it back. That was the only time his eyes got higher; they came clear up to mine, wildly astonished.

"Take it and beat it," I told him. "I just wanted a look. Wait a minute." I went to get the key from Mom and handed that to him too. "Don't lend it again without phoning me first. I'll lock up when I leave."

He was speechless. The poor goof didn't have enough wits left even to ask my name.

When he had gone Saul and I sat down again. "You see," I said genially, "we're easily satisfied as long as we get the truth. Now we know how you got in. What did you come for?"

Mom had it ready and waiting, having been warned it was going to be required. "You remember," she said, "that my husband thought Louis was a Communist."

I said I did.

"Well, we still thought so—I mean, after what Mr. Wolfe told us Monday afternoon. We still thought so."

"Who is we?"

"My son and I. We talked it over and we still thought

so. Today when my husband told us that Mr. Wolfe didn't believe what Webster said in his statement and it might mean more trouble about it, we thought if we came here and found something to prove that Louis was a Communist and showed it to Mr. Wolfe, then it would be all right."

"It would be all right," I asked, "because if he was a Communist Mr. Wolfe wouldn't care who or what killed him? Is that it?"

"Of course, don't you see?"

I asked Saul, "Do you want it?"

"Not even as a gift," he said emphatically.

I nodded. I switched to Jimmy. "Why don't you take a stab at it? The way your mother's mind works makes it hard for her. What have you got to offer?"

Jimmy's eyes still looked mean. They were straight at mine. "I think," he said glumly, "that I was a boob to stumble in here like this."

"Okay. And?"

"I think you've got us, damn you."

"And?"

"I think we've got to tell you the truth. If we don't—"

"Jimmy!" Mom gripped his arm. *"Jimmy!"*

He ignored her. "If we don't you'll only think it's something worse. You brought my sister's name into this, insinuating she had a key to this apartment. I'd like to push that down your throat, and maybe I will some day, but I think we've got to tell you the truth, and I can't help it if it concerns her. She wrote him some letters—not the kind you might think—but anyhow my mother and I knew about them and we didn't want them around. So we came here to get them."

Mom let go of his arm and beamed at me. "That was it!" she said eagerly. "They weren't really bad letters, but they were—personal. You know?"

If I had been Jimmy I would have strangled her. The way he had told it, at least it wasn't incredible, but her gasping at him when he said he was going to tell the truth, and then reacting that way when he went on to tell it, was enough to make you wonder how she ever got across a street. However, I met her beam with a deadpan. From the expression of Jimmy's eyes I doubted if another squeeze would produce more juice, and if not, it ought to be left that their truth was mine. So my deadpan was replaced with a sympathetic grin.

"About how many letters?" I asked Jimmy, just curious.

"I don't know exactly. About a dozen."

I nodded. "I can see why you wouldn't want them kicking around, no matter how innocent they were. But either he destroyed them or they're some place else. You won't find them here. Mr. Panzer and I have been looking for some papers—nothing to do with your sister or you—and we know how to look. We had just finished when you arrived, and you can take it from me that there's no letter from your sister here—let alone a dozen. If you want me to sign a statement on that I'd be glad to."

"You might have missed them," Jimmy objected.

"*You* might," I corrected him. "Not us."

"The papers you were looking for—did you find them?"

"No."

"What are they?"

"Oh, just something needed for settling his affairs."

"You say they don't concern—my family?"

"Nothing to do with your family as far as I know." I stood up. "So I guess that ends it. You leave empty-handed and so do we. I might add that there will be no point in my reporting this to Mr. Sperling, since he's no longer our client and since you seem to think it might disturb him."

"That's very nice of you, Andy," Mom said appreciatively. She arose to come to inspect me. "I'm so sorry about your face!"

"Don't mention it," I told her. "I shouldn't have startled you. It'll be okay in a couple of months." I turned. "You don't want that gun, do you, Saul?"

Saul took it from his pocket, shook the cartridges into his palm, and went to Jimmy and returned his property.

"I don't see," Mom said, "why we can't stay and

look around some more, just to make sure about those letters."

"Oh, come on," Jimmy said rudely.

They went.

Saul and I followed soon after. On our way down in the elevator he asked, "Did any of that stick at all?"

"Not on me. You?"

"Nope. It was hard to keep my face straight."

"Do you think I should have kept on trying?"

He shook his head. "There was nothing to pry him loose with. You saw his eyes and his jaw."

Before leaving I had gone to the bathroom for another look at my face, and it was a sight. But the blood had stopped coming, and I don't mind people staring at me if they're female, attractive, and between eighteen and thirty; and I had another errand in that part of town. Saul went with me because there was a bare possibility that he could help. It's always fun to be on a sidewalk with him because you know you are among those present at a remarkable performance. Look at him and all you see is just a guy walking along, but I honestly believe that if you had shown him any one of those people a month later and asked him if he had ever seen that man before, it would have taken him not more than five seconds to reply, "Yes, just once, on Wednesday, June twenty-second, on Madison Avenue between Thirty-ninth and Fortieth Streets." He has got me beat a mile.

As it turned out he wasn't needed for the errand. The building directory on the wall of the marble lobby told us that the offices of Murphy, Kearfot and Rony were on the twenty-eighth floor, and we took the express elevator. It was the suite overlooking the avenue, and everything was up to beehive standard. After one glance I had to reconsider my approach because I hadn't expected that kind of a setup. I told the receptionist, who was past my age limit and looked good and tough, that I wanted to see a member of the firm, and gave my name, and went to sit beside Saul on a leather couch that had known a million fannies. Before long another one, a good match for the receptionist only older, appeared to escort me down a hall and into a corner room with four big double windows.

A big broad-shouldered guy with white hair and deep-set blue eyes, seated at a desk even bigger than Wolfe's, got up to shake hands with me.

"Archie Goodwin?" he rumbled cordially, as if he had been waiting for this for years. "From Nero Wolfe's office? A pleasure. Sit down. I'm Aloysius Murphy. What can I do for you?"

Not having mentioned any name but mine to the receptionist, I felt famous. "I don't know," I told him, sitting. "I guess you can't do anything."

"I could try." He opened a drawer. "Have a cigar."

"No, thanks. Mr. Wolfe has been interested in the death of your junior partner, Louis Rony."

"So I understand." His face switched instantly from smiling welcome to solemn sorrow. "A brilliant career brutally snipped as it was bursting into flower."

That sounded to me like Confucius, but I skipped it. "A damn shame," I agreed. "Mr. Wolfe has a theory that the truth may be holding out on us."

"I know he has. A very interesting theory."

"Yeah, he's looking into it a little. I guess I might as well be frank. He thought there might be something around Rony's office—some papers, anything—that might give us a hint. The idea was for me to go and look. For instance, if there were two rooms and a stenographer in one of them, I could fold her up—probably gag her and tie her—if there was a safe I could stick pins under her nails until she gave me the combination—and really do a job. I brought a man along to help, but even with two of us I don't see how we can—"

I stopped because he was laughing so hard he couldn't hear me. You might have thought I was Bob Hope and had finally found a new one. When I thought it would reach him I protested modestly, "I don't deserve all that."

He tapered off to a chuckle. "I should have met you long ago," he declared. "I've been missing something. I want to tell you, Archie, and you can tell Wolfe, you can count on us here—all of us—for anything you want." He waved a hand. "The place is yours. You won't have to stick pins in us. Louis's secretary will show you anything, tell you anything—all of us will. We'll do everything we can to help you get at the truth. For a high-minded man truth is everything. Who scratched your face?"

He was getting on my nerves. He was so glad to have met me at last, and was so anxious to help, that it took me a full five minutes to break loose and get out of the room, but I finally made it.

I marched back to the reception room, beckoned to Saul, and, as soon as we were outside the suite, told him, "The wrong member of the firm got killed. Compared to Aloysius Murphy, Rony was the flower of truth."

16

The pictures came out pretty well, considering. Since Wolfe had told me to order four prints of each, there was about half a bushel. That evening after dinner, as Saul and I sat in the office inspecting and assorting them, it seemed to me there were more of Madeline than I remembered taking, and I left most of them out of the pile we were putting to one side for Wolfe. There were three good ones of Rony—one full-face, one three-quarters, and one profile—and one of the shots of the membership card was something to be proud of. That alone should have got me a job on *Life*. Webster Kane wasn't photogenic, but Paul Emerson was. I remarked on that fact to Wolfe as I went to put his collection on his desk. He grunted. I asked if he was ready for my report for the afternoon, and he said he would go through the pictures first.

Paul Emerson was one of the causes for the delay on my report. Saul and I had got back to the office shortly after six, but Wolfe's schedule had been shattered by the emergency on the roof, and he didn't come down until 6:28. At that minute he strode in, turned the radio on and dialed to WPIT, went to his chair behind the desk, and sat with his lips tightened.

The commercial came, and the introduction, and then Emerson's acid baritone:

This fine June afternoon it is no pleasure to have to report that the professors are at it again—but then they always are—oh, yes, you can count on the professors. One of them made a speech last night at Boston, and if you have anything left from last week's pay you'd better hide it under the mattress. He wants us not only to feed and clothe everybody on earth, but educate them also. . . .

Part of my education was watching Wolfe's face while Emerson was broadcasting. His lips, starting fairly tight, kept getting tighter and tighter until there was only a thin straight hairline and his cheeks were puffed and folded like a contour map. When the tension got to a certain point his mouth would pop open, and in a moment close, and it would start over again. I used to test my powers of observation, trying to spot the split second for the pop.

Minutes later Emerson was taking a crack at another of his pet targets:

. . . they call themselves World Federalists, this bunch of amateur statesmen, and they want us to give up the one thing we've got left—the right to make our own decisions about our own affairs. They think it would be fine if we had to ask permission of all the world's runts and funny-looking dimwits every time we wanted to move our furniture around a little, or even to leave it where it is. . . .

I anticipated the pop of Wolfe's mouth by three seconds, which was par. I couldn't expect to hit it right on the nose. Emerson developed that theme a while and then swung into his finale. He always closed with a snappy swat at some personality whose head was temporarily sticking up from the mob.

Well, friends and fellow citizens, a certain so-called genius has busted loose again right here in New York, where I live only because I have to. You may have heard of this fat fantastic creature who goes by the good old American name of Nero Wolfe. Just before I went on the air we received here at the studio a press release from a firm of midtown lawyers—a firm which is now minus a partner because one of them, a man named Louis Rony, got killed in an automobile accident Monday night. The authorities have investigated thoroughly and properly, and there is no question about its being an accident or about who was responsible. The authorities know all about it, and so does the public, which means you.

But this so-called genius knows more than everybody else put together—as usual. Since the regrettable accident took place on the property of a prominent citizen—a man whom I have the honor to know as a friend and as a great American—it was too good a chance for the genius to miss, to get some cheap publicity. The press release from the firm of lawyers states that Nero Wolfe intends to pursue his investigation of Rony's death until he learns the truth. How do you like that? What do you think of this insolent abuse of the machinery of justice in a free country like ours? If I may be permitted to express an opinion, I think we could get along very well without that kind of a genius in our America.

Among four-legged brutes there is a certain animal which neither works for its food nor fights for it. A squirrel earns its acorns, and a beast of prey earns its hard-won meal. But this animal skulks among the trees and rocks and tall grass, looking for misfortune and suffering. What a way to live! What a diet that is, to eat misfortune! How lucky we are that it is only among four-legged brutes that we may find such a scavenger as that!

Perhaps I should apologize, my friends and fellow citizens, for this digression into the field of natural history. Good-by for another ten days. Tomorrow, and for the remainder of my vacation, Robert Burr will be with you again in my place. I had to come to town today, and the temptation to come to the studio and talk to you was too much for me. Here is Mr. Griswold for my sponsor.

Another voice, as cordial and sunny as Emerson's was acid, began telling us of the part played by Continental Mines Corporation in the greatness of America. I got up and crossed to the radio to turn it off.

"I hope he spelled your name right," I remarked to Wolfe. "What do you know? He went to all that trouble right in the middle of his vacation just to give you a plug. Shall we write and thank him?"

No reply. Obviously that was no time to ask if he wanted our report for the afternoon, so I didn't. And later, after dinner, as I have said, he decided to do a survey of the pictures first.

He liked them so much that he practically suggested I should quit detective work and take up photography. There were thirty-eight different shots in the collection I put on his desk. He rejected nine of them, put six in his top drawer, and asked for all four prints of the other twenty-three. As Saul and I got them together I noticed that he had no outstanding favorites. All the family and guests were well represented, and of course the membership card was included. Then they all had to be labeled on the back and placed in separate envelopes, also labeled. He put a rubber band around them and put them in his top drawer.

Again the report got postponed, this time by the arrival of Doc Vollmer. He accepted Wolfe's offer of a bottle of beer, as he always did when he called in the evening, and after it had been brought by Fritz and his throat was wet he told his story. His reception at White Plains had been neither warm nor cold, he said, just businesslike, and after a phone call to Wolfe an Assistant DA had escorted him to the morgue. As for what he had found, the best he could do was a guess. The center of the impact of the car's wheels had been the fifth rib, and the only sign of injury higher on Rony than that was a bruise on the right side of his head, above the ear. Things that had happened to his hips and legs showed that they had been under the car, so his head and shoulders must have been projecting beyond the wheels. It was possible that the head bruise had been caused by contact with the gravel of the drive, but it was also possible that he had been struck on the head with something and knocked out before the car ran over him. If the latter, the instrument had not been something with a sharp edge, or with a limited area of impact like the head of a hammer or wrench, but neither had it had a smooth surface like a baseball bat. It had been blunt and rough and heavy.

Wolfe was frowning. "A golf club?"

"I shouldn't think so."

"A tennis racket?"

"Not heavy enough."

"A piece of iron pipe?"

"No. Too smooth."

"A piece of a branch from a tree with stubs of twigs on it?"

"That would be perfect if it were heavy enough." Vollmer swallowed some beer. "Of course all I had was a hand glass. With the hair and scalp under a microscope some evidence might be found. I suggested that to the Assistant District Attorney, but he showed no enthusiasm. If there had been an opportunity to snip off a piece I would have brought it home with me, but he didn't take his eyes off of me. Now it's too late because they were ready to prepare the body for burial."

"Was the skull cracked?"

"No. Intact. Apparently the medical examiner had been curious too. The scalp had been peeled back and replaced."

"You couldn't swear that he had probably been knocked down before the car struck him?"

"Not 'probably.' I could swear he had been hit on the head, and that the blow might have been struck while he was still erect—as far as my examination went."

"Confound it," Wolfe grumbled. "I hoped to simplify matters by forcing those people up there to do some work. You did all you could, Doctor, and I'm grateful." He turned his head. "Saul, I understand that Archie gave you some money for safekeeping the other evening?"

"Yes, sir."

"Have you got it with you?"

"Yes, sir."

"Please give it to Doctor Vollmer."

Saul got an envelope from his pocket, took some folded bills from it, and stepped to Vollmer to hand them over.

Doc was puzzled. "What's this for?" he asked Wolfe.

"For this afternoon, sir. I hope it's enough."

"But—I'll send a bill. As usual."

"If you prefer it, certainly. But if you don't mind I wish you'd take my word for it that it is peculiarly fitting to pay you with that money for examining Mr. Rony's head in an effort to learn the truth about his death. It pleases my fancy if it doesn't offend yours. Is it enough?"

Doc unfolded the bills and took a look. "It's too much."

"Keep it. It should be that money, and all of it."

Doc stuck it in his pocket. "Thanks. Anything to be mysterious." He picked up his beer glass. "As soon as I finish this, Archie, I'll take a look at your face. I knew you'd try to close in too fast some day."

I replied suitably.

After he had gone I finally reported for Saul and me. Wolfe leaned back and listened to the end without interrupting. In the middle of it Fred Durkin and Orrie Cather arrived, admitted by Fritz, and I waved them to seats and resumed. When I explained why I hadn't insisted on something better than Jimmy's corny tale about letters Gwenn had written Rony, in spite of the way Mom had scrambled it for him, Wolfe nodded in approval, and when I explained why I had walked out of the law office of Murphy, Kearfot and Rony without even trying to look in a wastebasket, he nodded again. One reason I like to work for him is that he never rides me for not acting the way he would act. He knows what I can do and that's all he ever expects; but he sure expects that.

When I got to the end I added, "If I may make a suggestion, why not have one of the boys find out where Aloysius Murphy was at nine-thirty Monday evening? I'd be glad to volunteer. I bet he's a D and a Commie both, and if he didn't kill Rony he ought to be framed for it. You ought to meet him."

Wolfe grunted. "At least the afternoon wasn't wasted. You didn't find the membership card."

"Yeah, I thought that was how you'd take it."

"And you met Mrs. Sperling and her son. How sure are you that he invented those letters?"

I shrugged. "You heard me describe it."

"You, Saul?"

"Yes, sir, I agree with Archie."

"Then that settles it." Wolfe sighed. "This is a devil of a mess." He looked at Fred and Orrie. "Come up closer, will you? I've got to say something."

Fred and Orrie moved together, but not alike. Fred was some bigger than Orrie. When he did anything at all, walk or talk or reach for something, you always expected him to trip or fumble, but he never did, and he could trail better than anybody I knew except Saul, which I would never understand. Fred moved like a bear, but Orrie like a cat. Orrie's strong point was getting people to tell him things. It wasn't so much the questions he asked. As a matter of fact, he wasn't very good at questions; it was just the way he looked at them. Something about him made people feel that he ought to be told things.

Wolfe's eyes took in the four of us. He spoke.

"As I said, we're in a mess. The man we were investigating has been killed, and I think he was murdered. He was an outlaw and a blackguard, and I owe him nothing. But I am committed, by circumstances I prefer not to disclose, to find out who killed him and why, and, if it was murder, to get satisfactory evidence. We may find that the murderer is one who, by the accepted standards, deserves to live as richly as Mr. Rony deserved to die. I can't help that; he must be found. Whether he must also be exposed I don't know. I'll answer that question when I am faced by it, and that will come only when I am also facing the murderer."

Wolfe turned a hand over. "Why am I giving you this lecture? Because I need your help and will take it only on my own terms. If you work with me on this and we find what we're looking for, a murderer, with the required evidence, any one or all of you may know all that I know, or at least enough to give you a right to share in the decision: what to do about it. That's what I won't accept. I reserve that right solely to myself. I alone shall decide whether to expose him, and if I decide not to, I shall expect you to concur; and if you concur you will be obligated to say or do nothing that will conflict with my decision. You'll have to keep your mouths shut, and that is a burden not to be lightly assumed. So before we get too far I'm giving you this chance to stay out of it."

He pressed a button on his desk. "I'll drink some beer while you think it over. Will you have some?"

Since it was the first group conference we had had for a long time, all five of us, I thought it should be done right, so I went to the kitchen, and Fritz and I collaborated. It was nothing fancy—a bourbon and soda for Saul, and gin fizzes for Orrie and me, and beer for Fred Durkin and Wolfe. Straight rye with no chaser was Fred's drink, but I had never been able to talk him out of the notion that he would offend Wolfe if he didn't take beer when invited. So while the rest of us sat and enjoyed what we liked, Fred sipped away at what I had heard him call slop.

Since they were supposed to be thinking something over, they tried to look thoughtful, and I tactfully filled in by giving Wolfe a few sidelights on the afternoon, such as the bottle of Scotch Rony had kept in the bond box. But it was too much for Saul, who hated to mark time. When his highball was half gone he lifted the glass, drained it, put it down, and spoke to Wolfe.

"What you were saying. If you want me to work on this, all I expect is to get paid. If I get anything for you, then it's yours. My mouth doesn't need any special arrangement to keep it shut."

Wolfe nodded. "I know you're discreet, Saul. All of you are. But this time what you'll get for me may be evidence that would convict a murderer if it were used, and there's a possibility that it may not be used. That would be a strain."

"Yes, sir. I'll make out all right. If you can stand it I can."

"What the hell," Fred blurted. "I don't get it. What do you think we'd do, play pattycake with the cops?"

"It's not that," Orrie told him impatiently. "He knows how we like cops. Maybe you never heard about having a conscience."

"Never did. Describe it to me."

"I can't. I'm too sophisticated to have one and you're too primitive."

"Then there's no problem."

"There certainly isn't." Orrie raised his glass. "Here's to crime, Mr. Wolfe. There's no problem." He drank.

Wolfe poured beer. "Well," he said, "now you know what this is like. The contingency I have described may never arise, but it had to be foreseen. With that understood we can proceed. Unless we have some luck this could drag on for weeks. Mr. Sperling's adroit stroke in persuading a man of standing to sign that confounded statement, not merely a chauffeur or other domestic employee, has made it excessively difficult. There is one possibility which I shall have explored by a specialist—none of you is equipped for it—but meanwhile we must see what we can find. Archie, tell Fred about the people who work there. All of them."

I did so, typing the names for him. If my week end at Stony Acres had been purely social I wouldn't have been able to give him a complete list, from the butler to the third assistant gardener, but during the examinations Monday night and Tuesday morning I had got well informed. As I briefed Fred on them he made notes on the typed list.

"Anyone special?" Fred asked Wolfe.

"No. Don't go to the house. Start at Chappaqua, in the village, wherever you can pick up a connection.

We know that someone in that house drugged a drink intended for Mr. Rony on Saturday evening, and we are assuming that someone wanted him to die enough to help it along. When an emotion as violent as that is loose in a group of people there are often indications of it that are heard or seen by servants. That's all I can tell you."

"What will I be in Chappaqua for?"

"Whatever you like. Have something break on your car, something that takes time, and have it towed to the local garage. Is there a garage in Chappaqua, Archie?"

"Yes, sir."

"That will do." Wolfe drank the last of his beer and used his handkerchief on his lips. "Now Saul. You met young Sperling today."

"Yes, sir. Archie introduced us."

"We want to know what he and his mother were looking for at Mr. Rony's apartment. It was almost certainly a paper, since they were looking in books, and probably one which had supported a threat held by Mr. Rony over young Sperling or his mother. That conjecture is obvious and even trite, but things get trite by occurring frequently. There is a clear pattern. A month ago Mrs. Sperling reversed herself and re-admitted Mr. Rony to her home as a friend of her daughter, and the son's attitude changed at the same time. A threat could have been responsible for that, especially since the main objection to Mr. Rony was then based on a mere surmise by Mr. Sperling. But Monday afternoon they were told something which so blackened Mr. Rony as to make him quite unacceptable. Yet the threat still existed. You see where that points."

"What blackened him?" Saul asked.

Wolfe shook his head. "I doubt if you need that, at least not now. We want to know what the threat was, if one existed. That's for you and Orrie, with you in charge. The place to look is here in New York, and the son is far more likely than the mother, so try him first—his associates, his habits—but for that you need no suggestions from me. It's as routine as Fred's job, but perhaps more promising. Report as usual."

That finished the conference. Fred got the rest of his beer down, not wanting to offend Wolfe by leaving some. I got money for them from the safe, from the cash drawer, not disturbing the contribution from our latest client. Fred had a couple of questions and got them answered, and I went to the front door to let them out.

Back in the office, Fritz had entered to remove glasses and bottles. I stood and stretched and yawned.

"Sit down," Wolfe said peevishly.

"You don't have to take it out on me," I complained, obeying. "I can't help it if you're a genius, as Paul Emerson says, but the best you can do is to sic Fred on the hired help and start Saul and Orrie hunting ratholes. God knows I have no bright suggestions, but then I'm not a genius. Who is my meat? Aloysius Murphy? Emerson?"

He grunted. "The others replied to the question I put. You didn't."

"Nuts. My worry about this murderer, if there is one, is not what you'll do with him after you get him, but whether you're going to get him." I gestured. "If you do, he's yours. Get him two thousand volts or a DSO—as you please. Will you need my help?"

"Yes. But you may be disqualified. I told you last week to establish a personal relationship."

"So you did. So I did."

"But not with the right person. I would like to take advantage of your acquaintance with the elder Miss Sperling, but you may balk. You may have scruples."

"Much obliged. It would depend on the kind of advantage. If all I'm after is facts, scruples are out. She knows I'm a detective and she knows where we stand, so it's up to her. If it turns out that she killed Rony I'll help you pin the medal on her. What is it you want?"

"I want you to go up there tomorrow morning."

"Glad to. What for?"

He told me.

17

Like all good drivers, I don't need my mind for country driving, just my eyes and ears and reflexes. So when we're on a case and I'm at the wheel of the car in the open, I'm usually gnawing away at the knots. But as I rolled north on the parkways that fine sunny June morning I had to find something else to gnaw on, because in that case I couldn't tell a knot from a doughnut. There was no puzzle to it; it was merely a grab bag. So I let my mind skip around as it pleased, now and then concentrating on the only puzzle in sight, which was this: had Wolfe sent me up here because he thought I might really get something, or merely to get me out of the way while he consulted his specialist? I didn't know. I took it for granted that the specialist was Mr. Jones, whom I had never been permitted to meet, though Wolfe had made use of him on two occasions that I knew of. Mr. Jones was merely the name he had given me offhand when I had had to make an entry in the expense book.

On the phone I had suggested to Madeline that it might be more tactful for me to park outside the entrance and meet her somewhere on the grounds, and she replied that when it got to where she had to sneak me in she would rather I stayed out. I didn't insist, because my errand would take me near the house anyway, and Sperling would be away, at his office in New York, and I doubted if Jimmy or Mom would care to raise a howl at sight of me since we were now better acquainted. So I turned in at the entrance and drove on up to the house, and parked on the plaza behind the shrubbery, at the exact spot I had chosen before.

The sun was shining and birds were twittering and

leaves and flowers were everywhere in their places, and Madeline, on the west terrace, had on a cotton print with big yellow butterflies on it. She came to meet me, but stopped ten feet off to stare.

"My Lord," she exclaimed, "that's exactly what I wanted to do! Who got ahead of me?"

"That's a swell attitude," I said bitterly. "It hurts."

"Certainly it does, that's why we do it." She had advanced and was inspecting my cheek at close range. "It was a darned good job. You look simply awful. Hadn't you better go and come back in a week or two?"

"No, ma'am."

"Who did it?"

"You'd be surprised." I tilted my head to whisper in her ear. "Your mother."

She laughed a nice little laugh. "She might do the other side, at that, if you get near her. You should have seen her face when I told her you were coming. How about a drink? Some coffee?"

"No, thanks. I've got work to do."

"So you said. What's this about a wallet?"

"It's not really a wallet, it's a card case. In summer clothes, without enough pockets, it's a problem. You told me it hadn't been found in the house, so it must be outdoors somewhere. When we were out looking for your sister Monday night it was in my hip pocket, or it was when we started, and in all the excitement I didn't miss it until yesterday. I've got to have it because my license is in it."

"Your driving license?"

I shook my head. "Detective license."

"That's right, you're a detective, aren't you? All right, come on." She moved. "We'll take the same route. What does it look like?"

Having her along wasn't part of my plan. "You're an angel," I told her. "You're a little cabbage. In that dress you remind me of a girl I knew in the fifth grade. I'm not going to let you ruin it scrambling around hunting that damn card case. Leave me but don't forget me. If and when I find it I'll let you know."

"Not a chance." She was smiling with a corner of

her mouth up. "I've always wanted to help a detective find something, especially you. Come on!"

She was either onto me or she wasn't, but in any case it was plain that she had decided to stay with me. I might as well pretend that nothing would please me better, so I did.

"What does it look like?" she asked as we circled the house and started to cross the lawn toward the border.

Since the card case was at that moment in my breast pocket, the simplest way would have been to show it to her, but under the circumstances I preferred to describe it. I told her it was pigskin, darkened by age, and four inches by six. It wasn't to be seen on the lawn. We argued about where we had gone through the shrubbery, and I let her win. It wasn't there either, and a twig whipped my wounded cheek as I searched beneath the branches. After we had passed through the gate into the field we had to go slower because the grass was tall enough to hide a small object like a card case. Naturally I felt foolish, kicking around three or four blocks away from where I wanted to be, but I had told my story and was stuck with it.

We finally finished with the field, including the route around the back of the outbuildings, and the inside of the barn. As we neared the vicinity of the house from the other direction, the southwest, I kept bearing left, and Madeline objected that we hadn't gone that way. I replied that I had been outdoors on other occasions than our joint night expedition, and went still further left. At last I was in bounds. Thirty paces off was a clump of trees, and just the other side of it was the graveled plaza where my car was parked. If someone had batted Rony on the head, for instance with a piece of a branch of a tree with stubs of twigs on it, before running the car over him, and if he had then put the branch in the car and it was still there when he drove back to the house to park, and if he had been in a hurry and the best he could do was give the branch a toss, it might have landed in the clump of trees or near by. That cluster of ifs will indicate the kind of errand Wolfe had picked for me. Searching the grounds for a likely weapon was a perfectly sound routine idea, but it needed ten trained men with no inhibitions, not a pretty girl in a cotton print looking for a card case and a born hero pretending he was doing likewise.

Somebody growled something that resembled "Good morning."

It was Paul Emerson. I was nearing the edge of the clump of trees, with Madeline not far off. When I looked up I could see only the top half of Emerson because he was standing on the other side of my car and the hood hit the rest of him. I told him hello, not expansively.

"This isn't the same car," he stated.

"That's right," I agreed. "The other one was a sedan. That's a convertible. You have a sharp eye. Why, did you like the sedan better?"

"I suppose," he said cuttingly, "you have Mr. Sperling's permission to wander around here?"

"I'm here, Paul," Madeline said sweetly. "Maybe you couldn't see me for the trees. My name's Sperling."

"I'm not wandering," I told him. "I'm looking for something."

"What?"

"You. Mr. Wolfe sent me to congratulate you on your broadcast yesterday. His phone's been busy ever since, people wanting to hire him. Would you mind lying down so I can run the car over you?"

He had stepped around the front of the hood and advanced, and I had emerged from the clump of trees. Within arm's reach he stood, his nose and a corner of his mouth twitching, and his eyes boring into me.

"There are restrictions on the air," he said, "that don't apply here. The animal I had in mind was the hyena. The ones with four legs are never fat, but those with two legs sometimes are. Your boss is. You're not."

"I'll count three," I said. "One, two, three." With an open palm I slapped him on the right cheek, and as he rocked I straightened him up with one on the left. The second one was a little harder, but not at all vicious. I turned and moved, not in haste, back among the trees. When I got to the other edge of the clump Madeline was beside me.

"That didn't impress me much," she declared, in a

voice that wanted to tremble but didn't. "He's not exactly Joe Louis."

I kept moving. "These things are relative," I explained. "When your sister called Mr. Wolfe a cheap filthy little worm I didn't even shake a finger at her, let alone slap her. But the impulse to wipe his sneer off would have been irresistible even if he hadn't said a word and even if he had been only half the size. Anyway, it didn't leave a mark on him. Look what your mother did to me, and I wasn't sneering."

She wasn't convinced. "Next time do it when I'm not there. Who did scratch you?"

"Paul Emerson. I was just getting even. We'll never find that card case if you don't help me look."

An hour later we were side by side on the grass at the edge of the brook, a little below the bridge, discussing lunch. Her polite position was that there was no reason why I shouldn't go to the house for it, and I was opposed. Lunching with Mrs. Sperling and Jimmy, whom I had caught technically breaking and entering, with Webster Kane, whom Wolfe had called a liar, and with Emerson, whom I had just smacked on both cheeks, didn't appeal to me on the whole. Besides, my errand now looked hopeless. I had covered, as well as I could with company along, all the territory from the house to the bridge, and some of it beyond the bridge, and I could take a look at the rest of it on the way out.

Madeline was manipulating a blade of grass with her teeth, which were even and white but not ostentatious. "I'm tired and hungry," she stated. "You'll have to carry me home."

"Okay." I got to my feet. "If it starts me breathing fast and deep don't misunderstand."

"I will." She tilted her head back to look up at me. "But first why don't you tell me what you've been looking for? Do you think for one minute I'd have kept panting around with you all morning if I had thought it was only a card case?"

"You haven't panted once. What's wrong with a card case?"

"Nothing." She spat out the blade of grass. "There's

nothing wrong with my eyes, either. Haven't I seen you? Half the time you've been darting into places where you couldn't possibly have lost a card case or anything else. When we came down the bank to the brook I expected you to start looking under stones." She waved a hand. "There's thousands of 'em. Go to it." She sprang to her feet and shook out her skirt. "But carry me home first. And on the way you'll tell me what you've been looking for or I'll tear your picture out of my scrapbook."

"Maybe we can make a deal," I offered. "I'll tell you what I've been looking for if you'll tell me what your idea was Tuesday afternoon. You may remember that you might have seen or heard something Monday evening that could have given you a notion about someone using my car, but you wouldn't tell me because you wanted to save your father some dough. That reason no longer holds, so why not tell me now?"

She smiled down at me. "You never let go, do you? Certainly I'll tell you. I saw Webster Kane on the terrace about that time, and if he hadn't used the car himself I thought he might have seen someone going to it or coming back."

"No sale. Try again."

"But that was it!"

"Oh, sure it was." I got to my feet. "It's lucky it happened to be Kane who signed that statement. You're a very lucky girl. I think I'll have to choke you. I'll count three. One, two—"

She sprinted up the bank and waited for me at the top. Going back up the drive, she got fairly caustic because I insisted that all I had come for was the card case, but when we reached the parking plaza and I had the door of the car open, she gave that up to end on the note she had greeted me with. She came close, ran a fingertip gently down the line of my scratch, and demanded, "Tell me who did that, Archie. I'm jealous!"

"Some day," I said, climbing in and pushing the starter button. "I'll tell you everything from the cradle on."

"Honest?"

"Yes, ma'am." I rolled away.

As I steered the curves down the drive my mind was on several things at once. One was a record just set by a woman. I had been with Madeline three hours and she hadn't tried to pump me with a single question about what Wolfe was up to. For that she deserved some kind of a mark, and I filed it under unfinished business. Another was a check on a point that Wolfe had raised. The brook made a good deal of noise. It wasn't the kind you noticed unless you listened, but it was loud enough so that if you were only twenty feet from the bridge, walking up the drive, and it was nearly dark, you might not hear a car coming down the drive until it was right on you. That was a point in support of Webster Kane's confession, and therefore a step backward instead of forward, but it would have to be reported to Wolfe.

However, the thing in the front of my mind was Madeline's remark that she had expected me to start looking under stones. It should have occurred to me before, but anyway it had now, and, not being prejudiced like Wolfe, I don't resent getting a tip from a woman. So I went on through the entrance onto the public highway, parked the car at the roadside, got a magnifying glass from the medicine case, walked back up the drive to the bridge, and stepped down the bank to the edge of the brook.

There certainly were thousands of stones, all shapes and sizes, some partly under water, more along the edge and on the bank. I shook my head. It was a perfectly good idea, but there was only one of me and I was no expert. I moved to a new position and looked some more. The stones that were in the water all had smooth surfaces, and the high ones were dry and light-colored, and the low ones were dark and wet and slippery. Those on the bank, beyond the water, were also smooth and dry and light-colored until they got up to a certain level, where there was an abrupt change and they were rough and much darker—a greenish gray. Of course the dividing line was the level of the water in the spring when the brook was up.

Good for you, I thought, you've made one hell of a

discovery and now you're a geologist. All you have to do now is put every damn rock under the glass, and along about Labor Day you'll be ready to report. Ignoring my sarcasm, I went on looking. I moved along the edge of the brook, stepping on stones, until I was underneath the bridge, stood there a while, and moved again, upstream from the bridge. By that time my eyes had caught onto the idea and I didn't have to keep reminding them.

It was there, ten feet up from the bridge, that I found it. It was only a few inches from the water's edge, and was cuddled in a nest of larger stones, half hidden, but when I had once spotted it it was as conspicuous as a scratched cheek. About the size of a coconut, and something like one in shape, it was rough and greenish gray, whereas all its neighbors were smooth and light-colored. I was so excited I stood and gawked at it for ten seconds, and when I moved, with my eyes glued on it for fear it would take a hop, I stepped on a wiggler and nearly took a header into the brook.

One thing sure, that rock hadn't been there long.

I bent over double so as to use both hands to pick it up, touching it only with the tips of four fingers, and straightened to take a look. The best bet would of course be prints, but one glance showed that to be an outside chance. It was rough all over, hundreds of little indentations, with not a smooth spot anywhere. But I still held it with my fingertips, because while prints had been the best bet they were by no means the only one. I was starting to turn, to move away from the brook to better footing, when a voice came from right behind me.

"Looking for hellgrammites?"

I swiveled my head. It was Connie Emerson. She was close enough to reach me with a stretched arm, which would have meant that she was an expert at the silent approach, if it hadn't been for the noise of the brook.

I grinned at the clear strong blue of her eyes. "No, I'm after gold."

"Really? Let me see—"

She took a step, lit on a stone with a bad angle, gave

a little squeal, and toppled into me. Not being firmly based, over I went, and I went clear down because I spent my first tenth of a second trying to keep my fingertip hold on my prize, but I lost it anyway. When I bounced up to a sitting position Connie was sprawled flat, but her head was up and she was stretching an arm in a long reach for something, and she was getting it. My greenish gray stone had landed less than a foot from the water, and her fingers were ready to close on it. I hate to suspect a blue-eyed blonde of guile, but if she had it in mind to toss that stone in the water to see it splash all she needed was another two seconds, so I did a headlong slide over the rocks and brought the side of my hand down on her forearm. She let out a yell and jerked the arm back. I scrambled up and got erect, with my left foot planted firmly in front of my stone.

She sat up, gripping her forearm with her other hand, glaring at me. "You big ape, are you crazy?" she demanded.

"Getting there," I told her. "Gold does it to you. Did you see that movie, *Treasure of Sierra Madre?*"

"Damn you." She clamped her jaw, held it a moment, and released it. "Damn you, I think you broke my arm."

"Then your bones must be chalk. I barely tapped it. Anyway, you nearly broke my back." I made my voice reasonable. "There's too much suspicion in this world. I'll agree not to suspect you of meaning to bump me if you'll agree not to suspect me of meaning to tap your arm. Why don't we move off of these rocks and sit on the grass and talk it over? Your eyes are simply beautiful. We could start from there."

She pulled her feet in, put a hand—not the one that had reached for my stone—on a rock for leverage, got to her feet, stepped carefully across the rocks to the grass, climbed the bank, and was gone.

My right elbow hurt, and my left hip. I didn't care for that, but there were other aspects of the situation that I liked even less. Counting the help, there were six or seven men in and around the house, and if Connie told them a tale that brought them all down to the brook it might get embarrassing. She had done enough harm as it was, making me drop my stone. I stooped and lifted it with my fingertips again, got clear of the rocks and negotiated the bank, walked down the drive and on out to the car, and made room for the stone in the medicine case, wedged so it wouldn't roll around.

I didn't stop for lunch in Westchester County, either. I took to the parkways and kept going. I didn't feel really elated, since I might have got merely a stray hunk of granite, not Exhibit A at all, and I didn't intend to start crowing unless and until. So when I left the West Side Highway at Forty-sixth Street, as usual, I drove first to an old brick building in the upper Thirties near Ninth Avenue. There I delivered the stone to a Mr. Weinbach, who promised they would do their best. Then I drove home, went in and found Fritz in the kitchen, ate four sandwiches—two sturgeon and two home-baked ham—and drank a quart of milk.

18

When I swallowed the last of the milk it wasn't five o'clock yet, and it would be more than an hour before Wolfe came down from the plant rooms, which was just as well since I needed to take time out for an overhaul. In my room up on the third floor I stripped. There was a long scrape on my left knee and a promising bruise on my left hip, and a square inch of skin was missing from my right elbow. The scratch on my cheek was developing nicely, getting new ideas about color every hour. Of course it might have been worse, at least nobody had run a car over me; but I was beginning to feel that it would be a welcome change to take on an enemy my own sex and size. I certainly wasn't doing so well with women. In addition to the damage to my hide, my best Palm Beach suit was ruined, with a big tear in the sleeve of the coat. I showered, iodined, bandaged, dressed, and went down to the office.

A look in the safe told me that if I was right in supposing that the specialist to be hired was Mr. Jones, he hadn't been hired yet, for the fifty grand was still all there. That was a deduction from a limited experience. I had never seen the guy, but I knew two things about him: that it was through him that Wolfe had got the dope on a couple of Commies that had sent them up the river, and that when you bought from him you paid in advance. So either it wasn't to be him or Wolfe hadn't been able to reach him yet.

I had been hoping for a phone call from Weinbach before Wolfe descended at six o'clock, but it didn't come. When Wolfe entered, got seated behind his desk, and said "Well?" I thought I was still undecided about including the stone in my report before hearing from Weinbach, but he had to know about Connie, so I kept on to the end. I did not, however, tell him that it was a remark of Madeline's that made me think of stones, thinking it might irritate him to know that a woman had helped out.

He sat frowning.

"I was a little surprised," I said smugly, "that you didn't think of a stone yourself. Doc Vollmer said something rough and heavy."

"Pfui. Certainly I thought of a stone. But if he used a stone all he had to do was walk ten paces to the bridge and toss it into the water."

"That's what he thought. But he missed the water. Lucky I didn't take the attitude you did. If I hadn't—"

The phone rang. A voice that hissed its esses was in my ear. Weinbach of the Fisher Laboratories hissed his esses. Not only that, he told me who he was. As I motioned to Wolfe to get on, I was holding my breath.

"That stone you left with me," Weinbach said. "Do you wish the technical terms?"

"I do not. I only want what I asked for. Is there anything on it to show it was used, or might have been used, to slam a man on the head?"

"There is."

"What!" I hadn't really expected it. "There is?"

"Yes. Everything is dried up, but there are four specks that are bloodstains, five more that may be bloodstains, one minute piece of skin, and two slightly larger pieces of skin. One of the larger pieces has an entire follicle. This is a preliminary report and none of it can be guaranteed. It will take forty-eight hours to complete all the tests."

"Go to it, brother! If I was there I'd kiss you."

"I beg your pardon?"

"Forget it. I'll get you a Nobel Prize. Write the report in red ink."

I hung up and turned to Wolfe. "Okay. He was murdered. Connie did it or knows who did. She knew about the stone. She stalked me. I should have established a personal relationship with her and brought her down here. Do you want her? I'll bet I can get her."

"Good heavens, no." His brows had gone up. "I must say, Archie, satisfactory."

"Don't strain yourself."

"I won't. But though you used your time well, to the purpose you were sent for, all you got was corroboration. The stone proves that Mr. Kane's statement was false, that Mr. Rony was killed deliberately, and that one of those people killed him, but there's nothing new in that for us."

"Excuse me," I said coldly, "for bringing in something that doesn't help."

"I don't say it doesn't help. If and when this gets to a courtroom, it will unquestionably help there. Tell me again what Mrs. Emerson said."

I did so, in a restrained manner. Looking back now, I can see that he was right, but at the time I was damn proud of that stone.

Since it gives the place an unpleasant atmosphere for one of us to be carrying a grudge, I thought it would be better if I got even immediately, and I did so by not eating dinner with him, giving as a reason my recent consumption of sandwiches. He loves to talk when he's eating, business being taboo, so as I sat alone in the office, catching up with the chores, my humor kept getting better, and by the time he rejoined me I was perfectly willing to speak to him—in fact, I had thought up a few comments about the importance of evidence in criminal cases which would have been timely and appropriate.

I had to put off making them because he was still getting himself arranged to his after-dinner position in his chair when the doorbell rang and, Fritz being busy with the dishes, I went to answer it. It was Saul Panzer and Orrie Cather. I ushered them into the office. Orrie got comfortable, with his legs crossed, and took out a pipe and filled it, while Saul sat erect on the front half of the big red leather chair.

"I could have phoned," Saul said, "but it's a little complicated and we need instructions. We may have something and we may not."

"The son or the mother?" Wolfe asked.

"The son. You said to take him first." Saul took out a notebook and glanced at a page. "He knows a lot of people. How do you want it, dates and details?"

"Sketch it first."

"Yes, sir." Saul closed the notebook. "He spends about half his time in New York and the rest all over. Owns his own airplane, a Mecklin, and keeps it in New Jersey. Belongs to only one club, the Harvard. Has been arrested for speeding twice in the past three years, once—"

"Not a biography," Wolfe protested. "Just items that might help."

"Yes, sir. You might possibly want this: he has a half interest in a restaurant in Boston called the New Frontier. It was started in nineteen forty-six by a college classmate, and young Sperling furnished the capital, around forty thousand, probably from his father, but that's not—"

"A night club?"

"No, sir. High-class, specializing in sea food."

"A failure?"

"No, sir. Successful. Not spectacular, but going ahead and showed a good profit in nineteen forty-eight."

Wolfe grunted. "Hardly a good basis for blackmail. What else?"

Saul looked at Orrie. "You tell him about the Manhattan Ballet."

"Well," Orrie said, "it's a bunch of dancers that started two years ago. Jimmy Sperling and two other guys put up the dough, and I haven't found out how much Jimmy's share was, but I can. They do modern stuff. The first season they quit town after three weeks in a dump on Forty-eighth Street, and tried it in the sticks, but that wasn't so good either. This last season they opened in November at the Herald Theater and kept going until the end of April. Everybody thinks the three angels got all their ante back and then some, but that will take checking. Anyhow they did all right."

It was beginning to sound to me as if we were up against a new one. I had heard of threats to tell a rich man how much his son had sunk, but not to tell how much his son was piling up. My opinion of Jimmy needed some shuffling.

"Of course," Orrie went on, "when you think of ballet you think of girls with legs. This ballet has got 'em all right; that's been checked. Jimmy is interested in ballet or why would he kick in? He goes twice a week when he's in New York. He also is personally interested in seeing that the girls get enough to eat. When I got that far I naturally thought I was on the way to something, and maybe I am but not yet. He likes the girls and they like him, but if that has led to anything he wouldn't want put in the paper it'll have to wait for another installment because I haven't caught up to it yet. Shall I keep trying?"

"You might as well." Wolfe went to Saul. "Is that all you have?"

"No, we've got plenty," Saul told him, "but nothing you might want except maybe the item I wanted to ask about. Last fall he contributed twenty thousand dollars to the CPBM."

"What's that?"

"Committee of Progressive Business Men. One of the funny fronts. It was for Henry A. Wallace for President."

"Indeed." Wolfe's eyes, which had been nearly closed, had opened a little. "Tell me about it."

"I can't tell you much, because it was afternoon when I scared it up. Apparently nobody was supposed to know about the contribution, but several people do, and I think I can get onto them if you say so. That's what I wanted to ask about. I had a break and got a line on a man in the furniture business who was pro-Wallace at first but later broke loose. He claims to know all about Sperling's contribution. He says Sperling made it in a personal check for twenty thousand, which he gave to a man named Caldecott one Thursday evening, and the next morning Sperling came to the CPBM office and wanted his check back. He wanted to give it in cash instead of a check. But he was too late because the check had already been deposited. And here's what I thought made it interesting; this man says that since the first of the year photostats of three different checks—contributions from three other people—have turned up in peculiar circumstances. One of them was his own check, for two thousand dollars, but he wouldn't give me the names of the other two."

Wolfe's brow was wrinkled. "Does he say that the people running the organization had the photostats made for later use—in peculiar circumstances?"

"No, sir. He thinks some clerk did it, either for personal use or as a Republican or Democratic spy. This man says he is now a political hermit. He doesn't like Wallace, but he doesn't like Republicans or Democrats either. He says he's going to vote the Vegetarian ticket next time but go on eating meat. I let him talk. I wanted to get all I could because if there was a photostat of young Sperling's check—"

"Certainly. Satisfactory."

"Shall I follow up?"

"By all means. Get all you can. The clerk who had the photostats made would be a find." Wolfe turned to me. "Archie. You know that young man better than we do. Is he a ninny?"

"If I thought so," I said emphatically, "I don't now. Not if he's raking in profits on a Boston restaurant and a Manhattan ballet. I misjudged him. Three to one I know where the photostat of Jimmy's check is. In a safe at the office of Murphy, Kearfot and Rony."

"I suppose so. Anything else, Saul?"

I wouldn't have been surprised if the next item had been that Jimmy had cleaned up a million playing the ponies or running a chicken farm, but evidently he hadn't tried them yet. Saul and Orrie stayed a while, long enough to have a drink and discuss ways and means of laying hands on the Republican or Democratic spy, and then left. When I returned to the office after letting them out I considered whether to get rid of the comments I had prepared regarding the importance of evidence in criminal cases, and decided to skip it.

I would just as soon have gone up to bed to give my bruises a rest, but it was only half past nine and my middle drawer was stuffed with memos and invoices connected with the repairs on the roof. I piled them on the desk and tackled them. It had begun to look as if Wolfe's estimate of the amount of the damage wasn't far off, and maybe too low if you included replacement of some of the rarer hybrids that had got rough treatment. Wolfe, seeing what I was at, offered to help, and I moved the papers over to his desk. But, as I had often discovered before, a man shouldn't try to run a detective business and an orchid factory at the same time. They're always tripping over each other. We hadn't been at the papers five minutes when the doorbell rang. I usually go when it's after nine o'clock, the hour when Fritz changes to his old slippers, so I went.

I switched on the stoop light, looked through the one-way glass panel, opened the door, said, "Hello, come in," and Gwenn Sperling crossed the threshold.

I closed the door and turned to her. "Want to see the worm?" I gestured. "That way."

"You don't seem surprised!" she blurted.

"It's my training. I hide it to impress you. Actually I'm overcome. That way?"

She moved and I followed. She entered the office, advanced three steps, and stopped, and I detoured around her.

"Good evening, Miss Sperling," Wolfe said pointedly. He indicated the red leather chair. "That's the best chair."

"Did I phone you I was coming?" she demanded.

"I don't think so. Did she, Archie?"

"No, sir. She's just surprised that we're not surprised."

"I see. Won't you sit down?"

For a second I thought she was going to turn and march out, as she had that afternoon in the library, but if the motion had been made she voted it down. Her eyes left Wolfe for a look at me, and I saw them stop at my scratched cheek, but she wasn't enough interested to ask who did it. She dropped her fur neckpiece onto a yellow chair, went to the red leather one and sat, and spoke.

"I came because I couldn't persuade myself not to. I want to confess something."

My God, I thought. I hope she hasn't already signed a statement. She looked harassed but not haggard, and her freckles showed hardly at all in that light.

"Confessions often help," Wolfe said, "but it's important to make them to the right person. Am I the one?"

"You're just being nice because I called you a worm!"

"That would be a strange reason for being nice. Anyhow, I'm not. I'm only trying to help you get started."

"You don't need to." Gwenn's hands were clasped tight. "I've decided. I'm a conceited nosy little fool!"

"You use too many adjectives," Wolfe said dryly. "For me it was cheap filthy little worm. Now, for you, it is conceited nosy little fool. Let's just say fool. Why? What about?"

"About everything. About Louis Rony. I knew darned well I wasn't really in love with him, but I thought I'd teach my father something. If I hadn't had him there he wouldn't have thought he could pique me by playing with Connie Emerson, and she wouldn't have played with him, and he wouldn't have got killed. Even if everything you said about him is true, it's my fault he got killed, and what am I going to do?"

Wolfe grunted. "I'm afraid I don't follow you. How was it your fault that Mr. Kane went to mail some letters and accidentally ran over Mr. Rony?"

She stared. "But you know that's not true!"

"Yes, but you don't—or do you?"

"Of course I do!" Her hands came unclasped. "I may be a fool, I guess I can't go back on that, but I've known Webster a long time and I know he couldn't possibly do such a thing!"

"Anyone can have an accident."

"I know they can; I don't mean that. But if he had run a car over Louis and saw he was dead, he would have gone back to the house, straight to a phone, and called a doctor and the police. You've met him. Couldn't you see he was like that?"

This was a new development, a Sperling trying to persuade Wolfe that Kane's statement was a phony.

"Yes," Wolfe said mildly. "I thought I saw he was like that. Does your father know you're here?"

"No. I—I didn't want to quarrel with him."

"It won't be easy to avoid it when he finds out. What made you decide to come?"

"I wanted to yesterday, and I didn't. I'm a coward."

"A fool and a coward." Wolfe shook his head. "Don't rub it in. And today?"

"I heard someone say something. Now I'm an eavesdropper too. I used to be when I was a child, but I thought I was completely over it. Today I heard Connie saying something to Paul, and I stayed outside the door and listened."

"What did she say?"

Gwenn's face drew together. I thought she was going to cry, and so did she. That would have been bad, because Wolfe's wits leave him when a woman cries.

I snapped at her. "What did you drive down here for?"

She pulled out of it and appealed to Wolfe. "Do I have to tell you?"

"No," he said curtly.

Naturally that settled it. She proceeded to tell. She looked as if she would rather eat soap, but she didn't stammer any.

"They were in their room and I was going by. But I didn't just happen to overhear it; I stopped and listened deliberately. She hit him or he hit her, I don't know which—with them you don't know who is doing the hitting unless you see it. But she was doing the talking. She told him that she saw Goodwin—" Gwenn looked at me. "That was you."

"My name's Goodwin," I admitted.

"She said she saw Goodwin finding a stone by the brook and she tried to get it and throw it in the water, but Goodwin knocked her down. She said Goodwin had the stone and would take it to Nero Wolfe, and she wanted to know what Paul was going to do, and he said he wasn't going to do anything. She said she didn't care what happened to him but she wasn't going to have her reputation ruined if she could help it, and then he hit her, or maybe she hit him. I thought one of them was coming to the door and I ran down the hall."

"When did this happen?" Wolfe growled.

"Just before dinner. Dad had just come home, and I was going to tell him about it, but I decided not to because I knew he must have got Webster to sign that statement, and he's so stubborn—I knew what he would say. But I couldn't just not do anything. I knew it was my fault Louis got killed, and after what you told us about him it didn't matter about him but it did about me. I guess that sounds selfish, but I've decided that from now on I'm going to be perfectly honest. I'm going to be honest to everyone about everything. I'm going to quit being a fake. Take the way I acted the day you came. I should have just phoned Louis and told him I didn't want to see him any more, that would have been the honest thing and that was what I really wanted to do; but no, I didn't do that, I had to phone him to come and meet me so I could tell him face to face—and what happened? I honestly believe I was hoping that someone would listen in on one of the extensions so they would know how fine and noble I was! I knew Connie did that all the time, and maybe others did too. Anyhow someone did, and you know what happened. It was just as if I had phoned him to come and get killed!"

She stopped for breath. Wolfe suggested, "You may be taking too much credit, Miss Sperling."

"That's a nasty crack." She wasn't through. "I couldn't say all this to my father or mother, not even to my sister, because—well, I couldn't. But I wasn't going to start being honest by hiding the worst thing I ever did. I thought it over very carefully, and I decided you were the one person who would know exactly what I meant. You knew I was afraid of you that afternoon, and you told me so. I think it was the first time anyone really understood me."

I had to keep back a snort. A fine freckled girl saying that to Wolfe with me present was approaching the limit. If there was anything on earth he didn't understand and I did, it was young women.

"So," Gwenn went on, "I had to come and tell you. I know you can't do anything about it, because Dad got Webster to sign that statement, and that ends it, but I felt I had to tell someone, and then when I heard what Paul and Connie said I knew I had to. But you've got to understand that I'm being absolutely honest. If this was me the way I was a year ago or a week ago I'd be pretending that I only came because I think I owe it to Louis to help to bring out the truth about how he died, but if he was the kind of man you said he was I don't really believe I owe him anything. It's only that if I'm going to be a genuine straightforward person I have to start now or I never will. I don't want ever to be afraid of anyone again, not even you."

Wolfe shook his head. "You're expecting a good deal of yourself. I'm more than twice your age, and up with you in self-esteem, but I'm afraid of someone. Don't overdo it. There are numerous layers of honesty, and the deepest should not have a monopoly. What else was said by Mr. and Mrs. Emerson?"

"Just what I told you."

"Nothing more—uh, informative?"

"I told you everything I heard. I don't—" She stopped, frowning. "Didn't I? About his calling her an idiot?"

"No."

"He did. When she said that about her reputation.

He said, 'You idiot, you might as well have told Goodwin you killed him, or that you knew I did.' Then she hit him—or he hit her."

"Anything else?"

"No. I ran."

"Had you already suspected that Mr. Emerson had murdered Mr. Rony?"

"Why I—" Gwenn was shocked. "I don't suspect that now. Do I?"

"Certainly you do. You merely hadn't put it so boldly. You may have got to honesty, Miss Sperling, but there is still sagacity. If I understand you, and you say I do, you think that Mr. Emerson killed Mr. Rony because he was philandering with Mrs. Emerson. I don't believe it. I've heard some of Mr. Emerson's broadcasts, and met him at your home, and I consider him incapable of an emotion so warm and direct and explosive. You said I can do nothing about Mr. Rony's death. I think I can, and I intend to try, but if I find myself reduced to so desperate an assumption as that Mr. Emerson was driven to kill by jealousy of his wife, I'll quit."

"Then—" Gwenn was frowning at him. "Then what?"

"I don't know. Yet." Wolfe put his hands on the edge of his desk, pushed his chair back, and arose. "Are you going to drive back home tonight?"

"Yes. But—"

"Then you'd better get started. It's late. Your newborn passion for honesty is admirable, but in that, as in everything, moderation is often best. It would have been honest to tell your father you were coming here; it would be honest to tell him where you have been when you get home; but if you do so he will think that you have helped me to discredit Mr. Kane's statement, and that would be false. So a better honesty would be to lie and tell him you went to see a friend."

"I did," Gwenn declared. "You *are* a friend. I want to stay and talk."

"Not tonight." Wolfe was emphatic. "I'm expecting a caller. Some other time." He added hastily, "By appointment, of course."

She didn't want to go, but what could the poor girl do? After I handed her her neckpiece she stood and prolonged it a little, with questions that got answers in one syllable, but finally made the best of it.

When she had gone I proceeded immediately to tell Wolfe what I thought of him. "You couldn't possibly ask for a better chance," I protested hotly. "She may not be Miss America 1949, but she's anything but an eyesore, and she'll inherit millions, and she's nuts about you. You could quit work and eat and drink all day. Evenings you could explain how well you understand her, which is apparently all she asks for. You're hooked at last, and it was about time." I extended a paw. "Congratulations!"

"Shut up." He glanced at the clock.

"In a minute. I approve of your lie about expecting a caller. That's the way to handle it, tease her on with the hard to get—"

"Go to bed. I *am* expecting a caller."

I eyed him. "Another one?"

"A man. I'll let him in. Put this stuff away and go to bed. At once."

That had happened not more than twice in five years. Once in a while I get sent out of the room, and frequently I am flagged to get off of my phone, when something is supposed to be too profound for me, but practically never am I actually chased upstairs to keep me from even catching a glimpse of a visitor.

"Mr. Jones?" I asked.

"Put this stuff away."

I gathered up the papers from his desk and returned them to my drawer before telling him, "I don't like it, and you know I don't. One of my functions is keeping you alive." I started for the safe. "What if I come down in the morning and find you?"

"Some morning you may. Not this one. Don't lock the safe."

"There's fifty grand it in."

"I know. Don't lock it."

"Okay, I heard you. The guns are in my second drawer but not loaded."

I told him good night and left him.

19

In the morning three-tenths of the fifty grand was no longer there. Fifteen thousand bucks. I told myself that before I died I must manage at least a look from a distance at Mr. Jones. A guy who could demand that kind of dough for piecework, and collect in advance, was something not to be missed.

When I arose at seven I had had only five hours' sleep. I had not imitated Gwenn and taken to eavesdropping, but I certainly didn't intend to snooze peacefully while Wolfe was down in the office with a character so mysterious I couldn't be allowed to see him or hear him. Therefore, not undressing, I got the gun I keep on my table and went to the hall and sat at the top of the stairs. From there, two flights up, I heard his arrival, and voices in the hall—Wolfe's and one other —and the office door closing, and then, for nearly three hours, a faint mumble that I had to strain my ears to catch at all. For the last hour of it I had to resort to measures to keep myself awake. Finally the office door opened and the voices were louder, and in half a minute he had gone and I heard Wolfe's elevator. I beat it to my room. After my head touched the pillow I tossed and turned for nearly three seconds.

In the morning my custom is not to enter the office until after my half an hour in the kitchen with Fritz and food and the morning paper, but that Friday I went there first and opened the safe. Wolfe is not the man to dish out fifteen grand of anybody's money without having a clear idea of what for, so it seemed likely that something might need attention at any moment, and when, a little after eight, Fritz came down from taking Wolfe's breakfast tray up to him, I fully expected to be told that I was wanted on the second floor. Nothing doing. According to Fritz, my name hadn't been mentioned. At the regular time, three minutes to nine, then at my desk in the office, I heard the sound of the elevator ascending. Apparently his sacred schedule, nine to eleven in the plant rooms, was not to be interrupted. He and Theodore were now handling the situation, no more outside help being needed.

There was one little cheep from him. Shortly after nine the house phone buzzed. He asked if any of the boys had called and I said no, and he said that when they did I was to call them off. I asked if that included Fred, and he said yes, all of them. I asked if there were fresh instructions, and he said no, just tell them to quit.

That was all for then. I spent two hours with the morning mail and the accumulation in my drawer. At 11:02 he entered, told me good morning as he always did no matter how much we had talked on the phone, got installed behind his desk, and inquired grumpily, "Is there anything you must ask me?"

"Nothing I can't hold, no, sir."

"Then I don't want to be interrupted. By anyone."

"Yes, sir. Are you in pain?"

"Yes. I know who killed Mr. Rony, and how and why."

"You do. Does it hurt?"

"Yes." He sighed deep. "It's the very devil. When you know all you need to know about a murderer, what is ordinarily the easiest thing to prove?"

"That's a cinch. Motive."

He nodded. "But not here. I doubt if it can be done. You have known me, in the past, to devise a stratagem that entailed a hazard. Haven't you?"

"That's understanding it. I have known you to take chances that have given me nightmares."

"They were nothing to this. I have devised a stratagem and spent fifteen thousand dollars on it. But if I can think of a better way I'm not going to risk it." He sighed again, leaned back, closed his eyes, and muttered, "I don't want to be disturbed."

That was the last of him for more than nine hours. I

don't think he uttered more than eighty words between 11:09 in the morning and 8:20 in the evening. While he was in the office he sat with eyes closed, his lips pushing out and in from time to time, and his chest expanding every now and then, I would say five inches, with a deep sigh. At the table, during lunch and dinner, there was nothing wrong with his appetite, but he had nothing to offer in the way of conversation. At four o'clock he went up to the plant rooms for his customary two hours, but when I had occasion to ascend to check on a few items with Theodore, Wolfe was planted in his chair in the potting room, and Theodore spoke to me only in a whisper. I have never been able to get it into Theodore's head that when Wolfe is concentrating on a business problem he wouldn't hear us yelling right across his nose, so long as we don't try to drag him into it.

Of the eighty words he used during those nine hours, only nine of them—one to an hour—had to do with the stratagem he was working on. Shortly before dinner he muttered at me, "What time is Mr. Cohen free in the evening?"

I told him a little before midnight.

When, in the office after dinner, he once more settled back and shut his eyes, I thought my God, this is going to be Nero Wolfe's last case. He's going to spend the rest of his life at it. I had myself done a good day's work and saw no sense in sitting on my fanny all evening listening to him breathe. Considering alternatives, and deciding for Phil's and a few games of pool, I was just opening my mouth to announce my intention when Wolfe opened his.

"Archie. Get Mr. Cohen down here as soon as possible. Ask him to bring a *Gazette* letterhead and envelope."

"Yes, sir. Is the ironing done?"

"I don't know. We'll see. Get him."

At last, I thought, we're off. I dialed the number, and after some waiting because that was a busy hour for a morning paper, got him.

His voice came. "Archie? Buy me a drink?"

"No," I said firmly. "Tonight you stay sober. What time can you get here?"

"Where is here?"

"Nero Wolfe's office. He thinks he wants to tell you something."

"Too late." Lon was crisp. "If it will rate the Late City, tell me now."

"It's not that kind. It hasn't come to a boil. But it's good enough so that instead of sending an errand boy, meaning me, he wants to see you himself, so when can you get here?"

"I can send a man."

"No. You."

"Is it worth it?"

"Yes. Possibly."

"In about three hours. Not less, maybe more."

"Okay. Don't stop for a drink, I'll have one ready, and a sandwich. Oh yes, bring along a *Gazette* letterhead and envelope. We've run out of stationery."

"What is it, a gag?"

"No, sir. Far from. It may even get you a raise."

I hung up and turned to Wolfe. "May I make a suggestion? If you want him tender and it's worth a steak, I'll tell Fritz to take one from the freezer and start it thawing."

He said to do so and I went to the kitchen and had a conference with Fritz. Then, back in the office, I sat and listened to Wolfe breathe some more. It went on for minutes that added up to an hour. Finally he opened his eyes, straightened up, and took from his pocket some folded papers which I recognized as sheets torn from his memo pad.

"Your notebook, Archie," he said like a man who has made up his mind.

I got it from the drawer and uncapped my pen.

"If this doesn't work," he growled at me, as if it were all my fault, "there will be no other recourse. I have tried to twist it so as to leave an alternative if it fails, but it can't be done. We'll either get him with this or not at all. On plain paper, double-spaced, two carbons."

"Heading or date?"

"None." He gazed, frowning, at the sheets he had taken from his pocket. "First paragraph:

"At eight o'clock in the evening of August 19, 1948, twenty men were gathered in a living room on the ninth floor of an apartment house on East 84th Street, Manhattan. All of them were high in the councils of the American Communist party, and this meeting was one of a series to decide strategy and tactics for controlling the election campaign of the Progressive party and its candidate for President of the United States, Henry Wallace. One of them, a tall lanky man with a clipped brown mustache, was saying:

" 'We must never forget that we can't trust Wallace. We can't trust either his character or his intelligence. We can count on his vanity, that's all right, but while we're playing him up we must remember that any minute he might pull something that will bring an order from Policy to let go of him.'

" 'Policy' is the word the top American Communists use when they mean Moscow or the Kremlin. It may be a precaution, though it's hard to see why they need one when they are in secret session, or it may be merely their habit of calling nothing by its right name.

"Another of them, a beefy man with a bald head and a pudgy face, spoke up:"

Wolfe, referring frequently to the sheets he had taken from his pocket, kept on until I had filled thirty-two pages of my notebook, then stopped, sat a while with his lips puckered, and told me to type it. I did so, double spacing as instructed. As I finished a page I handed it over to him and he went to work on it with a pencil. He rarely made changes in anything he had dictated and I had typed, but apparently he regarded this as something extra special. I fully agreed with him. That stuff, getting warmer as it went along, contained dozens of details that nobody lower than a Deputy Commissar had any right to know about—provided they were true. That was a point I would have liked to ask Wolfe about, but if the job was supposed to be finished when Lon Cohen arrived there was no time to spare, so I postponed it.

I had the last page out of the typewriter, but Wolfe was still fussing with it, when the bell rang and I went to the front and let Lon in.

Lon had been rank and file, or maybe only rank, when I first met him, but was now second in command at the *Gazette's* city desk. As far as I knew his elevation had gone to his head only in one little way: he kept a hairbrush in his desk, and every night when he was through, before making a dash for the refreshment counter he favored, he brushed his hair good. Except for that there wasn't a thing wrong with him.

He shook hands with Wolfe and turned on me.

"You crook, you told me if I didn't stop—oh, here it is. Hello, Fritz. You're the only one here I can trust." He lifted the highball from the tray, nodded at Wolfe, swallowed a third of it, and sat in the red leather chair.

"I brought the stationery," he announced. "Three sheets. You can have it and welcome if you'll give me a first on how someone named Sperling willfully and deliberately did one Louis Rony to death."

"That," Wolfe said, "is precisely what I have to offer."

Lon's head jerked up. "Someone named Sperling?" he snapped.

"No. I shouldn't have said 'precisely.' The name will have to wait. But the rest of it, yes."

"Damn it, it's midnight! You can't expect—"

"Not tonight. Nor tomorrow. But if and when I have it, you'll get it first."

Lon looked at him. He had entered the room loose and carefree and thirsty, but now he was back at work again. An exclusive on the murder of Louis Rony was nothing to relax about.

"For that," he said, "you'd want more than three letterheads, even with envelopes. What if I throw in postage stamps?"

Wolfe nodded. "That would be generous. But I have something else to offer. How would you like to have, for your paper only, a series of articles, authenticated for you, describing secret meetings of the group that controls the American Communist party, giving the details of discussions and decisions?"

Lon cocked his head to one side. "All you need," he declared, "is long white whiskers and a red suit."

"No, I'm too fat. Would that interest you?"

"It ought to. Who would do the authenticating?"

"I would."

"You mean with your by-line?"

"Good heavens, no. The articles would be anonymous. But I would give my warranty, in writing if desired, that the source of information is competent and reliable."

"Who would have to be paid and how much?"

"No one. Nothing."

"Hell, you don't even need whiskers. What would the details be like?"

Wolfe turned. "Let him read it, Archie."

I took Lon the original copy of what I had typed, and he put his glass down on the table at his elbow, to have two hands. There were seven pages. He started reading fast, then went slower, and when he reached the end returned to the first page and reread it. Meanwhile I refilled his glass and, knowing that Fritz was busy, went to the kitchen for beer for Wolfe. Also I thought I could stand a highball myself, and supplied one.

Lon put the sheets on the table, saw that his glass had been attended to, and helped himself.

"It's hot," he admitted.

"Fit to print, I think," Wolfe said modestly.

"Sure it is. How about libel?"

"There is none. There will be none. No names or addresses are used."

"Yeah, I know, but an action might be brought anyhow. Your source would have to be available for testimony."

"No, sir." Wolfe was emphatic. "My source is covered and will stay covered. You may have my warranty, and a bond for libel damages if you want it, but that's all."

"Well—" Lon drank. "I love it. But I've got bosses, and on a thing like this they would have to decide. Tomorrow is Friday, and they—good God, what's this? Don't tell me—Archie, come and look!"

I had to go anyway, to remove the papers so Fritz could put the tray on the table. It was really a handsome platter. The steak was thick and brown with charcoal braid, the grilled slices of sweet potato and sautéed mushrooms were just right, the watercress was high at one end out of danger, and the overall smell made me wish I had asked Fritz to make a carbon.

"Now I know," Lon said, "it's all a dream. Archie, I would have sworn you phoned me to come down here. Okay, I'll dream on." He sliced through the steak, letting the juice come, cut off a bite, and opened wide for it. Next came a bite of sweet potato, followed by a mushroom. I watched him the way I have seen dogs watch when they're allowed near the table. It was too much. I went to the kitchen, came back with two slices of bread on a plate, and thrust it at him.

"Come on, brother, divvy. You can't eat three pounds of steak."

"It's under two pounds."

"Like hell it is. Fix me up."

After all he was a guest, so he had to give in.

When he left a while later the platter was clean except for the bone, the level in the bottle of Scotch was down another three inches, the letterheads and envelopes were in my desk drawer, and the arrangement was all set, pending an okay by the *Gazette* high brass. Since the weekend was nearly on us, getting the okay might hold it up, but Lon thought there was a fair chance for Saturday and a good one for Sunday. The big drawback, in his opinion, was the fact that Wolfe would give no guarantee of the life of the series. He gave a firm promise for two articles, and said a third was likely, but that was as far as he would commit himself. Lon tried to get him to sign up for a minimum of six, but nothing doing.

Alone with Wolfe again, I gave him a look.

"Quit staring," he said gruffly.

"I beg your pardon. I was figuring something. Two pieces of two thousand words each, four thousand words. Fifteen thousand—that comes to three seventy-five a word. And he doesn't even write the pieces. If you're going to ghost—"

"It's bedtime."

"Yes, sir. Besides writing the second piece, what comes next?"

"Nothing. We sit and wait. Confound it, if this doesn't work . . ."

He told me good night and marched out to the elevator.

20

The next day, Friday, two more articles got dictated, typed, and revised. The second one was delivered to Lon Cohen and the third one was locked in our safe. They carried the story through Election Day up to the end of the year, and while they had no names or addresses they had about everything else. I even got interested in them myself, and was wondering what was going to come next.

Lon's bosses were glad to get them on Wolfe's terms, including the surety protection against libel suits, but decided not to start them until Sunday. They gave them a three-column play on the front page:

HOW THE AMERICAN COMMUNISTS PLAY IT
THE RED ARMY IN THE COLD WAR
THEIR GHQ IN THE USA

There was a preface in italics:

The Gazette *presents herewith the first of a series of articles showing how American Communists help Russia fight the cold war and get ready for the hot one if and when it comes. This is the real thing. For obvious reasons the name of the author of the articles cannot be given, but the* Gazette *has a satisfactory guaranty of their authenticity. We hope to continue the series up to the most recent activities of the Reds, including their secret meetings before, during, and after the famous trial in New York. The second article will appear tomorrow. Don't miss it!*

Then it started off just as Wolfe had dictated it.

I am perfectly willing to hold out on you so as to tell it in a way that will give Wolfe's stratagem the best possible build-up, as you may know by this time, but I am now giving you everything I myself had at the time. That goes for Friday, Saturday, Sunday, and Monday up to 8:30 P.M. You know all that I knew, or you will when I add that the third article was revised Sunday and delivered to Lon Monday noon for Tuesday's paper, that Weinbach's final report on the stone verified the first one, that nothing else was accomplished or even attempted, and that during those four days Wolfe was touchier than I had ever known him to be for so long a period. I had no idea what he expected to gain by becoming a ghost writer for Mr. Jones and telling the Commies' family secrets.

I admit I tried to catch up. For instance, when he was up in the plant rooms Friday morning I did a thorough check of the photographs in his desk drawer, but they were all there. Not one gone. I made a couple of other well-intentioned efforts to get a line on his script, and not a glimmer. By Monday I was grabbing the mail each time a delivery came for a quick look, and hoping it was a telegram whenever the doorbell rang, and answering the phone in a hurry, because I had decided that the articles were just a gob of bait on a hook and we were merely sitting on the bank, hoping against hope for a bite. But if the bite was expected in the form of a letter or telegram or phone call, no fish.

Then Monday evening, in the office right after dinner, Wolfe handed me a sheet from his memo pad covered with his handwriting, and asked, "Can you read that, Archie?"

The question was rhetorical, since his writing is almost as easy to read as print. I read it and told him, "Yes, sir, I can make it out."

"Type it on a *Gazette* letterhead, including the signature as indicated. Then I want to look at it. Address a *Gazette* envelope to Mr. Albert Enright, Communist Party of the USA, Thirty-five East Twelfth Street. One carbon, single-space."

"With a mistake or two, maybe?"

"Not necessarily. You are not the only one in New York who can type well."

I pulled the machine around, got the paper out and put it in, and hit the keys. When I took it out I read it over:

June 27, 1949.

Dear Mr. Enright:

I send this to you because I met you once and have heard you speak at meetings twice. You wouldn't know me if you saw me, and you wouldn't know my name.

I work at the *Gazette*. Of course you have seen the series that started on Sunday. I am not a Communist, but I approve of many things they stand for and I think they are getting a raw deal, and anyway I don't like traitors, and the man who is giving the *Gazette* the material for those articles is certainly a traitor. I think you have a right to know who he is. I have never seen him and I don't think he has ever come to the office, but I know the man here who is working with him on the articles, and I had a chance to get something which I believe will help you, and I am enclosing it in this letter. I have reason to know that it was in the folder that was sent to one of the executives to show him that the articles are authentic. If I told you more than that it might give you a hint of my identity, and I don't want you to know who I am.

More power to you in your fight with the imperialists and monopolists and warmakers.

A Friend.

I got up to hand it to Wolfe and returned to the typewriter to address the envelope. And, though I had done the whole letter without an error, on the envelope I fumbled and spelled Communist "Counimmst," and had to take another one. It didn't irritate me because I knew why: I was excited. In a moment I would know which photograph was going to be enclosed in that letter, unless the big bum dealt me out.

He didn't, but he might as well have. He opened his drawer and dug, held one out to me, and said, "That's the enclosure. Mail it where it will be collected tonight."

It was the picture, the best one, of the Communist party membership card of William Reynolds, Number 128-394. I withered him with a look, put the letter and picture in the envelope, sealed it and put a stamp on it, and left the house. In my frame of mind I thought a little air wouldn't hurt me any, so I walked to the Times Square Station.

I expected nothing more from Wolfe that evening, and that was what I got. We went to bed fairly early. Up in my room undressing, I was still trying to map it, having been unable to sketch one I would settle for. The main stratagem was now plain enough, but what was the follow up? Were we going to start sitting and waiting again? In that case, how was William Reynolds going to be given another name, and when and why and by whom? Under the sheet, I chased it out of my mind in order to get some sleep.

The next day, Tuesday, until noon and a little after, it looked like more sitting and waiting. It wasn't too dull, on account of the phone. The third article was in that morning's *Gazette,* and they were wild for more. My instructions were to stall. Lon called twice before ten o'clock, and after that it was practically chain phoning: city editor, managing editor, executive editor, publisher, everybody. They wanted it so bad that I had a notion to write one myself and peddle it for fifteen thousand bucks flat. By noon there would have been nothing to it.

When the phone rang again a little before lunchtime I took it for granted it was one of them, so instead of using my formula I merely said, "Yep?"

"Is this Nero Wolfe's office?" It was a voice I had never heard, a sort of an artificial squeak.

"Yes. Archie Goodwin speaking."

"Is Mr. Wolfe there?"

"Yes. He's engaged. Who is it, please?"

"Just tell him rectangle."

"Spell it, please?"

"R-e-c-t-a-n-g-l-e, rectangle. Tell him immediately. He'll want to know."

The connection went. I hung up and turned to Wolfe.

"Rectangle."

"What?"

"That's what he said, or rather squeaked. Just to tell you rectangle."

"Ah." Wolfe sat up and his eyes came clear open. "Get the national office of the Communist party, Algonquin four two two one five. I want Mr. Harvey or Mr. Stevens. Either one."

I swiveled and dialed. In a moment a pleasant feminine voice was in my ear. Its being pleasant was a shock, and also I was a little self-conscious, conversing for the first time with a female Commie, so I said, "My name's Goodwin, comrade. Is Mr. Harvey there? Mr. Nero Wolfe would like to speak to him."

"You say Nero Wolfe?"

"Yes. A detective."

"I've heard the name. I'll see. Hold the wire."

I waited. Accustomed to holding the wire while a switchboard girl or secretary saw, I leaned back and got comfortable, but it wasn't long before a man told me he was Harvey. I signaled to Wolfe and stayed on myself.

"How do you do, sir," Wolfe said politely. "I'm in a hole and you can help me if you want to. Will you call at my office at six o'clock today with one of your associates? Perhaps Mr. Stevens or Mr. Enright, if one of them is available."

"What makes you think we can help you out of a hole?" Harvey asked, not rudely. He had a middle bass, a little gruff.

"I'm pretty sure you can. At least I would like to ask

your advice. It concerns a man whom you know by the name of William Reynolds. He is involved in a case I'm working on, and the matter has become urgent. That's why I would like to see you as soon as possible. There isn't much time."

"What makes you think I know a man named William Reynolds?"

"Oh, come, Mr. Harvey. After you hear what I have to say you may of course deny that you know him if that's the way you want it. This can't be done on the telephone, or shouldn't be."

"Hold the wire."

That wait was longer. Wolfe sat patiently with the receiver at his ear, and I did likewise. In three or four minutes he started to frown, and by the time Harvey's voice came again he was tapping the arm of his chair with a forefinger.

"If we come," Harvey asked, "who will be there?"

"You will, of course, and I will. And Mr. Goodwin, my assistant."

"Nobody else?"

"No, sir."

"All right. We'll be there at six o'clock."

I hung up and asked Wolfe, "Does Mr. Jones always talk with that funny squeak? And did 'rectangle' mean merely that the letter from a friend had been received? Or something more, such as which commissars had read it?"

21

I never got to see the Albert Enright I had typed a letter to, because the associate that Mr. Harvey brought along was Mr. Stevens.

Having seen one or two high-ranking Commies in the flesh, and many published pictures of more than a dozen of them, I didn't expect our callers to look like wart hogs or puff adders, but even so they surprised me a little, especially Stevens. He was middle-aged, skinny, and pale, with thin brown hair that should have been trimmed a week ago, and he wore rimless spectacles. If I had had a daughter in high school, Stevens was the guy I would have wanted her to ask for directions in a strange neighborhood after dark. I wouldn't have gone so far with Harvey, who was younger and much huskier, with sharp greenish-brown eyes and a well-assembled face, but I certainly wouldn't have singled him out as the Menace of the Month.

They didn't want cocktails or any other liquid, and they didn't sit back in their chairs and get comfortable. Harvey announced in his gruff bass, but still not rude, that they had an engagement for a quarter to seven.

"I'll make it as brief as I can," Wolfe assured them. He reached in the drawer and got one of the pictures and extended his hand. "Will you glance at this?"

They arose, and Harvey took the picture, and they looked at it. I thought that was carrying things a little too far. What was I, a worm? So when Harvey dropped it on the desk I stepped over and got an eye on it, and then handed it to Wolfe. Some day he'll get so damn frolicsome that I'll cramp his style sure as hell. I was now caught up.

Harvey and Stevens sat down again, without exchanging a glance. That struck me as being overcautious, but I suppose Commies, especially on the upper levels, get the habit early and it becomes automatic.

Wolfe asked pleasantly, "It's an interesting face, isn't it?"

Stevens stayed deadpan and didn't speak.

"If you like that kind," Harvey said. "Who is it?"

"That will only prolong it." Wolfe was a little less pleasant. "If I had any doubt that you knew him, none was left after the mention of his name brought you here. Certainly you didn't come because you were grieved to learn that I'm in a hole. If you deny that you know that man as William Reynolds you will have had your trip for nothing, and we can't go on."

"Let's put it this way," Stevens said softly. "Proceed

hypothetically. If we say we do know him as William Reynolds, then what?"

Wolfe nodded approvingly. "That will do, I think. Then I talk. I tell you that when I met this man recently, for the first time, his name was not Reynolds. I assume you know his other name too, but since in his association with you and your colleagues he has been Reynolds, we'll use that. When I met him, a little more than a week ago, I didn't know he was a Communist; I learned that only yesterday."

"How?" Harvey snapped.

Wolfe shook his head. "I'm afraid I'll have to leave that out. In my years of work as a private detective I have formed many connections—the police, the press, all kinds of people. I will say this: I think Reynolds made a mistake. It's only a conjecture, but a good one I think, that he became frightened. He apprehended a mortal peril—I was responsible for that—and he did something foolish. The peril was a charge of murder. He knew the charge could be brought only if it could be shown that he was a Communist, and he thought I knew it too, and he decided to guard against that by making it appear that while pretending to be a Communist he was actually an enemy of communism and wanted to help destroy it. As I say, that is only a conjecture. But——"

"Wait a minute." Apparently Stevens never raised his voice, even when he was cutting in. "It hasn't quite got to where you can prove a man committed murder just by proving he's a Communist." Stevens smiled, and, seeing what he regarded as a smile, I decided to have my daughter ask someone else for directions. "Has it?"

"No," Wolfe conceded. "Rather the contrary. Communists are well advised to disapprove of private murders for private motives. But in this case that's how it stood. Since we're proceeding hypothetically, I may include in the hypothesis that you know about the death of a man named Louis Rony, run over by a car on the country estate of James U. Sperling, and that you know that William Reynolds was present. May I not?"

"Go on," Harvey rumbled.

"So we don't need to waste time on the facts that

have been made public. The situation is this: I know that Mr. Reynolds murdered Mr. Rony. I want to have him arrested and charged. But to get him convicted it is essential to show that he is a member of the Communist party, because only if that is done can his motive be established. You'll have to accept that statement as I give it; I'm not going to show you all my cards, for if I do so and you choose to support Mr. Reynolds I'll be in a deeper hole than I am now."

"We don't support murderers," Harvey declared virtuously.

Wolfe nodded. "I thought not. It would be not only blameworthy, but futile, to try to support this one. You understand that what I must prove is not that William Reynolds is a member of the Communist party; that can be done without much difficulty; but that this man who was at the scene of Mr. Rony's death is that William Reynolds—whatever else he may be. I know of only two ways to accomplish that. One would be to arrest and charge Mr. Reynolds and put him on trial, lay the ground by showing that membership in the Communist party is relevant to his guilt, subpoena you and your associates—fifty of them, a hundred—as witnesses for the State, and put the question to you. 'Is the defendant, or was he, a member of the Communist party?' Those of you who know him, and who answer no, will be committing perjury. Will all of you risk it —not most of you, but all of you? Would it be worth such a risk, to protect a man who murdered as a private enterprise? I doubt it. If you do risk it, I think we can catch you up. I shall certainly try, and my heart will be in it."

"We don't scare easy," Harvey stated.

"What's the other way?" Stevens asked.

"Much simpler for everybody." Wolfe picked up the photograph. "You write your names across this. I paste it on a sheet of paper. Below it you write, 'The man in the above photograph, on which we have written our names, is William Reynolds, whom we know to be a member of the Communist Party of the USA.' You both sign it. That's all."

For the first time they swapped glances.

"It's still a hypothesis," Stevens said. "As such, we'll be glad to think it over."

"For how long?"

"I don't know. Tomorrow or next day."

"I don't like it."

"The hell you don't." Harvey's manners were showing. "Do you have to?"

"I suppose not." Wolfe was regretful. "But I don't like to leave a man around loose when I know he's a murderer. If we do it the simple way, and do it now, we'll have him locked up before midnight. If we postpone it—" Wolfe shrugged. "I don't know what he'll be doing—possibly nothing that will block us—"

I had to keep a grin back. He might as well have asked them if they wanted to give Reynolds a day or two to do some more articles for the *Gazette,* because of course that was where he had them. Knowing that was in their minds, I tried to find some sign of it, any sign at all, in their faces, but they were old hands. They might have been merely a couple of guys looking over a hypothesis and not liking it much.

Stevens spoke, in the same soft voice. "Go ahead and arrest him. If you don't get it the simple way you can try the other one."

"No, sir," Wolfe said emphatically. "Without your statement it won't be easy to get him charged. It can be done, but not just by snapping my fingers."

"You said," Harvey objected, "that if we sign that thing that will be all, but it won't. We'd have to testify at the trial."

"Probably," Wolfe conceded. "But only you two, as friendly witnesses for the prosecution, helping to get a murderer punished. The other way it will be you two and many more, and, if you answer in the negative, you will be shielding a murderer merely because he is a fellow Communist, which will not raise you in public esteem—in addition to risking perjury."

Stevens stood up. "We'll let you know in half an hour, maybe less."

"Good. The front room is soundproofed, or you can go upstairs."

"There's more room outdoors. Come on, Jerry."

Stevens led the way. I went to the front to let them out and then returned to the office. What I saw, re-entering, gave me an excuse to use the grin I had squelched. Wolfe had opened a drawer and got out a sheet of paper and the tube of paste.

"Before they're hatched?" I inquired.

"Bah. The screw is down hard."

"Taking candy from a baby," I admitted. "Though I must say they're no babies, especially Stevens."

Wolfe grunted. "He's third from the top in the American Communist hierarchy."

"He doesn't look it but he acts it. I noticed they didn't even ask what evidence you've got that Reynolds did the killing, because they don't give a damn. All they want is to get the articles stopped and him burned. What I don't get, why did they just swallow the letter from a friend? Why didn't they give Reynolds a chance to answer a question?"

"They don't give chances." Wolfe was scornful. "Could he have proved the letter was a lie? How? Could he have explained the photograph of his membership card? He could only have denied it, and they wouldn't have believed him. They trust no one, especially not one another, and I don't blame them. I suppose I shouldn't put paste on this thing until they have written their names on it."

I wasn't quite as cocksure as he seemed to be. I thought they might have to take it to a meeting, and that couldn't be done in half an hour. But apparently he knew more than I did about Stevens' rank and authority. I had let them out at 6:34, and at 6:52 the bell rang and I went to let them in again. Only eighteen minutes, but the nearest phone booth was only half a block away.

They didn't sit. Harvey stood gazing at me as if there were something about me he didn't like, and Stevens advanced to the end of Wolfe's desk and announced, "We don't like the wording. We want it to read this way:

"As loyal American citizens, devoted to the public welfare and the ideals of true democracy, we believe that all lawbreakers should be punished, regardless of their political affiliations. Therefore, in the interest of justice, we have written our names on the above photograph, and we hereby attest that the man in that photograph is known to us as William Reynolds, and that to our knowledge he has been for eight years, until today, a member of the Communist Party of the USA. Upon learning that he was to be charged with murder, the Communist Party's Executive Committee immediately expelled him."

My opinion of Stevens went up a notch, technically. With nothing to refer to, not even a cuff, he rattled that off as if he had known it by heart for years.

Wolfe lifted his shoulders and dropped them. "If you like it better with all that folderol. Do you want Mr. Goodwin to type it, or will you write it by hand?"

I was just as well pleased that he preferred to use his pen. It would have been an honor to type such a patriotic paragraph, but I wouldn't put anything beneath a Commie, and what if one of them happened to take a notion to pull the letter from a friend out of his pocket and compare the typing? Even with the naked eye it would have been easy to spot the n slightly off line and the faint defect in the w. So I gladly let Stevens sit at my desk to write it. He did so, and signed it, and wrote his name on the picture. Then Harvey did likewise. Wolfe and I signed as witnesses, after Wolfe had read it over. Having the tube of paste at hand, as I have said, he proceeded to attach the photograph to the top of the sheet.

"May I see it a moment?" Stevens asked.

Wolfe handed it to him.

"There's a point," Stevens said. "We can't let you have this without some kind of guarantee that Reynolds will be locked up tonight. You said before midnight."

"That's right. He will be."

"You can have this as soon as he is."

I knew damn well they'd have a monkey wrench. If it had been something not tearable, a stone for instance,

I would simply have liberated it, and Harvey could have joined in if he felt like it.

"Then he won't be," Wolfe said, not upset.

"Why not?"

"Because that's the key I'm going to lock him in with. Otherwise, would I have gone to all this trouble to get it? Nonsense. I'm about to invite some people to come here this evening, but not unless I have that document. Please don't crumple it."

"Will Reynolds be here?"

"Yes."

"Then we'll come and bring this with us."

Wolfe shook his head. "You don't seem to listen to me. That paper stays here, or you're out of it until you get a subpoena. Give it to me, and I'll be glad to have you and Mr. Harvey come this evening. That's an excellent idea. You will be excluded from part of it, but you can be comfortable in the front room. Why don't you do that?"

That was the way it was finally compromised. They were plenty stubborn but, as Wolfe had said, the screw was down hard. They didn't know what Reynolds might spill in the next article, and they wanted him nailed quick, and Wolfe stood pat that he wouldn't move without the document. So he got it. It was arranged that they would return around ten o'clock and would stay put in the front room until invited to join the party.

When they had gone Wolfe put the document in his middle drawer.

"We're overstocked on photographs," I remarked. "So that's why Mr. Jones didn't need to load up. He knew him and one look was all he needed. Huh?"

"Dinner's waiting."

"Yes, sir. It would be a funny coincidence if Harvey or Stevens happened to be Mr. Jones. Wouldn't it?"

"No. You can find coincidence in the dictionary. Get Mr. Archer on the phone."

"Now? Dinner's waiting."

"Get him."

That wasn't so simple. At my first try, the District Attorney's office in White Plains, someone answered but couldn't help me any. I then got Archer's home and was told that he was out for the evening, but I wasn't to know where, and I had to press even to sell the idea that he should be informed immediately that Nero Wolfe wanted him to call. I hung up and settled back to wait for anything from five minutes to an hour. Wolfe was sitting up straight, frowning, with his lips tight; a meal was spoiling. After a while the sight of him was getting on my nerves, and I was about to suggest that we move to the dining room and start, when the phone rang. It was Archer.

"What is it?" He was crisp and indignant.

Wolfe said he needed his advice.

"What about? I'm dining with friends. Can't it wait until morning?"

"No, sir. I've got the murderer of Louis Rony, with evidence to convict, and I want to get rid of him."

"The murderer—" A short silence. Then, "I don't believe it!"

"Of course you don't, but it's true. He'll be at my office this evening. I want your advice on how to handle it. I can ask Inspector Cramer of the New York Police to send men to take him into custody, or I can—"

"No! Now listen, Wolfe—"

"No, listen to me. If your dinner is waiting, so is mine. I would prefer that you take him, for two reasons. First, he belongs to you. Second, I would like to clean it up this evening, and in order to do that the matter of Mr. Kane's statement will have to be disposed of. That will require the presence not only of Mr. Sperling and Mr. Kane, but also of the others who were there the evening Mr. Rony was killed. If you come or send someone, they'll have to come too. All of them, if possible; under the circumstances I don't think they'll be reluctant. Can you have them here by ten o'clock?"

"But my God, this is incredible! I need a minute to think—"

"You've had a week to think but preferred to let me do it for you. I have, and acted. Can you have them here by ten o'clock?"

"I don't know, damn it! You fire this at me point-blank!"

"Would you rather have had me hold it a day or two? I'll expect you at ten, or as close to that as you can make it. If you don't bring them along you won't get in; after all, in this jurisdiction you're merely visitors. If ends have to be left dangling I'll let the New York Police have him."

Wolfe and I hung up. He pushed his chair back and arose.

"You can't dawdle over your dinner, Archie. If we're to keep our promise to Mr. Cohen, and we must, you'll have to go to see him."

22

As I understand it, the Commies think that they get too little and capitalists get too much of the good things in life. They sure played hell with that theory that Tuesday evening. A table in the office was loaded with liquids, cheese, nuts, homemade pâté, and crackers, and not a drop or a crumb was taken by any of the thirteen people there, including Wolfe and me. On a table in the front room there was a similar assortment in smaller quantities, and Harvey and Stevens, just two of them, practically cleaned it up. If I had noticed it before the Commies left I would have called it to their attention. I admit they had more time, having arrived first, at ten sharp, and also they had nothing to do most of the evening but sit and wait.

I don't think I have ever seen the office more crowded, unless it was at the meeting of the League of Frightened Men. Either Archer had thought pressure was called for or Wolfe had been correct in assuming that none of the Stony Acres bunch would be reluctant about coming, for they were all there. I had let them choose seats as they pleased, and the three Sperling women—Mom, Madeline, and Gwenn—were on the big yellow couch in the corner, which meant that my back was to them when I faced Wolfe. Paul and Connie Emerson were on chairs side by side over by the globe, and Jimmy Sperling was seated near them. Webster Kane and Sperling were closer to Wolfe's desk. District Attorney Archer was in the red leather chair; I had put him there because I thought he rated it. What made it thirteen was the fact that two dicks were present: Ben Dykes, brought by Archer, and Sergeant Purley Stebbins of Manhattan Homicide, who had informed me that Westchester had invited him. Purley, my old friend and even older enemy, sat over by the door.

It started off with a bang. When they were all in and greetings, such as they were, had been attended to, and everyone was seated, Wolfe began his preamble. He had got only four words out when Archer blurted, "You said the man that murdered Rony would be here!"

"He is."

"Where?"

"You brought him."

After that beginning it was only natural that no one felt like having a slice of cheese or a handful of nuts. I didn't blame any of them, least of all William Reynolds. Several of them made noises, and Sperling and Paul Emerson both said something, but I didn't catch either of them because Gwenn's voice, clear and strong but with a tremble under it, came from behind my back.

"I told my father what I told you that evening!"

Wolfe ignored her. "This will go faster," he told Archer, "if you let me do it."

"The perfect mountebank!" Emerson sneered.

Sperling and Archer spoke together. A growl from the side made their heads turn. It was Sergeant Stebbins, raising his voice from his seat near the door. He got all eyes.

"If you take my advice," he told them, "you'll let

him tell it. I'm from the New York Police, and this is New York. I've heard him before. If you pester him he'll string it out just to show you."

"I have no desire to string it out," Wolfe said crossly. His eyes went from left to right and back. "This shouldn't take long if you'll let me get on. I wanted you all here because of what I said to you up there in my bedroom eight days ago, the evening Mr. Rony was killed. I thereby assumed an obligation, and I want you to know that I have fulfilled it."

He took the audience in again. "First I'll tell you why I assumed that Mr. Rony was killed not accidentally but deliberately. While it was credible that the driver of the car might not have seen him until too late, it was hard to believe that Mr. Rony had not been aware of the car's approach, even in the twilight, and even if the noise of the brook had covered the noise of the car, which could not have been going fast. Nor was there any mark on the front of the car. If it had hit him when he was upright there would probably, though not certainly, have been a mark or marks."

"You said all this before," Archer cut in impatiently.

"Yes, sir. The repetition will take less time if you don't interrupt. Another point, better than either of those, why was the body dragged more than fifty feet to be concealed behind a shrub? If it had been an accident, and the driver decided not to disclose his part in it, what would he have done? Drag the body off the road, yes, but surely not fifty feet to find a hiding place."

"You said that before too," Ben Dykes objected. "And I said the same argument would apply just as well to a murderer."

"Yes," Wolfe agreed, "but you were wrong. The murderer had a sound reason for moving the body where it couldn't be seen from the drive if someone happened to pass."

"What?"

"To search the body. We are now coming to things I *haven't* said before. You preferred not to show me the list of articles found on the body, so I preferred not to tell you that I knew something had been taken from it. The way I knew it was that Mr. Goodwin had himself made an inventory when he found the body."

"The hell he had!"

"It would have been better," Archer said in a nasty voice for him, "to tell us that. What had been taken?"

"A membership card, in the name of William Reynolds, in the American Communist party."

"By God!" Sperling cried, and left his chair. There were exclamations from others. Sperling was following his up, but Archer's voice cut through.

"How did you know he had one?"

"Mr. Goodwin had seen it, and I had seen a photograph of it." Wolfe pointed a finger. "Please let me tell this without yanking me around with questions. I have to go back to Saturday evening a week ago. Mr. Goodwin was there ostensibly as a guest, but actually representing me in behalf of my client, Mr. Sperling. He had reasons to believe that Mr. Rony was carefully guarding some small object, not letting it leave his person. There were refreshments in the living room. Mr. Goodwin drugged his own drink and exchanged it for Mr. Rony's. He drank Mr. Rony's. But it had been drugged by someone else, as he found to his sorrow."

"Oh!" A little cry came from behind me, in the voice of the little cabbage. Wolfe frowned past my shoulder.

"Mr. Goodwin had intended to enter Mr. Rony's room that night to learn what the object was, but didn't, because he was himself drugged and Mr. Rony was not. Instead of swallowing his drink, Mr. Rony had poured it into the ice bucket. I am still giving reasons why I assumed that he was not killed by accident, and that's one of them: his drink had been drugged and he either knew it or suspected it. Mr. Goodwin was mortified, and he is not one to take mortification lightly; also he wanted to see the object. The next day, Sunday, he arranged to have Mr. Rony return to New York in his car, and he also arranged for a man and woman—both of them have often worked for me—to waylay them and blackjack Mr. Rony."

That got a reaction from practically everybody. The loudest, from Purley Stebbins, reached me through the others from twenty feet off. "Jesus! Can you beat him?"

Wolfe sat and let them react. In a moment he put up a hand.

"That's a felony, I know, Mr. Archer. You can decide what to do about it at your leisure, when it's all over. Your decision may be influenced by the fact that if it hadn't been committed the killer of Mr. Rony wouldn't have been caught."

He took in the audience, now quiet again. "All they took from him was the money in his wallet. That was necessary in order to validate it as a holdup—and by the way, the money has been spent in my investigation of his death, which I think he would regard as fitting. But Mr. Goodwin did something else. He found on Mr. Rony the object he had been guarding, and took some photographs of it, not taking the object itself. It was a membership card, in the name of William Reynolds, in the American Communist party."

"Then I was right!" Sperling was so excited and triumphant that he yelled it. "I was right all the time!" He glared indignantly, sputtering. "Why didn't you tell me? Why didn't—"

"You were as wrong," Wolfe said rudely, "as a man can get. You may be a good businessman, Mr. Sperling, but you had better leave the exposure of disguised Communists to competent persons. It's a task for which you are disqualified by mental astigmatism."

"But," Sperling insisted, "you admit he had a membership card—"

"I don't admit it, I announce it. But it would have been witless to assume that William Reynolds was necessarily Louis Rony. In fact, I had knowledge of Rony that made it unlikely. Anyway, we have the testimony of three persons that the card was in his possession—you'll find that a help in the courtroom, Mr. Archer. So at the time the identity of William Reynolds—whether it was Mr. Rony or another person—was an open question."

Wolfe turned a hand up. "But twenty-four hours later it was no longer open. Whoever William Reynolds was, almost certainly he wasn't Louis Rony. Not only that, it was a workable assumption that he had murdered Rony, since it was better than a conjecture that he had dragged the body behind a bush in order to search it, had found the membership card, and had taken it. I made that assumption, tentatively. Then the next day, Tuesday, I was carried a step further by the news that it was my car that had killed Rony. So if William Reynolds had murdered Rony and taken the card, he was one of the people there present. One of those now in this room."

A murmur went around, but only a murmur.

"You've skipped something," Ben Dykes protested. "Why did it have to be Reynolds who murdered and took the card?"

"It didn't," Wolfe admitted. "These were assumptions, not conclusions. But they were a whole; if one was good, all were: if one was not, none. If the murderer had killed and searched the body to get that card, surely it was to prevent the disclosure that he had joined the Communist party under the name of William Reynolds, a disclosure threatened by Rony—who was by no means above such threats. That's where I stood Tuesday noon. But I was under an obligation to my client, Mr. Sperling, which would be ill met if I gave all this to the police—at least without trying my own hand at it first. That was what I had decided to do"—Wolfe's eyes went straight at Sperling—"when you jumped in with that confounded statement you had coerced Mr. Kane to sign. And satisfied Mr. Archer, and fired me."

His eyes darted at Kane. "I wanted you here for this, to repudiate that statement. Will you? Now?"

"Don't be a fool, Web," Sperling snapped. And to Wolfe, "I didn't coerce him!"

Poor Kane, not knowing what to say, said nothing. In spite of all the trouble he had caused us, I nearly felt sorry for him.

Wolfe shrugged. "So I came home. I had to get my assumptions either established or discredited. It was possible that Mr. Rony had not had the membership card on his person when he was killed. On Wednesday Mr. Goodwin went to his apartment and made a thorough search—not breaking and entering, Mr. Stebbins."

"You say," Purley muttered.

"He had a key," Wolfe asserted, which was quite true. "The card wasn't there; if it had been, Mr. Goodwin would have found it. But he did find evidence, no matter how or what, that Mr. Rony had had in his possession one or more objects, probably a paper or papers, which he had used as a tool of coercion on one or more persons here present. It doesn't matter what his demands were, but in passing let me say that I doubt that they were for money; I think what he required, and was getting, was support for his courtship of the younger Miss Sperling—or at least neutrality. Another—"

"What was the evidence?" Archer demanded.

Wolfe shook his head. "You may not need it; if you do, you may have it when the time comes. Another assumption, that Mr. Rony was not upright when the car hit him, also got confirmed. Although the car had not struck his head, there was a severe bruise above his right ear; a doctor hired by me saw it, and it is recorded on the official report. That helped to acquit the murderer of so slapdash a method as trying to kill a lively and vigorous young man by hitting him with a car. Obviously it would have been more workmanlike to ambush him as he walked up the drive, knock him out, and then run the car over him. If that—"

"You can't ambush a man," Ben Dykes objected, "unless you know he'll be there to ambush."

"No," agreed Wolfe, "nor can you expect me ever to finish if you take no probabilities along with facts. Besides the private telephone lines in Mr. Sperling's library there are twelve extensions in that house, and Miss Sperling's talk with Mr. Rony, arranging for his arrival at a certain hour for a rendezvous on the grounds, could have been listened to by anyone. William Reynolds could certainly have heard it; let him prove he didn't. Anyhow, the ambush itself is no longer a mere probability. By a brilliant stroke of Mr. Goodwin's, it was established as a fact. On Thursday he searched the grounds for the instrument used for laying Mr. Rony out, and he found it, in the presence of a witness."

"He didn't!" It was Madeline's voice from behind me. "I was with him every minute and he didn't find anything!"

"But he did," Wolfe said dryly. "On his way out he stopped at the brook and found a stone. The question of the witness, and of the evidence that the stone had been in contact with a man's head, can wait, but I assure you there's no doubt about it. Even if the witness prefers to risk perjury we'll manage quite well without her."

His eyes made an arc to take them in. "For while such details as the head bruise and the stone will be most helpful and Mr. Archer will be glad to have them, what clinches the matter is a detail of a different sort. I have hinted at it before and I now declare it: William Reynolds, the owner of that card, the Communist, is in this room. You won't mind, I hope, if I don't tell you how I learned it, so long as I tell you how I can prove it, but before I do so I would like if possible to get rid of a serious embarrassment. Mr. Kane. You're an intelligent man and you see my predicament. If the man who murdered Mr. Rony is charged and put on trial, and if that statement you signed is put in evidence by the defense, and you refuse to repudiate it, there can be no conviction. I appeal to you: do you want to furnish that shield to a Communist and a murderer? No matter who he is. If you are reluctant to credit my assertion that he is a Communist, consider that unless that can be proven to the satisfaction of a judge and jury he will not be in jeopardy, for that is essential to the case against him. But as long as your statement stands it would be foolhardy even to arrest him; Mr. Archer wouldn't dare to move for an indictment."

Wolfe got a paper from a desk drawer. "I wish you would sign this. It was typed by Mr. Goodwin this evening before you came. It is dated today and reads, 'I, Webster Kane, hereby declare that the statement signed by me on June twenty-first, nineteen forty-nine, to the effect that I had killed Louis Rony accidentally by driving an automobile over him, was false. I signed it at the suggestion of James U. Sperling, Senior, and I hereby retract it.' Archie?"

I got up to reach for the paper and offer it to Kane, but he didn't move a hand to take it. The outstanding economist was in a hole, and his face showed that he realized it.

"Take out the last sentence," Sperling demanded. "It isn't necessary." He didn't look happy either.

Wolfe shook his head. "Naturally you don't like to face it, but you'll have to. On the witness stand you can't possibly evade it, so why evade it now?"

"Good God." Sperling was grim. "The witness stand. Damn it, if this isn't just an act, who is Reynolds?"

"I'll tell you when Mr. Kane has signed that, not before—and you have witnessed it."

"I won't witness it."

"Yes, sir, you will. This thing started with your desire to expose a Communist. Now's your chance. You won't take it?"

Sperling glowered at Wolfe, then at me, then at Kane. I thought to myself how different this was from smiling like an angel. Mrs. Sperling murmured something, but no one paid any attention.

"Sign it, Web," Sperling growled.

Kane's hand came out for it, not wanting to. With it I gave him a magazine to firm it, and my pen. He signed, big and sprawly, and I passed it along to the Chairman of the Board. His signature, as witness, was something to see. It could have been James U. Sperling, or it could have been Lawson N. Spiffshill. I accepted it without prejudice and handed it to Wolfe, who gave it a glance and put it under a paperweight.

He sighed. "Bring them in, Archie."

I crossed to the door to the front room and called out, "Come in, gentlemen!"

I would have given a nickel to know how much time and effort they had wasted trying to hear something through the soundproofed door. It couldn't be done. They entered in character. Harvey, self-conscious and aggressive in the presence of so much capitalism, strode across nearly to Wolfe's desk, turned, and gave each of them in turn a hard straight eye. Stevens was interested in only one of them, the man he knew as William Reynolds; as far as he was concerned the others were dummies, including even the District Attorney. His eyes too were hard and straight, but they had only one target. They both ignored the chairs I had reserved for them.

"I think," Wolfe said, "we needn't bother with introductions. One of you knows these gentlemen well; the others won't care to, nor will they care to know you. They are avowed members of the American Communist party, and prominent ones. I have here a document"—he fluttered it—"which they signed early this evening, with a photograph of a man pasted on it. The writing on it, in Mr. Stevens' hand, states that for eight years the man in the photograph has been a fellow Communist under the name of William Reynolds. The document is itself conclusive, but these gentlemen and I agreed that it would be helpful for them to appear and identify Reynolds in person. You're looking at him, are you, Mr. Stevens?"

"I am," said Stevens, gazing at Webster Kane with cold hate.

"You goddam rat," rumbled Harvey, also at Kane.

The economist was returning their gaze, now at Stevens, now at Harvey, stunned and incredulous. His first confession had required words, written down and signed, but this one didn't. That stunned look was his second confession, and everybody there, looking at him, could see it was the real thing.

He wasn't the only stunned one.

"Web!" roared Sperling. "For God's sake—*Web!*"

"You're in for it, Mr. Kane," Wolfe said icily. "You've got no one left. You're done as Kane, with the Communist brand showing at last. You're done as Reynolds, with your comrades spitting you out as only they can spit. You're done even as a two-legged animal, with a murder to answer for. The last was my job—the rest was only incidental—and thank heaven it's over, for it wasn't easy. He's yours, Mr. Archer."

I wasn't needed to watch a possible outburst, since both Ben Dykes and Purley Stebbins were there and had closed in, and I had an errand to attend to. I pulled my phone over to me and dialed the *Gazette,* and got Lon Cohen.

"Archie?" He sounded desperate. "Twelve minutes to go! Well?"

"Okay, son," I said patronizingly. "Shoot it."

"As is? Webster Kane? Pinched?"

"As specified. We guarantee materials and workmanship. If you're a leading economist I know where there's a vacancy."

23

Later, long after midnight, after everyone else had gone, James U. Sperling was still there. He sat in the red leather chair, eating nuts, drinking Scotch, and getting things clear.

What kept him, of course, was the need to get his self-respect back in condition before he went home and to bed, and after the terrific jolt of learning that he had nurtured a Commie in his bosom for years it wasn't so simple. The detail that seemed to hurt most of all was the first confession—the one he had got Kane to sign. He had drafted it himself—he admitted it; he had thought it was a masterpiece that even a Chairman of the Board could be proud of; and now it turned out that, except for the minor item that Rony had been flat instead of erect when the car hit him, it had been the truth! No wonder he had trouble getting it down.

He insisted on going back over everything. He even wanted answers to questions such as whether Kane had seen Rony pour his doped drink in the ice bucket, which of course we couldn't give him. Wolfe generously supplied answers when he had them. For instance, why had Kane signed the repudiation of his statement that he had killed Rony accidentally? Because, Wolfe explained, Sperling had told him to, and Kane's only hope had been to stick to the role of Webster Kane in spite of hell. True, within ten breaths he was going to be torn loose from it by the cold malign stares of his former comrades, but he didn't know that when he took the pen to sign his name.

When Sperling finally left he was more himself again, but I suspected he would need more than one night's sleep before anyone would see him smiling like an angel.

That was all except the tail. Every murder case, like a kite, has a tail. The tail to this one had three sections, the first one public and the other two private.

Section One became public the first week in July, when it was announced that Paul Emerson's contract was not being renewed. I happened to know about it in advance because I was in the office when, one day the preceding week, James U. Sperling phoned Wolfe to say that the Continental Mines Corporation was grateful to him for removing a Communist tumor from its internal organs and would be glad to pay a bill if he sent one. Wolfe said he would like to send a bill but didn't know how to word it, and Sperling asked him why. Because, Wolfe said, the bill would ask for payment not in dollars but in kind. Sperling wanted to know what he meant.

"As you put it," Wolfe explained, "I removed a tumor from your staff. What I would want in return is the removal of a tumor from my radio. Six-thirty is a convenient time for me to listen to the radio, and even if I don't turn it to that station I know that Paul Emerson is there, only a few notches away, and it annoys me. Remove him. He might get another sponsor, but I doubt it. Stop paying him for that malicious gibberish."

"He has a high rating," Sperling objected.

"So had Goebbels," Wolfe snapped. "And Mussolini."

A short silence.

"I admit," Sperling conceded, "that he irritates me. I think it's chiefly his ulcers."

"Then find someone without them. You'll be saving money, too. If I sent you a bill in dollars it wouldn't be modest, in view of the difficulties you made."

"His contract expires next week."

"Good. Let it."

"Well—I'll see. We'll talk it over here."

That was how it happened.

The tail's second section, private, was also in the form of a phone call, some weeks later. Just yesterday, the day after Webster Kane, alias William Reynolds, was sentenced on his conviction for the first degree murder of Louis Rony, I put the receiver to my ear and once more heard a hard cold precise voice that used only the best grammar. I told Wolfe who it was and he got on.

"How are you, Mr. Wolfe?"

"Well, thank you."

"I'm glad to hear it. I'm calling to congratulate you. I have ways of learning things, so I know how superbly you handled it. I am highly gratified that the killer of that fine young man will be properly punished, thanks to you."

"My purpose was not to gratify you."

"Of course not. All the same, I warmly appreciate it, and my admiration of your talents has increased. I wanted to tell you that, and also that you will receive another package tomorrow morning. In view of the turn events took the damage your property suffered is all the more regrettable."

The connection went dead. I turned to Wolfe.

"He sure likes to keep a call down to a nickel. By the way, do you mind if I call him Whosis instead of X? It reminds me of algebra and I was rotten at it."

"I sincerely hope," Wolfe muttered, "that there will never be another occasion to refer to him."

But one came the very next day, this morning, when the package arrived, and its contents raised a question that has not been answered and probably never will be. Did X have so many ways of learning things that he knew how much had been shelled out to Mr. Jones, or was it just a coincidence that the package contained exactly fifteen grand? Anyhow, tomorrow I'll make my second trip to a certain city in New Jersey, and then the total in the safe deposit box will be a nice round figure. The name I go by there need not be told, but I can say that it is not William Reynolds.

The tail's third section is not only private but strictly personal, and it goes beyond phone calls, though there are those too. This coming week end at Stony Acres I expect no complications like dope in the drinks, and I won't have to bother with a camera. Recently I quit calling her ma'am.

ABOUT THE AUTHOR

REX STOUT, the creator of Nero Wolfe, was born in Noblesville, Indiana, in 1886, the sixth of nine children of John and Lucetta Todhunter Stout, both Quakers. Shortly after his birth, the family moved to Wakarusa, Kansas. He was educated in a country school, but, by the age of nine, was recognized throughout the state as a prodigy in arithmetic. Mr. Stout briefly attended the University of Kansas, but left to enlist in the Navy, and spent the next two years as a warrant officer on board President Theodore Roosevelt's yacht. When he left the Navy in 1908, Rex Stout began to write freelance articles, worked as a sightseeing guide and as an itinerant bookkeeper. Later he devised and implemented a school banking system which was installed in four hundred cities and towns throughout the country. In 1927 Mr. Stout retired from the world of finance and, with the proceeds of his banking scheme, left for Paris to write serious fiction. He wrote three novels that received favorable reviews before turning to detective fiction. His first Nero Wolfe novel, *Fer-de-Lance,* appeared in 1934. It was followed by many others, among them, *Too Many Cooks, The Silent Speaker, If Death Ever Slept, The Doorbell Rang* and *Please Pass the Guilt,* which established Nero Wolfe as a leading character on a par with Earle Stanley Gardner's famous protagonist, Perry Mason. During World War II, Rex Stout waged a personal campaign against Nazism as chairman of the War Writers' Board, master of ceremonies of the radio program "Speaking of Liberty" and as a member of several national committees. After the war, he turned his attention to mobilizing public opinion against the wartime use of thermonuclear devices, was an active leader in the Authors' Guild and resumed writing his Nero Wolfe novels. All together, his Nero Wolfe novels have been translated into twenty-two languages and have sold more than forty-five million copies. Rex Stout died in 1975 at the age of eighty-eight. A month before his death, he published his forty-sixth Nero Wolfe novel, *A Family Affair.*

REX STOUT
&
NERO WOLFE

Rex Stout created Nero Wolfe, that Falstaff in girth and wit, that serious eater, devoted orchidologist and acknowledged agoraphobe. Nero solved crimes by sheer brain-power and with more than a little help from the brash but efficient Archie Goodwin.

Nero Wolfe made his dazzling debut in 1934, when his creator was 47 years of age. And from then on the 286 pound, sedentary sleuth triumphed over a variety of evil forces that even included the F.B.I. Wolfe accomplished these feats between beers in a brownstone on West 35th Street in New York. Dispensing with crime laboratories and the like, he relied on old-fashioned logic of the sort practiced by Sherlock Holmes (the vowels in whose name were identical to Nero Wolfe's, even in their order).

Mr. Stout's Nero Wolfe books have appeared in over 22 languages and have sold more than forty-five million copies. Mr. Stout had completed forty-six mysteries starring Wolfe at the time of his death at 88. The first was *Fer de Lance,* the last *A Family Affair*. In between, there were forty-four other mysteries, each one of them a brilliant display of the talents of Rex Stout and the expert sleuth Nero Wolfe.